MAY 1 1 2021

THE NOWHERE

A Novel

CHRIS GILL

Published by PRNTD Publishing 2019

1 3 4 5 7 9 10 8 6 4 2

ISBN 9780994462060

First published in Australia in 2019 by PRNTD Publishing

Typeset in Baskerville

www.prntdpublishing.com

In loving memory of Dad

"Sometimes you find yourself in the
middle of nowhere, and sometimes, in the middle of
nowhere you find yourself."

– Unknown

Prologue

As the first wave of teenagers poured out the school gate in a hyperactive frenzy, it dawned on me I should have already left. That would have been the only hope of avoiding gridlock somewhere along the city's spine. But there was something about the air of adolescent enthusiasm that kept me stationary. Their chorus of shouts and laughter a reminder it wasn't just the start of the weekend, but the beginning of another long, hot summer.

A tall girl strutted ahead of the crowd with her blonde mane pulled away from her face. Two brunettes walked with her, one on either side. Close behind were a group of guys – a pack of hyenas chattering rowdily. The leader chanted, grinning, yearning for attention with his arms outstretched. Another blasted out the repetitive sound of thumping dance music through a portable speaker.

The second surge soon appeared. A girl dressed all in black contrasted the vivid blue, cloudless sky. An overweight boy looked far more forlorn than he should have on the last day of term. Two older guys walked with an attractive girl between them – her arms draped loosely around their shoulders. Their shirts were covered in signatures, a sign they'd finished high school for good. The girl's smile beamed brighter than the sun. A summer lay ahead, filled with excitement, sex and energy. The start of a new life filled with opportunity and success, and, no doubt, eventual disappointment. It would go fast. It would go slow. She would try and control it, but it would turn out to be unpredictable anyway.

That's when my phone started to vibrate.

Quickly pulling it out the pocket of my scrubs before the annoying ringtone kicked in, I was greeted with an anonymous number. Must be a bloody sales call. Why did I bother answering?

'Hello?'

'Hey, Seb. It's me.'

I froze. Even though it took me a few moments to process it, it was surprising how quickly I recognised the voice. I asked anyway: 'Who is this?'

'It's Jake, Seb. Don't you remember?'

Of course I remembered. How could I forget? 'Sure, I remember.'

'I remember a lot.'

Jake's voice was deeper and more gravelly with age. What sort of stories could he tell me with those worn words? He would have lived a full life. I'd thought about it a lot over the years. Much more than I should have. Sadness enveloped me at the thought of all we'd missed out on. Of all the years we'd never get back.

'How much do you remember?' he asked.

I swallowed and stayed silent. He was testing me. The same way he used to when I spoke to him on that dusty old landline, standing in the narrow hallway of the farmhouse.

'I remember everything.'

There was a pregnant pause before Jake finally spoke again. 'I had to go through a few hurdles to find your number. I hope you don't mind me calling you out the blue. You're kind of elusive online. Not on Facebook or anything. Not that I blame you. That stuff screws with your head.' He hesitated again. 'I can't even remember the last time I saw you.'

I could. The salty tears. His flared nostrils and pale lips. We'd both known deep down we wouldn't be seeing each other again for a very long time, if ever. It had to be that way. We had no choice. And we only had ourselves to blame.

'Anyway, you live in Perth, right? I live in Sydney these days, but I'm coming your way for work next month. Do you wanna meet for coffee or something?'

A chill crept down my spine. Was I ready to see him again? Would I ever be?

You can't keep it secret forever. The truth always comes out eventually.

It was time to change the subject: 'Are you coming to surf?'

Jake let out a raspy laugh. It wasn't a laugh I recognised.

'Hell no. I'm a marketing director, Seb. That was just a teenage dream – you know that.' I didn't. That's what I'd pictured him doing ever since we last saw each other.

'In fact,' he continued, 'I never did get back into surfing after... well, you know. After The Nowhere.'

Hearing the words made me shudder. Not that a day went by I didn't think about that place at least once. But hearing it said aloud was like being kicked in the stomach. It caught me off guard. I sure as hell wasn't ready for it.

There was tension now. He must have decided he'd made

3

a mistake calling me.

'Well, do you wanna meet or not?'

That sounded more like the blunt, know-it-all Jake I once knew.

Just like the day I smoked the first cigarette he'd given me without thinking, I spoke without thought: 'Sure.'

'Great. Do me a favour and save my number, Seb. I'll be in touch soon.'

The line went dead. As did my pulse.

Did that really just happen? Did Jake really call me after all those years? Could I meet him and face all those memories? It would be the first time I'd have to confront exactly what had happened that summer. The summer I never spoke about to anyone, but one that continued to smoulder in the back of my mind.

The sound of teenage naivety completely disappeared. The school directly opposite was now completely empty. Soon, the next set of hospital staff would be climbing into their cars around me, ready to drive off into the day's golden hour. When the sunset would swathe the city with that deep, burnt amber before draping it in darkness. Then, I'd be alone. There was no going back now, and there could be no more running away. I had to face my past. I had to meet with Jake. Leaning my head back, I closed my eyes and transported myself back there. Back to The Nowhere.

20th January 1997

It was the fly that woke me. Its faint buzzing like a lawn-mower in the distance, growing louder as it flew closer to my face. My eyes still closed, I wrinkled my nose and reached out to grab the glass on my bedside table. The temperature of the water a stark reminder it was the height of summer. My eyelids fluttered a few times as they opened. Turning to the digital clock beside my bed, I was instantly reminded of what day it was. Not that it made much difference. It would be like every other. *Slam.* The fly dropped to the floor. My palm caked in sweat and fly guts.

To my surprise, Dad and Jeremy were already at the kitchen table. In lieu of my usual bowl of cornflakes sat a chocolate cake with a seventeen-shaped candle poking out the middle.

'Happy birthday to you, happy birthday to you…'

Dad must've been making up for last year. You would have thought my sixteenth would have been more significant.

'…happy birthday, dear Sebastian…'

But that was the first birthday without Mum. He must've had other things on his mind.

'…happy birthday to you.'

Cheers and applause followed as I blew out the candle. Dad was wearing his favourite denim shirt he reserved for special occasions. It made a change from seeing him in his grubby red plaid shirt he wore most days. He picked up a small wrapped box as he stood to face me. Running a hand through his thick, greasy hair that was much darker than mine, he extended his arm to offer me the gift. 'Happy birthday, Seb.'

Overlooking the tiny pictures of Santa and Rudolph, who were making an appearance a couple of weeks too late, I smiled at the gesture. 'Thanks, Dad. You shouldn't have.'

'That's where you're wrong, Son. It's about time I bought you something to say thank you for all your hard work. I know it's been… difficult for you out here at times.'

Talk about an understatement. But I didn't want to ruin the moment. Especially as I knew what was waiting for me beneath the wrapping.

Breaking into a huge smile, I tore the paper away to reveal a navy box. Was I right? Were there keys inside? Trembling with excitement, I opened it, only to be met with a small, thin, golden chain.

'It's a necklace,' Dad stated the obvious. 'It belonged to your grandfather who left it for me when he died. I want it to be yours.'

Disappointment tore through me. Was it too much to have wanted a car? Nothing flash, just a beaten-up banger he could have used to teach me how to drive. Any old car that would've given me the freedom to leave when the time was right. To reverse out the driveway, floor the pedal and never look back. But all those hopes and dreams were gone, crushed in front of me like the fly between my hands.

'Well… aren't you going to say something?' Dad's caterpillar moustache twitched.

'Wow… thanks, Dad.' I tried my best to sound enthusiastic. 'I really love it.'

He knew I was lying. The last thing I wanted to do was wind him up. Not on my birthday. I didn't want to have to deal with his temper.

'He doesn't like it,' Jeremy chimed in. He had a habit of doing that. Stirring Dad up to get mad at me to keep the attention away from him. It was a stupid strategy that always backfired. Once Dad was riled up, he'd end up taking his rage out on us both. My brother never seemed to learn that. Or if he did, he had a very short memory.

'I can see that.' Dad's words were stern now. I knew that tone all too well.

His eyes narrowed. I hated that I could see my own in his. They were the same mahogany hue. Jeremy had my mother's steely eyes, which I'd always been jealous of. They were a gift from her that only he'd been lucky enough to inherit.

'Always been fuckin' ungrateful, Seb.' Dad's words were spat with malice as he sat back down. His face turned red, and a thin purple vein zigzagged down the side of his neck. It only surfaced when he was especially mad, and the sight of it was enough to induce fear in my brother and me. It was like seeing a redback scuttle out from underneath a plant pot.

'I do like it, Dad, honestly. I guess I'd just hoped…'

'You'd just hoped what? That I'd bought you a car?'

My silence confirmed he was right.

'And why would I have done that? You've got everything you need right here, haven't you? Or are you planning to drive off and leave me and your brother here?'

I held my nerve. 'Of course not.'

Jeremy got up to walk away. Just as I'd predicted, he'd dropped the bomb and then planned to scamper off. Dad wasn't having any of it.

'Stay right where you are, Jeremy. It's important you hear this too.'

My blood ran cold. Why would Dad choose to have one of his turns on my birthday? Couldn't I have just acted more convincing?

'I know we never speak about your mother's passing, boys. But you must understand how hard it is for me too, raising you both on my own. I know I don't have a lot to give you, but this cattle station, it's my pride and joy. It's the one thing I have in the world, aside from you two, that I truly care about.' He turned and looked directly at me. 'Now why would you want to go running away from that?'

I shook my head. 'I don't.'

This time I sounded more decisive. Dad's temper slowly started to subside. His face turned from pink back to its sandy, tanned tone and the vein disappeared.

'Don't wind me up on your birthday, Seb.' He clumsily thumbed the delicate gold chain out of its box. 'May I?'

I nodded.

His warm breath brushed the back of my neck as he fastened the clasp. Black coffee, blended with his morning cigarette. 'There.'

I humoured him with a smile. It was as much enthusiasm as I could muster. 'Thanks, Dad. I really do love it.'

'That's my boy. Now c'mon, it might be your birthday, but you've still got work to do. Jeremy, it's time to go.'

My brother looked half relieved the argument was over and half disappointed it hadn't escalated enough for him to be late for summer school. Within minutes, he and Dad rushed out the house and climbed into the ute. Stepping outside to feed Scampi, I followed the vehicle pounding along the dusty red road with my eyes until it was out of sight. I breathed a sigh of relief. Although the break from Dad wouldn't last long, it was always the highlight of my day.

I scooped chunks of dog food into Scampi's bowl. The flies soon began to circle with their metallic drone. Before they had a chance to descend onto the thick, gelatinous outer-layer of the low-grade beef, Scampi bounded over. I gave his back a rub as he began to devour his meal. His coat was a firework display of black, grey and brown across a white canvas. Dad always said he was handsome for a cattle dog, maybe because the markings on his face were almost symmetrical. I grinned as he licked up the last of his food. I loved seeing him happy. It was contagious, even if only for a moment.

With Scampi on my heels, I made my way towards the quad bikes. I decided I'd ease my way into the morning slowly. Surely I owed that to myself on my birthday. I leaned back against the windmill, which, like me, was bronzed from too much sun. Scampi quickly followed my lead and perched beside me. His eyes never strayed from the cows that roamed nearby. It wasn't even nine o'clock and the temperature must've been in the late twenties. The humidity was low, the heat drier than dirt. Scanning the cloudless sky, the milky moon caught my attention. Although faint in the daylight, its craters were still visible. Was there someone out there looking down on me? Were they just as alone? Were they sitting underneath an empty sky, getting ready to spend another day herding cows when they should have been getting ready to go meet their friends?

Scampi's sharp bark brought me back from my daydream. Dad would be on his way home soon and wouldn't be happy to find me lazing around, gazing into space.

'C'mon then, Scamp. Let's get on with it.'

30th January 1997

Puffing on a self-rolled cigarette, Dad adjusted his wide-brimmed hat. Beads of sweat formed along the length of his moustache, as they did every summer's day. I wiped my brow, staring up at the sun's unforgiving glare. Its bold outline stained my eyes in three places, forming a triangle of iridescent circles.

'How're you going, Seb?' He took a long, deep drag of smoke.

My heart sank. We'd been getting on much better since my birthday, so I really didn't want to provoke him again. Normally when Dad asked how I was feeling, it turned into an interrogation. If I told him how unhappy I was, he'd call me ungrateful. If I didn't tell him anything, he'd say I was being aloof. Either way, he'd get angry. Either way, I'd lose.

'I'm doing pretty well actually, Dad. Thanks for asking.'

He seemed to believe my lie. 'Glad to hear it, Son. You've seemed in good spirits lately and you're working hard, which you know I appreciate.'

I smiled meekly and said nothing.

'Y'know, I've been thinking about our conversation the other week. On your birthday. About the car.'

Here we go.

'I'm gonna buy you one, Seb.'

Dynamite in my chest. Was he serious? Was I actually going to get my wish? Maybe this meant he was warming to the idea of me eventually leaving The Nowhere. I wasn't holding my breath. There had to be a catch.

'Seriously?'

'Seriously. You've more than earned it recently. You've shown your maturity, and I feel I've built up enough trust in you to know you're not going to go running away as soon as you get your license.'

There it was. The guilt trip. That would be the catch. But I wasn't going to miss out on the opportunity by appearing ungrateful.

'Wow. Thanks, Dad. That means the world to me.'

I almost reached out to hug him but resisted. That was something we never did. Instead, I settled for a wide smile that showed my gratitude. He patted me on the back, threw the butt of his cigarette on the ground and stamped it out. Scampi barked – as if to remind us we had work to do.

'We know, Scamp.' Dad climbed back onto his quad bike. 'We know.'

The grin remained on my face throughout the rest of the day and well into the evening, long after Jeremy got home.

'What are you so happy about?' My brother's eyes focused on mine suspiciously. He'd been staring at me for at least five minutes, spinning the spaghetti in circles on the tip of his fork.

'Never you mind.' Dad's stern tone. He probably didn't want to make Jeremy feel jealous, especially if it meant he'd have to buy him something too.

Jeremy looked annoyed, but his face soon relaxed. He

clearly thought he'd just get it out of me later anyway. But I wouldn't tell him. I worried that if I did, I'd risk losing the car altogether. It was a risk I wasn't willing to take.

After dinner, Dad cracked open a bottle of beer and spread out on the couch watching highlights of the day's cricket. I washed the dishes as Jeremy dried. I preferred to dry, but my brother wasn't quite tall enough to reach into the sink. I always joked that his time would come. As I scrubbed off the resilient pieces of bolognese that were stuck to the bottom of the pan, our conversation somehow morphed from meaningless banter to Mum.

'Why don't we talk about her anymore?' Jeremy sounded so innocent that it made my heart hurt.

'You know it's hard for Dad, J. He gets upset, so he reacts in the only way he knows how to deal with those emotions.'

Jeremy nodded. It was so easy to forget how young he was. After everything he'd been through in his brief seven years, he'd matured early. His eyes seemed to hide so much. Perhaps it was the same pain and longing I felt.

'But if you ever want to talk about her, you can talk about her with me. When it's just the two of us together.' I offered my brother a warm smile in support.

The tension in his eyes relaxed, and his face gave way to a smile. 'Thanks, Seb. I'd love to go visit her sometime.'

Mum's ashes had been buried back in Perth, near where she grew up. Dad would've liked to have brought them with him, but there's no way my grandmother would have allowed that. Perth was where her daughter belonged. Deep down, Dad knew too. She hadn't been a country person, despite how he'd tried to convince her to become one.

'When?'

I wasn't ready for all the questions. There's nothing I wanted more than to be able to jump on the next plane to Perth to escape the misery of The Nowhere. But I barely had a dollar to my name, so that was out the question. 'I'm not sure, J. All in good time.'

He scrunched up his face.

'I'm sorry, Jeremy. It's just not that easy.'

'Why can't we just ask Dad?'

'Dad doesn't have the money right now, J.' It was the truth. My father's big dream of moving to the country and living off the land was all well and good in theory, but it hadn't gone as smoothly as he'd planned. He owed the bank a lot of money.

Jeremy looked up at me with bleary eyes, bloodshot with tears and tiredness.

'Come on then.' I slipped into my big brother tone. 'It's time to get ready for bed.'

We crept past Dad, who was out cold on the couch. The cricket highlights blared as a blowfly landed directly on the rim of his beer bottle.

As I tucked my brother in, his eyes wandered to the photo of him and Mum beside his bed.

'Tell me the story.' He nestled into his doona. 'The one about the picture.'

I picked up the small frame and smiled. A two-year-old Jeremy had chocolate cake smeared all over his face and hands. Mum was crouching next to his highchair, bursting with laughter, her youthful beauty frozen in time.

'It was your second birthday and everyone was around you. Me, Mum, Dad and Grandma. Mum wanted to take a photo of you with your birthday cake, so she quickly went to grab her camera. By the time she returned you'd nosedived into the cake, getting chocolate all over your face.'

Jeremy erupted into a fit of giggles, just like he always did when I recited the story. It put him at ease, transporting him to a different time. One filled with fun, with too much sugar, with Mum.

After my brother finally fell asleep, I stepped out into the back yard. The sound of crickets was deafening, and the warm air was thick and heavy, shrouded with the sweet, familiar scent of eucalyptus. Narrowing my eyes, I adjusted my vision to the darkness. The brittle grass crunched beneath my bare feet as I looked around for Scampi, who came running quietly towards me. I crouched down and squeezed him tighter than usual. His amber eyes stared back at me. They held a mixture of sadness and adoration. They mirrored my own.

'Today was a good day, Scamp. You don't even know but there's a whole world out there I'm going to show you. As soon as I can, I'm going to pack us up and drive us as far away from here as possible.'

11th February 1997

Once the last cow was loaded onto the truck, Mitch slammed the door. His skin was ruddy from too much time spent in the sun and an unkempt beard coated his bloated face. 'Cheers, mate. See you next time.'

'See ya then.' Dad tipped his hat.

We watched the truck reverse out the driveway and follow the road towards Westonia before getting back onto our quad bikes. I dreaded pick-up days. We didn't have many cows for a cattle station, never more than eighty at a time. Although I knew they paid the bills, it was hard not to get attached to them. Watching them graze in the sun every day, without a care in the world, was strangely cathartic. They had no idea what awaited them when they were loaded into the truck. I often wondered if the slaughterhouse would be a better fate than a life spent in The Nowhere. At least they got to escape.

Today felt different, though. Nothing could have dampened my spirits now I knew I was getting a car. Soon I'd be leaving the farm behind, and the cows and the slaughterhouse and Dad would be nothing more than fading memories.

The quad bike chugged a few times before the engine fired up. It was the same sound it always made as it got started – a croaky cough. Following Dad through the vast fields of coarse, sun-bleached grass, I visualised myself sitting in my car, gliding down the highway with the windows down and the fresh air blowing against my face. Driving towards the city – any city. Further and further away from the farm with every second that passed.

We pulled up beside one of the few silver gum trees that littered the landscape and hopped off our bikes. It was time for Dad's ciggie break. The tree gave us a little shelter from the sun's harsh rays. It was hard to get used to the heat in The Nowhere. The dry, blistering swelter of the midday summer sun was all-encompassing. That's not to say it didn't get hot back in Perth – far from it. Some days it got so warm we'd spend the whole day inside with the air con on full blast. But there was no refuge in The Nowhere. No air con, either.

I lifted Scampi's collar and gave the patch underneath a scratch, which he loved. Dad rolled his cigarette, humming one of his favourite old songs. I had no idea what it was, but he hummed it whenever he was in a good mood. This made it one of my favourite songs too.

That's when I heard the vehicle.

Dad heard it too. There was no way he couldn't have, seeing as it was such an unfamiliar sound on the farm. Aside from the occasional cawing of a crow, magpie or cockatoo, The Nowhere remained silent. Dad instantly stopped humming as his eyes locked with mine.

'You hear that, Son?'

'Yeah.'

'Must be trespassers.'

Was he angry? Intimidated? Excited?

A mustard ute rolled down the road running alongside

our farm. It didn't make sense. We never had guests in The Nowhere. In the entire time we'd lived here, we'd never even had a single visitor. It was Mum who'd been the socialite of the family. She always had heaps of friends coming in and out the house, while Dad was more of an introvert. Mum's friends still called from time to time to check in on him, but they never made the epic trip out to see us. Not that I blamed them. Not that Dad would ever think to invite them.

The ute ground to a halt and three figures jumped out. They made their way towards us. A man and woman walked in front, perhaps slightly younger than Dad. Behind them was a boy who must have been around my age.

'What do you think they want?' I asked.

He remained silent, as if deep in thought. It was rare to see my father speechless. He was the king of our castle, so I worried he wouldn't take kindly to strangers. But my heartbeat quickened in excitement. How refreshing would it be to have a conversation with someone other than Dad or Jeremy?

The trio finally reached us. The man spoke first, offering a friendly wave as he did so.

'G'day, I'm Rob.' He had a country accent, but it wasn't as strong as my father's. He sounded laid-back, which suited his long blonde-grey hair and beard. 'We're your new neighbours.'

Neighbours? We'd never had neighbours in The Nowhere.

Dad was visibly confused. 'You mean... you've moved into that old place behind the bush?'

Rob nodded and smiled. 'We sure have.'

The other farm. I'd completely forgotten it existed. Dad had told me about it a long time ago when I'd asked what was beyond the bushland at the end of our property. He'd heard a family of crop farmers had once occupied it. But as the summers grew drier and the land infertile, they sold up and moved away, leaving it derelict.

Rob turned to me and held my focus. 'And what's your name?'

'It's Sebastian, sir.'

'Mate, call me Rob. I hope we didn't wake you guys earlier. We'd made such momentum after leaving Adelaide we kept going. Didn't get here 'til the early hours.'

'We didn't hear a thing,' I said, trying to catch the boy's eye.

'Yeah, good job we didn't buy this little fella as a guard dog.' Dad patted Scampi on the head in a display of affection that was out of character. 'So, Adelaide, eh? Never been. Least you'll be used to the dry heat in these parts. What business do you have here anyway?'

'We're from Byron actually, did the drive over the past four days. We owned a company that turned sour, then one day we just thought, why not? Let's sell up, buy a farm and move away.'

That sounded familiar.

The boy, who I assumed to be their son, shook his head and muttered something inaudible under his breath. Was he upset he'd been dragged away from all his friends, the same way I had? Or was it something else? A fleeting glance offered nothing conclusive.

'We thought we'd just do something completely different,' the woman said in a soft tone. Her long, wispy hair was plaited messily, and sat over her shoulder, cascading down her front. 'So, we're planning to grow canola.'

I didn't even need to look at Dad to know what his expression would be.

'You're planning to grow canola? With no previous experience on a farm?'

The woman smiled and bobbed her head. Her expression remained the same, not giving anything away. They were handling Dad well.

'Well, I don't mean to sound disrespectful, but you've got quite the challenge ahead of you. I mean, we tried growing crops here, but it just didn't happen. It barely rains at all these days. And when it does, during the storms, it's not enough to grow the kind of crops you'd need to make a living.'

After a brief pause, Rob replied: 'Thanks for your concern, mate. But we're not worried.'

The certainty in his tone was enough to stun not only me but my father too.

'Anyway, I didn't catch your name, mate.' He reached his hand out towards my father. Would he reciprocate?

'You're right, how rude of me. My name's Stu, pleasure to meet you all.' He shook Rob's hand.

I sighed with relief.

'And I'm Alison. And this here is our son, Jake. Jake, say hello, darling.'

Jake remained silent, his eyes focused on the ground. His thick lips were pursed. His ashy hair, pushed to the side, created a weighty fringe. Poor guy. I knew exactly how he was feeling. Should I say something? Let him know he's not alone? It wasn't the right time.

'Teenagers,' Dad said.

As insensitive as he could be sometimes, he knew how to break an awkward silence.

Alison turned back to face us. 'I'm sorry. My son has been through a lot these past few weeks, saying goodbye to his home and friends.'

'Of course. Don't worry – he'll get used to it. They always do.'

I winced at my father's words, at the way he talked about Jake and me like we weren't even there. I wanted the ground to crack open and swallow me whole. Now there was no chance Jake would ever want to hang out with me. Not with my patronising father around.

'Yeah, you're right,' Rob said. 'Anyway, you better excuse us. We just wanted to introduce ourselves, but we should continue getting settled. By the sound of things, we have some hard yakka ahead of us.'

'No worries. You'll have to come over one night for your first farmyard barbie.'

I cringed again. I tried to remember the last time we'd even had a barbecue.

'For sure, we'd love that,' Alison said.

Knowing Dad, the barbecue would never happen.

The couple said goodbye, before leading their sullen son

back towards their ute.

I waited until our neighbours were out of earshot until I spoke: 'They seemed nice.'

'Yeah, nice. A bit airy-fairy though, if you ask me. Typical Byron folk. And there's no way they're going to be able to grow crops on that farm. Should've forked out a little extra to buy further back in the Wheatbelt.'

He was just bitter. Dad was extremely competitive and a sore loser. I hoped they'd be able to get the crops to grow. Not only to spite my dad, but because I wanted them to stay. I wanted to hear more about Byron Bay. I'd never even been outside of Western Australia. The only holidays we ever went on were along the west coast or to Grandma's place in Fremantle, but I'd always wanted to visit the other states.

Dad slapped the back of my head. 'Come on, Seb. Get your head outta the clouds. We've got a lot to get done.' He was already revving up his quad bike.

I reluctantly hopped onto mine and we continued our checks. As we drove across the cracked red earth, I daydreamed of the beautiful beaches that lined the east coast. Countless questions clouded my head. What had Jake whispered to himself? And why on earth would his parents leave paradise to live *here*?

23rd February 1997

'You definitely have a temperature.' Dad held the back of his hand against my forehead. It had hurt, holding the light bulb so close to it, but my lie had to be believable. 'Well, it's a shame you're crook. I know how much you enjoy coming to church. But it's more important you rest up and get better for tomorrow. I'll need help getting those hay bales out.'

He was right, I did enjoy church, but only because it got me away from the farm for a few hours.

I nodded. 'I know. Don't worry – I'll be there.'

Since our new neighbours had arrived in The Nowhere, my mind was plagued with one question. Would I ever get to see them again? Every day I'd ride my quad bike around the property, gazing into the distance, hoping to see a sign of them coming to visit or a hint of them beyond the bush. There was nothing. No trace of Jake, or his parents. Why had Jake tried so hard to avoid eye contact with me? Was he just shy? Or was it something more than that? Behind their broad, friendly smiles, his parents could have been just as controlling and cruel as my father.

At first, I'd reminded Dad about the barbecue idea at least once every couple of days. Like an echidna weaving its way through a tunnel of balloons, I'd carefully pick the best times to bring it up. But in the end, I knew better than to keep asking. The first few times he simply ignored me, but by the fourth time, he gave me a glare that signalled a warning.

Why didn't he want me to make a friend? He should have encouraged it. Surely he'd seen how miserable I was on the farm. Maybe he didn't want me to have any distractions from work. If I were ever going to see Alison, Rob and Jake again, and have any chance of forging a friendship, I'd have to take matters into my own hands. I'd have to go visit them myself.

We attended Westonia's church the last Sunday of every month. Dad's school run each morning wasn't long enough, and we worked most weekends, so this was the perfect time for me to feign illness and go visit our neighbours. Once the ute disappeared out of sight, I set off through the bushland that separated our farms, counting my steps along the way. Perhaps I wanted to work out exactly how far our neighbours were from us. Maybe I just wanted to control the nerves in my stomach that really were making me feel sick. What was I so nervous about? I certainly worried that Dad would re- alise he'd forgotten something and turn back. It wasn't even worth imagining his reaction if he found me anywhere but in bed resting. Or perhaps it was because I was concerned the neighbours wouldn't want to see me. *Two hundred and five, two hundred and six…* My questions melted away as I counted. *Two hundred and seven, two hundred and eight…*

Being in the scrub was so different to being on the farm. The sounds were different. The feeling was different. Bushes rustled as I pushed my way through, and I could feel birds watching me from above in the towering eucalyptus. Every- thing around me teemed with life as I counted. *Three hundred and twenty-eight, three hundred and twenty-nine…*

By the time I reached four hundred, the front of the neighbours' farm was in full sight. It wasn't what I was expecting. Considering Dad had said it'd been abandoned, the farmhouse looked in much better condition than ours. It had a thick coating of warm taupe across its wooden walls. The family must have painted it already. Canola seedlings had sprouted from the soil that surrounded the property. A smile grew across my face. Did this mean they would be sticking around?

That was when I realised Jake was standing directly ahead of me, side on, digging into the dirt with a pitchfork. He was wearing the same t-shirt and denim shorts as the last time I'd seen him, as well as a pair of gardening gloves that were covered in dirt. He threw his pitchfork to the ground and pulled off his gloves, wiping his brow with the back of his hand. He turned towards me. For the first time, our eyes made direct contact. He looked shocked to see me. I instinctively recoiled. He lowered his eyes, turned back around and headed inside the house.

Alison was also working outside. This time there was no floaty, floral dress. She was in an old white shirt covered in black smears, cargo trousers covered in dirt and grass stains, and beaten up Doc Martens. Rob was nowhere to be seen.

'Sebastian!' There was no going back now. 'What a pleasant surprise.'

'Hi, Alison.' I slowly walked over. A cold trickle of sweat dripped down my back.

'Come, come,' she beckoned. 'Sit down. I could do with a break. Let me go fetch some lemonade.'

Was this really a good idea? If I got talking to Alison, perhaps it would be difficult to leave. But before I had a chance to decline, she disappeared inside to fetch our drinks. This was my chance to take a better look at my surroundings. The size of the house was like ours, and their land stretched back the way ours did, except there weren't any cows grazing on the scorched grass. In fact, most of their land wasn't being used at all. The crops were growing in a small patch behind the house. They must have been testing the waters, which was no surprise after Dad's warning.

'Here you go.' Alison reappeared clutching a tray of lemonade. She placed it down on the white cast iron table, the kind Grandma had back in Fremantle. The ice audibly cracked as she poured three glasses. Would Jake be joining us? She pointed towards the chair beside her. 'Sit down, dear.'

I did as I was told. Two red-capped parrots flew overhead.

'Where's your father, Sebastian?'

I stiffened. Was my cover blown? I'd lied to Dad and now I'd need to lie to Alison. There's no way I could tell her I was ill.

'He's gone to church with my brother. I didn't feel like it today.'

Alison smirked. 'I don't blame you. They're all just stories anyway.'

Had I heard her right? It was unusual to hear an adult reject the notion of religion so casually.

'Rob and I should probably start going anyway. It would

be good to get to know some people in the community. But when it comes to religion, the only thing we worship is the ground beneath our feet.' She gave me a quick wink and a smile.

Alison was likeable. She had a presence about her. An aura. Perhaps it was heightened by the lack of feminine energy in my life, but there was something comforting about her.

'So tell me, where's your mother?'

It was as if she'd read my mind. I hesitated for a moment, purely out of habit. It would be the first time in a long while I'd have to explain to someone she was no longer with us. Before I had the chance to reply, Alison had once again tapped my thoughts.

'Don't worry, darl. You don't have to talk about it.'

This time it was my turn to ask a question. 'Where's Rob?'

'Oh, Rob's a late riser. Particularly on Sundays. Jake and I tend to get up and get as much of the work done as we can, don't we Jake?' Alison looked around for a response, but as soon as she realised her son was nowhere to be seen, she went on. 'Then Rob swaps with me for the afternoon. Past noon I'm no help anyway.' She chuckled to herself before taking a sip of lemonade.

Realising I'd yet to try it, I sipped the quickly warming drink. It was just the right amount of sweet and sour.

'You like it?'

'I love it, thank you. It's been a long time since I've had homemade lemonade.'

Alison stared into my eyes as if she was trying to unravel me. She studied my gaze, perhaps looking for clues. Were my scars really that visible? It was time to change the subject.

'I can't believe you managed to get crops to grow. Dad will be so impressed. How'd you manage it?'

Alison's expression evolved into one of pride. Beaming, she said simply: 'Call it a woman's touch.'

It might have been meant as a joke, but there was probably a lot of truth behind it. Was that what was lacking on our farm? Maybe the dynamics within the house would benefit from a female presence.

'Oh dear, Jake's drink's getting warm. I'm sorry he's being so antisocial. He's taken the move badly, but he'll come around. You can both be friends, once he's ready.'

Once again, Alison had proven her telepathic powers. If it was so obvious to a stranger that I needed social interaction, why couldn't it be obvious to Dad? Perhaps he just chose to ignore it.

'It's okay. I completely get how he's feeling. It definitely takes some getting used to out here.'

Alison averted her gaze to her canola seedlings. 'I can relate to that too. I think it's going to take some getting used to for all of us.'

Was Jake not the only one missing home? Maybe Alison really *was* like my mum. Had she been dragged away from her friends and family and the city she loved? And what about Rob? Was he the reason they'd moved to The Nowhere? Dad and Jake would be home soon, so I'd have to leave with all my questions left unanswered, my thirst unquenched.

The last drop of lemonade seemed to evaporate before it reached my mouth. 'Thanks again, Alison. But I really must be going – I've got lots of chores to do.'

'What a good boy you are. I do hope your positive attitude rubs off on Jake.' She offered me one final smile. 'Make sure you drop by again soon, darl.'

I nodded and stood up from the table. 'See ya.'

I wandered back towards the bush, picking up the pace as soon as I was out of sight. My jog became a sprint as I raced through the scrub. Branches reached out and scratched my bare arms and legs. They couldn't be home yet, could they? Surely there still had to be time. *Two hundred and eighty, two hundred and eighty-one.* The prospect of an aggressive confrontation was mere minutes away. *Three hundred and six, three hundred and seven.* The house was in sight. Just one last push and I'd be home.

Suddenly the back door swung open to reveal Dad standing directly ahead of me. Shit.

'Sebastian!'

Jeremy peered out from behind my father, waiting to see what would happen next. Why were they back so early? How could I be so unlucky?

'Sebastian, get your fucking arse over here right now.'

There was nowhere to run. What was he going to say or do this time? I'd overstepped the line. Lying to my dad was the worst thing I could possibly do.

'I'm sorry, Dad,' I mumbled as I got closer.

He turned to Jeremy. 'Get inside.'

My brother paused for a moment. He was scared for me. He knew what Dad was capable of.

'Now.'

Jeremy scampered inside. Dad turned back to look at me. Furrowed eyebrows. Heavy breathing. The purple vein. The eruption was due any second.

'You lied to me, Seb. I understand you want to make a friend. I don't have an issue with that. But I have an issue with you lying.'

I swallowed sawdust. This wasn't going to end well.

Dad launched forward and before I had a chance to move, his hands were clasped around my neck. I gagged and tried to prise them away, but it was no good. He was possessed. Was he going to finish me off this time?

His grip finally loosened as the anger drained away. Gasping for air, I tried to get the words out. To apologise again. But it was too late. The back of his hand met my face with such force it sent me falling backwards. I hit the ground, stunned, the side of my face in flames.

I held my breath for a few moments. Should I get up? Or should I wait to be told to get up? My face throbbed. I could have cried, but I didn't. I wouldn't allow myself to. I wouldn't let him win.

My father towered above me, my blood visible on his wedding band. He didn't show any sign of remorse. Perhaps he enjoyed the feeling of power. Maybe he got a kick out of making me feel afraid. The throbbing had been replaced with a lingering sting.

'You worry me, Son.' He shook his head in disgust. 'And

you want me to believe you're ready for a car? Well, I'm sorry, mate. Looks like you've got another thing coming.'

There it was. The excuse he'd been waiting for. Any reason to go back on his word and deny me the one thing in the world I truly wanted. The only thing. The sting turned to sadness. Maybe I just wasn't meant to escape The Nowhere. The sun's unsympathetic glare exposed the disappointment on my face.

'Maybe you'll think about it a little harder next time before you decide to lie to your father.' He disappeared inside, slamming the fly screen shut.

Slumped on the floor, I lay in silence. Scampi crept over and began licking the side of my face. He loved the taste of blood.

8ᵗʰ March 2017

I could just make out the stern expression of the news presenter reading the evening headlines as I drove into the driveway. The deep crease etched into his forehead as he delivered
the gloomy news. Dad must have fallen asleep in front of the
television again. As I pushed open the front door, I was met
with the smell of a microwaved meal. He couldn't have been
asleep for long. Pacing towards the television to switch it off,
Dad's voice stopped me in my tracks.

'I was watching that.'

Had he even been asleep? If he had, he must have woken up when I walked in and waited to see if I'd turn off his
programme, which must have finished long ago. He'd never
cared for the news. I switched it back on.

'Sorry, Dad.'

He scratched the side of his head, nails running through
his peppery hair. He rubbed his face and tried to focus his
faded eyes on me. He had on the same plaid shirt and jeans
he'd worn for the past twenty years. You could take the man
out of the farm, but there's no way you could take him out
of his worn-out denim. Dirty plates, mugs, cutlery and glasses lined the kitchen sink. Too lazy to even bother loading
the dishwasher, I began washing them up as I stared out the
window that overlooked the neatly manicured backyard. It'd
been given a fresh cut. Funny how Dad always managed to
get that done despite leaving dishes in the sink and the house

in a mess. His love for the outdoors had stayed with him since The Nowhere. He'd take any chance he got to be out in the garden. He kept it looking beautiful.

Stacking the dishes to drip-dry, I put some pasta on to boil. Dad never waited until I got home to have dinner. He preferred to comfort eat his way through those garish late-afternoon game shows. I'd lost count of how many days I'd made pasta for dinner, but I could never be bothered to be adventurous with my cooking since it was just for me. How long had it been like that? At least the last decade.

Full, I scraped the surplus into the bin before making my way to my room. Peering past the smear marks and dust on my bedroom mirror, I stared at my tired reflection. How kind had the years been to me? At a few years short of forty, I hadn't aged too badly. There were creases in all the obvious places. Smile lines, crow's feet. I kept my hair short. Long enough on top to style and the sides sharply shaved. Dark circles seemed to have moved in under my eyes somewhere in my mid-thirties and decided to stick around. It was just one of the many joys of being a shift worker.

Once my pale blue scrubs were off, I dropped my undies and jumped into the shower. Dad hadn't seen the point of having an en-suite installed, but I liked the privacy. It also saved me walking down the hallway to the main bathroom and risking waking him up. I'd managed to renovate most of the house, but there were still patches of dated décor I hadn't got around to updating. I'd been hanging on for that pay rise that was taking its sweet time.

I lathered my weary skin with shower gel. The parts of

my body less exposed to the sun were understandably paler, but even the visible parts could do with seeing a few more rays. It wasn't that I was out of shape as such, but I needed to get back into the routine of going to the gym. I'd had a good thing going for a few years, but like most phases of my life, it had dwindled before completely disappearing.

Despite it being summer, I turned up the temperature of the shower so it slightly scalded my skin. My heat tolerance had remained high since The Nowhere, and summers in Perth seemed like nothing compared to those long, sweaty days. My eyes scrunched closed, I moved closer to the showerhead, my face directly under the stream of hot water, and opened my mouth.

You can't keep it secret forever. The truth always comes out eventually.

11th March 1997

Gasping for air, I stretched my arm out the shower and fumbled for the towel to quickly dry my face. Had I been trying to drown myself? It was hard to tell. I'd spent the past few weeks in a complete daze, keeping quiet and doing my best to stay out of Dad's way. He knew I was despondent. But I had every right to be. The bruise on the side of my face had granted me that privilege, but it had now faded to nothing more than a yellow stain.

Once dry, I quickly dressed and made my way towards the kitchen for breakfast. The smell of eggs frying floated down the hallway. That was unusual for a Tuesday. Eggs and bacon were normally reserved for Saturdays. Dad was plating up as I entered the kitchen, but Jeremy wasn't there.

'Where's J?'

'I took him early this morning, remember?'

I suddenly did. Jeremy's class was off on a day trip to an old gold mine that shut down a few years back to learn about its history. Thank god I never had to do anything like that when I was his age. The idea of sitting in a hot bus to go look at some big hole in the ground would not have been my idea of fun as a seven-year-old boy. Or at any age, for that matter.

'Ah yeah, I remember.'

'Sit down. I've made brekkie.'

His tone suggested he was in good spirits, which was a huge relief. Despite how angry I still was with him, my mood was so easily influenced by his. He had such a hold over my emotions. I'm sure he realised it too.

'Son, I know I was hard on you a few weeks back. I shouldn't have lashed out the way I did.'

I remained silent as I pierced the yolk and watched the liquid gold ooze down the toast. He'd made them just the way I liked.

'Now, I know how much you want that damn car, but I'm afraid after what happened I need to build up my trust in you again. Right now, I simply can't give you the opportunity to leave the farm, because I know you would in a heartbeat.'

Dad's face took on an expression I'd never seen him use before. He looked vulnerable. Scared, even. Did I feel sorry for him? Maybe I would if he wasn't manipulating me. Or if he didn't insist on keeping me captive in The Nowhere when I was only a year away from officially becoming an adult, old enough to take control of my life and make my own decisions. Did he want me to remain on the farm forever?

'But I do want you to be happy, Seb. I want you to have a friend. Which is why I'm going to keep my promise and invite the neighbours over for that barbie.'

It wasn't a car, but it was the next best thing. Had he simply had enough of my sulking for the last few weeks? Whatever his reason, I didn't want to jinx it with my questions. Instead, I mustered a smile. 'Really?'

'Yes, really. Like I said before, it's not the fact you went next door I was hurt by. It was that you lied to me.'

Hurt? I'd heard Dad describe his feelings in many ways before. Angry, frustrated, exhausted even. But never hurt.

The word stood out like a rainbow lorikeet flying through an overcast sky.

'But you know that. And you've been punished for that. Preventing you from making a friend out here would just be unfair.'

Another word I hadn't thought Dad was familiar with. It was my turn to say something. 'Thanks, Dad. I'd love that.'

'I thought you would.' He mopped up what was left of his eggs with the remaining finger of toast before necking the last of his coffee. 'Let's get through our morning checks, and we'll head up there after lunch.'

The silence stretched on for as long as the road that led to our neighbours' farm. Was Dad doing this purely for me, or because he also wanted to make friends? Had he ever even had friends? There was Nick, a carpenter who he'd used to meet up with down the local in Perth. He was a tall man who I probably only heard utter two or three sentences in all the times I'd met him. He'd stand in silence behind Dad, following him around like a dog. Maybe that's what Dad had liked about him. Then one evening that all changed. Dad got home late from the pub and was louder than normal. He'd woken both Jeremy and me up. My brother had been sleeping in the bottom bunk in my room. Bursting through the front door, his incoherent ramblings were barely muffled by the thin walls. He was picking an argument with my mother, again. Quietly creeping out of bed, I pressed my ear against the wall, trying desperately to decipher his slurs. Soon after the angry voice ceased ranting, Dad had passed out. The next day I found the right time to bring the incident up with Mum, who quickly brushed it off. All she said was that he wouldn't be going to the pub with Nick again anytime soon.

As we approached the property, I could make out two figures working outside. Rob and Alison. No sign of Jake this time. I hadn't told Dad about the seedlings. There hadn't really been a good time. It was worth not telling him just to see the reaction on his face as the ute rolled up to the driveway. He was gobsmacked.

'What the... How the hell did they manage that?'

'I dunno, Dad. Why don't you ask them?' It wasn't often I got to see someone get the upper hand over him, so I was going to enjoy every minute.

His competitive eyes darted from side to side at the crops that were sprouting through thick and fast. We climbed out the vehicle and were immediately greeted by our neighbours.

'G'day,' Rob called out, the same friendly smile on his face he'd had the day we met him. 'What a nice surprise.'

'I'm in shock. How did you get all this to grow?'

Rob's cheeks pushed his deep-set eyes closed as he let out a loud, single-syllable laugh. 'I might not have been completely honest when I said I had no previous experience on a farm. I actually grew up on one down in Tassie. I just didn't think I'd remember what to do.'

Dad looked at him suspiciously. 'The conditions up here are a little bit different to the ones down in Tas. I'm impressed.' He sounded genuine, which appeared to flatter the couple.

'Thank you,' Alison grinned. 'This means we'll be sticking around. Can I offer you both some lemonade?'

A rush of fear pulsated through me. Was she going to bring up my visit? In doing so, would she remind Dad I'd lied? If she did, would that make him change his mind about the barbecue?

'No, thanks. That does sound tempting, but we've got heaps of work to get done today.' Dad's response gave me instant respite. 'We actually just stopped by to see if you guys wanna come over for that barbie I mentioned.'

'We would love that,' Alison replied, without pausing for thought. 'You just pick a time and we'll be there.'

Dad was taken aback by her quick decision. 'How about this Saturday?'

I was shocked Dad had chosen a date so soon. But then again, why wouldn't he? It's not like we ever had any plans, so if he was serious about having the family over, there was no need to wait. After a brief silence, Rob chimed in: 'Perfect. We'll see you then. What time do you want us round?'

'Does six-ish work for you?'

'Six sounds great.' Alison pushed her delicate hair out of her face. 'What can we bring? I make a mean potato salad.'

'Sounds great.' Dad smiled. 'And how about some of that homemade lemonade?'

As we rolled out the driveway, Jake emerged from the shadows of the porch and threw me a glance. Before I had a chance to wave, he disappeared back into the house. Why was he so despondent? He couldn't have just been pissed off about the move. There must have been more to it. Something about the way he was acting troubled me. Saturday would be my chance to find out why.

19th May 2017

'One… two… three… clear!'

Still nothing. That wasn't a good sign.

'One… two… three… clear!'

An eerie silence filled the room, one we knew all too well. It was the silence that arose when we all knew what was about to happen but didn't want to accept it.

'One… two… three… clear!'

Sandra's eyes said it all. We'd lost him. We'd lost another one.

Half an hour after the patient died, Sandra found me sitting in the staff room. My shift was over, but I was still in my scrubs, staring blankly at the wall.

'Seb?'

Turning around slowly, I presented my colleague the warmest smile I could manage.

She walked over and pulled the chair out beside me to sit down. 'Do you want a coffee or anything?'

I shook my head. 'No, thank you.'

After a brief pause, she spoke again. 'There's nothing you could have done, Seb. I mean… we did all we could.'

I held her focus. 'I know. It just never gets any easier, does it?'

She shook her head. 'But you can't keep torturing yourself every time. It's too much to carry.'

If only she knew.

'What are you doing tonight?' The question took me by surprise.

Sandra was an attractive woman. Not the prettiest, but there was something about her that made her stand out. Her long, mousey hair was pulled back into a bun, and she wore minimal makeup. Her eyes were an unnoticeable colour and her skin not as dark as it would be if she got to spend more time in the sun. I'd never seen her wear anything other than her scrubs, so I had no idea what she looked like outside the hospital walls. She was probably a completely different person. Maybe she was married. It's not as if she'd wear her wedding ring at work. But she'd never spoken about a man in her life.

I hesitated for a moment. What excuse could I use to get out of her proposition? I'd spent my whole life finding reasons to get out of these sorts of things, anything to prevent myself getting too close to someone. But in this case, I was either too slow on the uptake or Sandra could see right through me.

'It's okay, Seb. You can just say you're busy.'

Guilt surged to my heart. It was all too obvious that I was trying to think of a convincing lie, and I felt bad for it. I also knew I was preventing myself from getting to know someone purely through fear. It was time to break the cycle. In reality, I'd be spending my Friday night like every other night of my miserable existence, heading home and cooking a meal for myself that I didn't even want to eat while my miserable father sat in front of the TV. I'd then spend the evening dodging bullets he'd fire at me in an attempt to avoid an argument before he'd pass out on the couch and I'd head to bed with a book – one that would help me escape my grim reality. As soon as I'd close my eyes, they'd be there again. The memories I could never let go of.

But not this Friday, I decided with resolve. This Friday, everything would change, and it would all begin with the kind woman standing before me. She was the closest thing I had to a friend. Someone who might actually give a shit about how I felt.

'No, I've got nothing planned. What do you have in mind?'

*

Sandra picked a humble BYO Thai restaurant on the city fringe. She'd told me their massaman curry was to die for, and I couldn't say no.

'So, tell me something about yourself that I don't already know,' Sandra challenged, pouring us both a large glass of chardonnay.

She looked more radiant than usual. Her hair was tied up in a loose bun with strands falling across her face and a dark green dress that accentuated her figure in all the right places. She looked dressed up, but not overdressed. It was strange seeing her wear something other than her scrubs. Strange, in a good way.

'What a question.'

'Okay, well I'll start. I've been married once.'

I hadn't known that, which wasn't really a surprise. I'd

never tried to find out anything about Sandra's life outside the hospital. I gave very little away about myself so expected the same in return. Our conversations usually revolved around the latest shows we were bingeing on Netflix.

Sandra's eyes locked on mine. 'Your turn.'

What could I offer? I hadn't opened up to anyone in a very long time. I hadn't really opened up to anyone since my mother died. Besides Jake, that is.

'I'm a Capricorn.'

Pulling up to Sandra's driveway, she shifted her body to face me. I stopped the vehicle but decided to keep the engine running.

'I had a lovely time tonight, Seb.'

'So did I.' It *had* been nice to get out my own head, even for just a few hours.

Sandra's expression changed from one of content to concern. 'Why do you find it so hard to... talk?'

That wasn't fair. I talked all the time. But not the way she meant. And it wasn't the time to even try answering that question, so I remained quiet.

You can't keep it secret forever. The truth always comes out eventually.

The silence started to feel awkward. Was she waiting for me to kiss her? Why had I led her on? Surely I was too old to be making those same mistakes.

'Would you like to come in?'

Because I'd anticipated the invitation, I already had my answer ready. 'I had a lovely night, Sandra. But I think it's best we remain just friends. I'm worried it wouldn't be very… professional.'

This time Sandra's expression was easy to read. She was over it. 'Goodnight, Sebastian.'

She climbed out the car and slammed the door.

29th January 1994

The bottle spun seven times until it finally slowed and stopped completely. Its open neck pointed straight towards me, leaving no uncertainty. It was my turn. My turn to kiss Kylie. She'd already pashed two other guys tonight, so she knew exactly what she was doing. It would be my first kiss. What a way to remember it. Playing spin the bottle on a skate ramp in the middle of the night.

'Your turn!' Mick cheered before swigging back another mouthful of beer. This prompted all the others to start cheering too. Why had we even bothered coming tonight? It's not like Kylie and I were even friends with any of these idiots. The thought of both our parents discovering we were out was also freaking me out. I'd told Mum and Dad I was crashing at Kylie's, while Kylie had said the same to her mum. All it would take was one of them calling the other to find out we weren't telling the truth.

Kylie looked at me with her frosty eyes. The eyes that never hung on to anyone's focus long enough to give anything away. The ginger hair I'd never seen in its natural, frizzy state. Only ever doused in mousse creating big, bouncy ringlets. She was that one girl in school who all the girls wanted to be friends with and all the guys wanted to be with. But it didn't seem to matter. She chose me. I had no idea why, but she chose me. So why were we wasting our time with these losers?

'Guess Mick's right,' she finally said. 'It's our turn.'

It was hard to even recognise my friend. Her face was so plastered with makeup I couldn't even make out her freckles, which usually covered her face this time of year.

'I guess it is,' I said quietly.

It's not that I didn't want to kiss her. Of course I did. Kylie was gorgeous – every guy wanted to pash her. I guess I was just nervous. I didn't want to fuck it up. And she was my best friend. I didn't want to fuck that up either.

She reached across the empty bottle. I could smell her perfume. It was much stronger than usual. So strong it could have given me a headache if I had to breathe it in for too long. I closed my eyes and felt her kiss me. It felt soft and wet, sort of how I'd imagined, while at the same time feeling completely different. I opened my mouth and felt her tongue massage mine. She tasted of Passion Pop. It was an awkward kiss, not the fireworks I'd expected. Within moments it was over and Kylie sat back down. The crowd of drunken teens around us began jeering like animals. I wanted to disappear.

'Your turn,' Mick said again, this time to Kylie. It was obvious he was waiting for the bottle to land on him. Kylie was the hottest of all the girls playing the game, and he had that horny, possessed look about him. I'd seen enough. I scooped up my backpack and bottle of beer and walked away. None of them cared.

I found a quiet space behind the opposite end of the skate ramp. I needed to be alone with my thoughts. Why did I feel so disappointed? So empty? I'd finally had my first kiss. It didn't matter it had been with my best friend; I should have been over the moon. So, what was my problem?

Kylie suddenly appeared around the corner of the ramp, struggling to walk in her cheap heels. Why had she even bothered wearing them? It's not like we were going out nightclubbing. Seeing her caked in makeup and stumbling around in her tacky shoes under a skate ramp seemed kind of depressing.

'Seb, are you all right?'

'I'm fine. Why don't you go back to the game?'

Kylie sat down beside me. 'Are you pissed off at me?'

'No, of course not. I'm just... not into it. Not into this.'

'We can go home if you like. Back to mine? Mum will be asleep anyway – she won't notice us come in.'

We had planned to stay up all night, and then sneak back to our homes in the early hours before anyone awoke. But the idea of staying up until then was hardly appealing right now.

'Yeah, maybe in a bit. Might be a good idea.'

Kylie reached out and held my hand. 'Was it bad?'

'Was what bad?' I knew what she meant.

'The kiss, dummy. You kinda stormed off right after. I was worried it'd been bad.'

'What? No. It wasn't bad. It was just... I dunno. Not really how I'd imagined it.'

Kylie looked curious. 'How did you imagine it?'

'Not in front of a heap of losers, for one.'

'Seb, they're not losers. Not everyone's a loser just because they're different to us.'

From the moment Kylie and I had met at the beginning

of high school, we'd hit it off and been inseparable. We just seemed to be on the same page. She'd come over to my house in the afternoons during the week, and we'd spend weekends at hers. Kylie's father had left when she was young, and she'd grown up with her mum and sister, but this didn't seem to affect the atmosphere in Kylie's home. It was always somewhere happy for me to escape to when Mum and Dad were arguing, or when Dad was having a bad turn.

Something was different with her lately. She was changing, right in front of my eyes. It had always been me and her – no one else. But now she wanted to invite others into our space. Outsiders. She'd never even shown interest in male attention until she'd turned fourteen. Suddenly, it was as if there was this whole other side of her. She was turning into someone I didn't know.

'Do you want to try again?' she suddenly asked.

'What? No. That's not what I meant.'

'You might like it more this time. Without everyone sitting around watching.'

What game was she trying to play? Was she making a move on me? Is that what this was? Was she willing to jeopardise our friendship over some stupid drunken kiss in a skate park? I wasn't having any of it.

'No, Kylie. I don't want to try it again. We're just friends, okay? That's all we're ever going to be.'

'Seb, what's wrong with you? I'm not saying we have to be any more than just friends. It's just a kiss. You know what, do what you want.' She got up and walked back towards the crowd.

'Go on,' I called out. 'Why don't you kiss every bloody one of them?'

But she didn't hear me. She was already back with the animals.

I downed the rest of my beer, before dropping the empty bottle onto the concrete. It broke into pieces. I picked up my backpack and disappeared. I'd had enough for one night.

15ᵗʰ March 1997

I woke to the sound of two kookaburras laughing outside my bedroom window. Excitement swept through me as I realised what day it was. It'd felt like Saturday would never come. Each day had dragged by longer than the one before, and I couldn't stop myself from constantly checking my watch. Dad caught me doing it a couple of times, but didn't say anything. He could tell how excited I was, so I was grateful he wasn't trying to dampen my spirits. He'd done more than enough of that already. I'd been cautious not to provoke his temper during the week, focusing on completing all my duties on the farm quickly and efficiently. Maybe he'd finally realise that to get the best out of me he would need to give a little back. But I wouldn't hold my breath.

When was the last time we'd even had a barbecue? It must have been back in Perth, about a year before Mum got sick. We hadn't been spending much time together as a family. Both Mum and Dad were working late, and I spent all my free time at Kylie's house, leaving it up to my grandmother to look after Jeremy. The barbie ended up being one of the happier memories with my family. Why hadn't I treasured it more at the time?

After showering, I threw on the only shirt I could find in my wardrobe. It was lightweight, crafted from powder-blue cotton. Mum had bought it for me years ago. Luckily, it still fit. It was nice to wear something that made me feel a little smarter for a change. The late summer heat was still roasting, so I rolled the sleeves up and teamed it with a pair of grey denim shorts.

'Morning, Seb,' Dad said through a mouth full of cornflakes. 'You gonna help me set up today?'

'Yeah, sure.' What did we need to set up? It was just a barbecue.

'I'm going into town with Jeremy to pick up the meat from the butcher's and some veggies for you to make a salad. This should give you enough time to clean the house and yard.'

Of course that's what he'd meant. Nothing good ever came without a price.

Something stuck out about Dad's behaviour this morning. He was nervous. I'd been so caught up in my own excitement about our neighbours' visit that I'd totally overlooked that he also wanted to make a good impression.

It was about four-thirty when the doorbell rang. I'd finished cleaning hours earlier, and the Waldorf salad I'd made was chilling in the fridge. Dad was already outside getting the barbecue going. I opened the door.

'Hey! Welcome!' I cringed at how enthusiastic I sounded, but I couldn't hide my excitement.

'Hi, Seb,' Alison's plump lips curved into a smile. She was holding a bottle of white wine in one hand and a bottle of red in the other. 'We have no idea what your dad drinks, so we brought options.'

It didn't matter that he drank neither – it was a kind

gesture all the same.

Alison stepped inside, followed by Rob, with a six-pack under his right arm. 'If your dad's anything like me, he'll have one of these.'

It was as if Rob had heard my thoughts.

Hiding behind his parents, perpetually sulking, was Jake, who walked into the house, eyes downcast, clutching a book in one hand and a bowl of potato salad in the other. He momentarily looked up and caught my eyes with his own. They were a clear, bright blue.

Over the next hour, Dad and Rob worked the barbecue, while I helped Alison serve some of her homemade lemonade and set up the table. Jeremy had worn both himself and Scampi out racing around the yard, so the pair were snoozing on the grass.

Jake sat alone by the water tank at the back of the house reading the book he'd brought with him. Although I couldn't make out the title, its length suggested it wasn't an easy read. How long had it been since I'd read something? Reading had been my main salvation when we first moved to The Nowhere. It had been the perfect escape. Maybe it was the same for Jake. The difference was, I'd had no one to talk to but Jeremy, and he was much too young at the time for a meaningful conversation. At least Jake had the option of talking to me. It was an option he appeared to have no interest in.

I approached him, a glass of lemonade in hand. He looked up at me for a second, before turning his attention to the glass. He looked at it like it was poison.

'I'm all right.'

I knew he wasn't.

The next time I approached Jake was to let him know the food was ready. We all took our places around the table as Dad dished up the burger patties and sausages. We helped ourselves to buns, onions, tomato sauce and mustard. The conversation was light. Dad spoke to Rob at length about cricket. Alison spoke to me about my time on the farm, genuinely intrigued as to how I'd found the adjustment from city life. Jeremy was giggling at a fly stuck in his tomato sauce while secretly feeding Scampi his entire burger pattie under the table. Scampi happily swallowed it whole, patiently waiting for more. Jake didn't utter a single word the whole time. He ate half a pattie and quarter of a sausage, leaving the rest on the table in front of him.

'Would you like a beer, boys?' Dad asked.

Jake's face lit up. 'Sure, thanks.'

'He speaks.' Dad toyed, breaking the beer cap off on the table. He passed the beer over to Jake. The froth poured out the top, like a geyser releasing hot steam.

'Seb?'

It was the first time Dad had ever offered me a beer.

'Yes, please. Thanks.'

I watched as Dad carried out the same treatment for me. Holding the cold bottle in my hand, I felt a rush of acceptance.

'Tell me about your cattle, Stu,' Alison said, shifting her almond eyes from the distant paddocks to my father.

'Yeah, we've got mostly Murray Greys I bought off a guy near Warralakin when we first got here. I want to invest in some purebred Angus but bloody hell those bulls are pricey.'

It was clear how happy Dad was to be discussing his cattle. Alison had worked him out so quickly.

As the sun dipped into the horizon the conversation moved on to money, loans and the hardships of rural living. My brother, Jake and I quickly spread out across the yard. Jeremy had apparently gained a second wind, as he was back to chasing Scampi. I considered approaching Jake again to attempt a conversation but instead decided to take my beer and sit underneath the rusty windmill at the side of the house. I'd hoped the barbecue would provide the perfect opportunity to get to know him, but I was starting to realise there was no chance of this ever happening. For whatever reason, Jake didn't want to have anything to do with me. Swigging my beer alone, I decided I was going to at least savour that. Savour the moment Dad had offered me his approval.

That was when Jake sat down beside me.

Beer splashed to the ground as I jolted, pivoting to face him.

'Careful,' he said, 'you don't wanna waste it.'

Shyness seeped through me. I'd always been socially awkward, but there was more at stake here in The Nowhere next to the one person who could actually become my friend. What if I said something that sounded stupid? Chewing the inside of my cheek, I decided to remain quiet.

'You all right? Cat got your tongue or somethin'?'

His voice was different to how I'd imagined. It was deeper and didn't rise at the end. It was as if he'd trained himself to sound less country Australia than his parents.

'Sorry, yeah. I'm all good, thanks.'

'How long have you lived out here?'

'Two years now.' The words hit me as soon as I'd spoken them out loud. Two years I'd never be getting back.

'Woah, that sucks.'

'Yeah, it does.' I placed my bottle of beer on a patch of cracked, reddish earth between the dry clusters of grass. 'But it gets easier,' I lied.

Jake turned and looked towards the horizon, narrowing his eyes. 'Have you ever thought about leaving?'

He made it sound so easy. As if there hadn't been a day gone by I hadn't dreamt about escape. 'Yeah. I've thought about it.'

It went quiet.

To avoid the silence turning awkward, I quickly changed the subject. 'Your mum mentioned you surfed back in Byron?'

His eyes widened. It must have been a subject he was happy to talk about. 'It was my life back home. I'm gonna – I mean, I *was* gonna be a professional surfer.'

'You still could be?'

'Nah, not if I'm gonna be stuck out here now. I'll miss my window.' His tone was laced with disappointment. It was a feeling I knew only too well. 'But I don't plan to stick around for long. I just gotta get hold of some wheels, and I'm outta here.'

'You drive?'

'Yeah. You?'

'No, not yet. Maybe you could teach me.'

The sound of crickets in the scrub grew louder – as if they were competing with us.

'Where's your mum?'

The question hit me like a rock against the side of my head. The same way it had when Alison had asked. Jake sensed my discomfort.

'I'm sorry, mate. I shouldn't have asked.'

'No, no – it's okay.' I didn't want to make him feel awkward. It had taken long enough to get him talking to me. 'She died before we moved out here.' I spoke the words with such lack of emotion, I surprised myself.

'I'm sorry.' Another silence, which this time he broke. 'I won heaps of championships back home.'

'For surfing?' I already knew the answer, but I wanted to keep the conversation moving.

'Yeah, it's all I've ever wanted. It gives – I mean, it gave my life purpose.'

Something about his words got to me. Was it jealousy? Was that what I was feeling? Maybe it was because I'd never known what I'd wanted to be. I'd never found something I was good enough at or something I cared about enough to pursue. I was no good at maths, slightly better at English but average at everything else. Sometimes I thought I could be a tradie of some kind, but Dad always reminded me I wasn't built for it. I was more lean than skinny, but he was referring more to my character than my physical strength.

'It's all their fault.' Jake's head flicked in the direction of his parents, his fringe momentarily airborne before landing perfectly back in place. 'Stupid pair of hippies.'

It shocked me to hear him speak so negatively about his parents. That was when I realised why he was acting up. To punish them.

This time it was my turn to be sympathetic. 'I'm sorry you've been taken away from your dreams.'

Jake turned to look at me. I couldn't predict his response. He had an unnerving coldness about him, which made him impossible to read. He'd probably just shrug it off before falling silent again.

'It's all right. I'm sorry for blanking you, mate.'

Another surprise. Not just the acknowledgement, but also the apology itself.

'It's fine. Want another beer?'

Jake's eyes lit up, the same way they had earlier, and a mischievous smile broke across his face.

'Bloody oath.'

16th April 1997

My first spoonful of cornflakes was an inch away from my mouth when the doorbell rang. Dad glared at me suspiciously.

'You got a guest?' A half-chewed cornflake flew from his mouth as he spoke, landing on his chin.

'What? No. Why would I?'

'Seb's got a guest,' Jeremy piped up.

The doorbell rang again. Scampi barked.

'Well, you gonna go answer it or just sit there gawping into space?'

I leapt from the kitchen table and quickly strode towards the front door. Could it be him? I kept my fingers crossed as I swung the door open.

There he was. The chunky fringe. The thick lips. The intense eyes.

'Jake, hey. What brings you over here?'

'Hey, mate. I'm ahead on all my chores this week, so Mum said I could come see if you wanted to hang out.'

He wanted to hang out with me? Inside I was glowing, but outside I had to remain composed. He didn't know my dad at all. He couldn't just turn up unannounced and hang out with me on a weekday. Or even on the weekend, for that matter.

'G'day, Jake.' Dad appeared behind me. 'How's it going, mate?'

'It's going good.'

There was an absurdity to the moment. But I had to keep calm and think fast. I white lied: 'Jake just dropped by to see if we wanted any help on the farm today. He's ahead on all his chores.'

Jake's face dropped. Swapping his duties with mine was evidently not what he had in mind.

'Ahead on all your chores are you, mate?' Dad asked rhetorically. 'That canola's just coming on easy for you guys, isn't it?'

I held my breath, terrified Jake would give away my lie. But he remained quiet.

'Well,' Dad continued, 'I can't see why not. We're definitely not ahead with our work right now so we could do with an extra pair of hands. Come on in.'

Jake smiled and did as he was told.

What was I getting myself into?

Once the sound of Dad's ute had faded into nothing more than a distant hum as he took Jeremy to school, I took the chance to brief Jake on a few things.

'I'm really glad you came around. It'd be awesome to hang out. But Dad's unpredictable, and he won't let me slack off during the week.'

'He seems pretty cool to me.' Jake looked around the house, picking up an embarrassing photo of me from the mantelpiece while eyeing up our ugly carpet and cigarette smoke-stained wallpaper that belonged in the 1970s. 'Anyway, I'm fine with helping you guys out. I just wanted a change of scenery.'

My sigh exposed my relief. I really hadn't expected him to be okay with helping out on the farm. But I wasn't going to complain.

'Great. Come on then – I'll show you where the quad bikes are.' We had a couple spare in case ours ever broke down.

'Awesome!' Jake's face brightened like a child's. 'I didn't realise we got to ride bikes.'

If only I were as enthused by the notion.

It had been two hours of uneventful cow checking before we stopped for Dad's ciggie break. A near-invisible haze distorted the horizon, and the sweat dripping down our faces attracted a cloud of flies. Jake pulled off his t-shirt and used it to mop his brow as we moved into the shade. My eyes were immediately drawn to the large, bright white scar running across his chest.

'Christ, mate,' Dad blurted out. 'How the hell did ya get that?'

Normally I'd cringe at his tactlessness, but in this case, I stomached it. I wanted to know too.

Jake smiled proudly as he peered down at the blemish. 'Some dickhead tried to jump me, so I pushed him backwards and he fell and hit his head. He got all riled up, and when I left school one day, he was waiting for me at the gate with a chain wrapped round his fist. He whacked me right in the chest. Blood gushed out everywhere. It was pretty intense. I knocked him out afterwards, though. Broke his nose.'

I wondered whether my astonishment was written across my face. Jake's story unnerved me. Not just the violent nature of his actions, but how frankly he spoke about them. He seemed devoid of any empathy.

Dad smirked as he rolled his cigarette. 'Good on ya, mate. Bet he didn't bother you again.'

'Sure didn't.'

As soon as Dad stamped out his cigarette, we clambered back onto our quad bikes and continued our checks. I rode just behind Jake, who still had his t-shirt off. The ridges of his spine were visible through the flesh of his curved back. His story repeatedly replayed in my mind, but something didn't add up. What made the guy want to jump him in the first place? There was something about the way he acted that was just… off. I couldn't put my finger on it, but I was determined to figure it out. Not yet though. One day at a time.

11th May 1997

The cotton-wool clouds drifted by at a casual pace as Jake and I lay on our backs in the scrub. It had become a place of solace for us both, a neutral ground between both our worlds. The air was crisp, so we both rugged up with an extra layer. The relentless heat of the summer had continued longer than it should have, so we'd welcome winter tying its knot around The Nowhere. We lay side by side in silence, but it wasn't awkward. It was refreshing to be in the company of someone my own age. I knew he felt the same.

After Jake's first surprise visit, he'd started popping over unannounced to help us out on the farm. Soon, he began coming around simply to hang out. He chose his time wisely. He knew exactly when Dad dropped Jeremy off at school and picked him up, so he'd either pop over briefly during those times or call on the landline. It was as if he'd already sussed Dad out and knew better than to distract me when he was around. He also often came over during lunchtimes, which traditionally Dad and I would spend wolfing down sandwiches and Coke before getting back to our chores. Dad didn't seem to have a problem with Jake visiting on our lunch break. He'd make him a sandwich too, and tell us to take a break for half an hour or so. He also didn't seem to have too much of a problem with us hanging out on weekends, as long as I didn't miss church.

I began to see that Dad was actually glad I was making

a friend. He must have seen my unhappiness these past two years. He undoubtedly took a share of the blame for that, so if sacrificing a bit of my work time each day meant I was happier and more productive, he wasn't going to discourage it. If it was good for business, it was good for him.

Jake suddenly sat up, pulling a crumpled pack of Marlboro Lights out from his jeans pocket.

'Where'd you get those?' I asked.

'They were in the bin. Dad always chucks 'em every time he decides to give up. Or he stashes them around the house in odd places and forgets about 'em. I don't like letting them go to waste.'

I'd never tried a cigarette before. I'd never wanted to – I'd never seen the appeal. Kids smoked all the time at school. Even Kylie tried it once and offered me a drag, but it just hadn't interested me. Maybe it was because I'd watched Dad puffing away on them my whole life. I'd been put off. He'd always told me never to start. It's probably when he sounded his most compassionate. Perhaps he'd just been worried I'd pinch his.

After a brief pause, Jake's expression changed from excitement to realisation. 'You haven't tried it before, have you?'

I considered lying for a second but decided there was no point. 'Nope. Never really wanted to.'

He grinned. 'Well, I'm glad I get to do the honours.' He pulled a cherry red lighter out of his back pocket.

Why did I suddenly feel lucky? Was it acceptance? Approval? Probably a combination of both. I'd never had a friend like Jake before. He definitely would have been one of the cooler kids in school. I'd always been a drifter. I wasn't disliked by anyone, but I'd never exactly belonged to any tribe. I would've described myself as a misfit, but I was never quite edgy enough to really justify that title. As Jake proffered the pack of cigarettes, I felt cooler than I ever had before. I felt part of a tribe. Jake's tribe.

I slid out a cigarette. When Jake passed me his lighter with a devilish smirk, I was instantly reminded of how his eyes had brightened at the barbecue when I offered him the second beer. It was his self-destructive streak. Or, at least, his love of danger. I'd heard it in his stories about his life back in Byron and the things he'd got up to with his mates. It made me feel inadequate at times. I'd always been someone to play it safe. I'd never broken the rules.

Inhaling the toxic air, I was hit with an extreme head rush before breaking into a coughing fit. Jake looked on and smiled, drawing back on his cigarette with sophistication and experience. He made it look so effortless.

He grinned. 'It gets better.'

14ᵗʰ June 1997

By the time Jake appeared from amidst the bush, I had already started setting up our picnic in the small clearing. He'd told me to bring the food, and he'd bring the beer and cigarettes. I'd made cheese and ham sandwiches and grabbed a few pieces of fruit to stuff in Mum's old hamper I'd found buried away in the loft.

'You poof,' Jake laughed as he pointed at the checked picnic blanket I'd laid out on the ground.

'Shut up, dick.' I pulled the sandwiches and fruit from the hamper.

'I knew I couldn't rely on you for any decent snacks,' Jake said, reaching into his own bag. He threw a handful of lollies across the blanket. 'Here you go, mate. Want a beer?'

'Sure.'

He pulled out a couple of cold tinnies and threw one my way before fishing out a stolen pouch of tobacco. 'Dad's again,' he said, winking.

I cracked open my beer, then reached back into the hamper and pulled out a couple of books. 'Hey, I saw you reading that book when you came over for the barbie. I thought you might wanna try these if you get bored. If you haven't read them already.'

Jake began rolling two cigarettes without looking up. 'Nah, you're all right, mate. I was just being a dick bringing that round, so I had an excuse not to talk to you.'

Ouch. That hurt. I shoved the books back in the hamper.

'Chill out, mate. We're cool now. But yeah, you'd be wasting your time giving those to me. I can't read.'

'Serious?'

'Yep, well, not a novel anyway. I'm a bit dyslexic. I really struggled at school. I think that's why I was always getting myself into trouble.'

Bingo. The pieces were starting to fit together.

'I see. Sorry to hear that.'

'You're all right, mate. Wouldn't do me much good out here anyway, would it?'

'No, I suppose not. Well, if you ever want to learn, maybe I could teach you?'

Jake sneered as he passed me one of the cigarettes and the lighter. 'I bet you were top of the class at school, right?'

I sparked up and drew back. 'Nah, I was pretty average. But I know the basics. I can read a book.'

That sounded harsher than I'd meant it too. Would he be offended?

'Well, we can't be good at everything, can we?' Jake lit his cigarette and inhaled as if the smoke would make all his frustrations disappear. He angled his eyes to suss out what was going on in my head. 'You think I'm an idiot?'

'Course not. I don't think you're an idiot at all. And besides, you're going to be a champion surfer. As if anyone will care then if you can read or not.'

I was worried he'd think I was taking the piss, but he seemed satisfied with my answer. I'd meant it.

'I used to be so jealous of the clever kids at school. Guess that's why I was always starting fights.'

This was my chance. 'Is that how you ended up with that?' I pointed to the area where his scar would be under his sweater.

'Nah, I told you how I got that. I was jumped. But the guy who jumped me, I kicked the shit out of his brainy little brother.'

I winced. I was disappointed to hear Jake had targeted someone weaker than him just because they were intelligent. Maybe he deserved the scar.

'But yeah, I ended up getting expelled from three schools. In the end, my folks let me drop out. Which is why I focused on my surfing. It's all I ever loved anyway.'

At least he'd found his calling. At least his parents had encouraged him to pursue it. Until they moved to The Nowhere, that is.

'So why did you really leave Byron? You've obviously got a talent for surfing. Didn't your parents want you to continue with it?'

Jake took one long final drag of his cigarette before stubbing it out in the dirt. He looked up towards the crisp blue sky and exhaled the remainder of the smoke.

'Unfortunately, old habits die hard, mate. There was this one dude on my squad who hated me. I was a better surfer than him and he knew it. We were up in Brissy for a tournament, and he tried to pick a fight with me the night before the match. I beat the shit outta him. Let's just say, neither of us competed the next day.'

'Shit, Jake.'

'Yeah, I know. It was a poor move. I should have risen above it. We both got slung off the team, and that was it for my parents. It's true that Dad's business was going down the dunny, so me getting kicked off the surfing team was the last straw. They decided it was time for a fresh start. I guess me being dragged along with them is their idea of punishment.'

As I swallowed the chilled beer, I visualised Jake's violent stories in my head. As much as I wanted to, I couldn't quite believe everything he was telling me. After all, it was his word against those of the other guys. What if it had been him who'd picked the fight with the surfer? There seemed to be a thread of violence running through his past.

'Anyway, enough of my old shit. As much as it sucks being out here, at least I've made a mate. I guess it *is* a fresh start.' He reached out his can.

Stretching my arm out towards his, our cans collided. The aluminium slam was less satisfying than the clink of our bottles at the barbecue, but it made me feel good.

'Cheers, Seb.'

'Cheers.'

We ate the sandwiches and lollies and finished the rest of the beer. The fruit remained untouched and the novels unread.

Who was this guy?

25th June 1997

Rat-tat-tat.

Was it a branch rattling against the window?

Rat-tat-tat.

It was louder that time.

Rat-tat-tat.

My vision blurred, I made out 2:33 am on the luminous screen of my clock. Wearing just my undies, I leapt towards the window. Squinting into the inky night, I instantly recognised the form standing outside.

'Jake? Are you crazy?' I whispered loudly, carefully opening the window. I sounded as confused as I must have looked. 'What are you doing here?'

That's when I noticed the smile on his face. It was a change from the usual sulkiness. 'Can I come in?'

There was no way he could. Dad might've already woken up. Or Jeremy. It would only be a matter of time before Scampi would start barking. But if I went outside, I risked getting caught and being in even deeper trouble. I took another look at Jake. His eyes seemed to be challenging me – as if they were portals into a dimension so different to mine. A dimension that was unpredictable. Dangerous. Exciting.

'You'd better not, Jake,' I said finally. 'But hang on. I'm coming out there with you.'

After throwing on some jeans and a t-shirt, I quickly climbed out my window, leaving a slight gap so I'd easily be able to get back in. The cool air clasped my body, making me wish I'd grabbed a jumper. I paced away from the house, signalling for Jake to follow. Scampi was out back, so I led us to the front of the house and up the driveway.

Once we reached the main road, we walked about five hundred metres south, away from both our farms. Finding a scatter of bushes we could hide behind, we sat down on the grass, which was still dry from the harsh summer months. Jake pulled out a plastic carrier bag with a bottle inside it.

'Here you go, mate. This'll warm you up.'

It suddenly all made sense. I should have been furious about the early morning disruption, but I couldn't be more excited. Jake tore the plastic bag away to reveal a bottle with a quarter already missing. Russian script was wrapped around its label. Vodka.

'It's Mum's. We won't drink it all – we can just have a bit and then fill the rest with water. She'll never notice. I'm sure of it.'

Any average seventeen-year-old would have been going to pubs by now. Maybe even sneaking into the odd night-club. But we weren't average seventeen-year-olds, and The Nowhere wasn't an average place. Throwing back neat vod-ka behind the bush on the side of the road in the early hours of the morning would have to do.

Jake took the first swig. He tried to play it cool for a few seconds, but the burn kicked in and his face recoiled.

'Gross.' He stuck out his tongue.

'You're really selling this to me.'

The grimace on Jake's face was replaced with the same

mischievous grin I'd seen earlier. 'Your turn.'

Hesitantly, I took the bottle of vodka from his hands. This would be my first taste of the spirit. Dad had given me a drop of whiskey before, but he wasn't a fan of vodka. I closed my eyes and took a large gulp. It burnt my throat like I'd just swallowed acid. I gagged, before coughing a few times as my mouth went numb.

Jake burst into a fit of laughter. 'Your face. If only you could see it.'

Euphoria surged through me, partly because of the vodka and partly because of my excitement at being out so late with Jake. Before I knew it, I was laughing too. Jake took the bottle back and had another swig.

We sat for at least half an hour talking and taking it in turns to swig the neat spirit. My vision started to blur and I knew I should slow down.

'Nah, I'm good. I'll skip.'

'Pussy.' There was a vein of malice in Jake's tone, which I ignored.

As I sat on the parched blades of grass next to my friend, I couldn't help but stare at his delicate features. His high cheekbones. His masculine jawline. His vivid eyes. He was so genetically blessed. Why hadn't I been so lucky? I was so average looking compared to him. My oily skin. My wide nose. My thin lips. I studied his, comparing how much thicker they were. What would it feel like to kiss them?

You faggot.

'Are you all right?' Jake asked, before taking another swill. Was I that easy to read? 'Yeah, I'm good. Just feeling a bit pissed.'

Jake smiled back at me. 'So, I was thinking… about what you said at your barbie. About how you'd thought about running away.'

Did I even say that? The alcohol was doing its job. 'Uh, yeah. What about it?'

Jake took another sip of the vodka, this time a little smaller, before passing it back to me. He pulled out a crumpled pack of tobacco from his jeans pocket and began speedily rolling two ciggies. 'Well, once I get my hands on some wheels… why don't you come with me?'

Was he serious? I'd only known him a couple of months, and he wanted me to be part of his escape plan? It didn't matter that it sounded crazy. It also sounded bloody exciting.

'Sounds awesome.'

'Sweet. Now we just gotta get our hands on a ride.'

He passed me a perfectly rolled cigarette, before lighting his own. Turns out he was right – smoking did get better. Or at least it got easier. We'd made a habit of meeting on Saturdays and smoking. Since Jake had found a large packet of tobacco amongst his dad's things, we'd both become experts at rolling. I was particularly good after watching Dad do it for so many years. A couple of times Jake suggested I take some of Dad's tobacco, but I quickly explained to him why that was such a bad idea. I was lucky he hadn't noticed I was smoking at all. It was probably because his own clothes stunk so badly.

Carefully placing the cigarette in my mouth, the paper clung to the wet of my lips, which were cracked from the cold. My vision became hazier the more the booze kicked in. Jake reached over and lit it for me. I drew back, visualising a different existence to the one I was living. One where the sun shone, but I could enjoy it. One where the waves lapped against the sand, and I would never stop appreciating them. One where I'd be watching Jake surf, and he'd look so happy because that's all he longed to do. As the smoke drifted from our mouths into the clear night's sky, thoughts of Jake clouded my head. His toned, tanned torso. His bright blue boardies and wet hair. Watching him paddle out past where the waves break before battling against the foam. His upper arms tensing as he pulled himself upright. His body now a shimmering statue atop a surfboard, gliding through the water. It was then I realised.

It had to be the vodka. It just had to be the vodka.

I realised what had been so painfully obvious, but I hadn't allowed myself to face.

There's no way it couldn't be the bloody vodka.

'Seb?' Jake broke my train of thought as the world suddenly came back into motion. It occurred to me I'd been sitting in silence, holding my lower lip between my teeth. Like I'd gone into a trance. I wanted to peel all my thoughts away like scabs. I stared down at my tingling hands. They were red and swollen from the night's chill.

'I think that vodka's hit you pretty hard, mate,' Jake continued, taking one last drag on his cigarette before stamping it out. His moonlit eyes glistened.

'Yeah, I think you're right… mate. I reckon I should go to bed. I'm feeling pretty beat.'

Jake laughed again. 'No worries. We can talk about this another time.'

Standing up slowly, I began pacing back towards the house.

'See ya, then!' Jake shouted from behind me.

But I didn't look back.

22nd May 2017

'Morning, Seb.' Sophie peeled her eyes away from her phone. 'How was your weekend?'

'Yeah, not too bad thanks. Yours?'

'Pretty good, thanks. Over too fast. But then they always are, right?'

I nodded. 'They sure are. Hey, do you know if Sandra's still here?'

'Yeah, she's in the staff room now. You've just caught her.'

After a weekend of hardly any sleep, I'd been dreading going to work and facing her. Why had I agreed to go on a date with her in the first place? I should've known better than to lead her on. It must have been my yearning for friendship. Why was I always so selfish?

Sandra was thankfully still in the staff room when I entered, sitting at the table on her own with a mug of coffee.

'Hey, Sandra. Can we talk?'

She paused for a few moments, before tilting her head up to look at me. 'Sure.'

Breathing slowly, I sat down next to my colleague and readied myself to tell her the truth. What did I have to lose?

'Okay. So I had a lovely time on Friday night. Thank you for that. But I should have been upfront with you from the start. I'm… I'm gay. And I know, it's 2017 and it's not a big deal, but I don't have many people in my life that I'm close to these days. So I never really talk about it. But I should have told you by now, just to avoid the sort of awkwardness we ended up having after dinner. So I'm sorry. I hope I haven't messed up our chance of being friends.'

There was a brief break as Sandra processed my words.

'Are you done?'

'I think so.'

She smiled. 'Well, first of all, that's the most I've heard you talk about yourself. Ever. So for that, I'm grateful. And I'm also happy you were finally able to let me in. It means a lot, Seb.'

Instant relief. Our conversation could have gone two ways, so thankfully she took the softer approach.

'And you're right – it *is* 2017. This means a girl can ask a guy out for dinner but not mean for it to be romantic.'

I cringed. How had I been so presumptuous?

'But I guess that's a relief,' she continued. 'If you had thought I was making a move and you rejected me, I'm glad it was because you're into guys.'

She started laughing, which prompted me to do the same.

'I just wish you could have told me sooner. I might not be able to be your girlfriend, but I'd love to be your friend.'

I nodded, still smiling. 'I'd like that too. Very much.'

There was so much more I wanted to tell her. But one thing at a time.

You can't keep it secret forever. The truth always comes out eventually.

14th July 1997

It was a fresh, still morning. The kind where the sky is clear and the weak winter sun casts sharp shadows across the landscape. The bitter air blew against the back of my neck as I walked down to the bush to meet Jake. It was the first time we were hanging out since the vodka incident. I'd pushed my confusion to the back of my mind and decided I'd just pick up where we left off. My friendship with him meant too much to me to jeopardise over some bizarre drunken thoughts.

Jake was wearing his classic t-shirt and jeans, but with a heavy denim jacket thrown over the top. I wore a chunky knit to protect me from the bitter chill. We were only meeting briefly while Dad dropped Jeremy off at school, so I walked quickly to make the most of the time.

'Hey, stranger,' he said, kicking off the conversation without an ounce of awkwardness. Fog drifted from his mouth as he spoke.

'Hey, sorry. It's been full-on on the farm.' I sounded convincing.

'No worries, mate. Same on mine. You all right?' He was obviously referring to my drunken episode.

'Yeah, sorry about the other night. I hadn't drunk anything that strong in a long time, think I had a weird reaction to it.'

'No drama, mate. Long as we're all good.'

'Course we are.'

'Sweet. So, you thought about what I said? That's if you remember.'

Of course I remembered. And of course I'd been thinking about it. I hadn't been able to stop imagining what it would be like to run away with Jake and never return. Away from Dad, away from the isolation, away from The Nowhere. It would be a new beginning. One I'd been dreaming about for the last two years. But it was the thought of leaving my brother behind that held me back. How could I live with myself? Dad could be violent, but I copped the worst of it. This shielded my brother. With me out the picture, would Jeremy be the new target? Dad would have lost the only other person able to work on the farm, so he'd be even angrier. I didn't doubt for a second he'd have Jeremy helping him out as soon as physically possible.

As difficult as it was, I had to accept Jeremy couldn't keep me from leaving. I'd managed to come to terms with this when Dad had agreed to buy me a car. Deep down, I knew that my longing to escape was enough to keep my guilt at bay. And it wasn't like Jeremy would be far behind me. As soon as he reached a legal age, he'd be driving away from The Nowhere himself as fast as his car could take him. Or I'd be coming back to get him.

'I do remember. And I still wanna come.' I couldn't see any reason why I would say no to Jake. Not only was he my only friend, he also offered a real chance for me to escape the farm. He knew how to drive. He had a licence. All we needed was a ride, and that would be it. The Nowhere would be a distant memory, disappearing into the red dirt behind us.

His face gleamed. 'Awesome. Now we just gotta get our hands on some wheels.'

Excitement fluttered inside my stomach like bats frantically hitting the sides of a cave. 'For sure. This, as you know with my dad, could be a problem from my side.'

Jake had never explained why getting a car would be difficult for him. His parents seemed so nice and chilled. Surely it wouldn't be an issue?

'Yeah, that sucks. It's the same for me. My folks say they'll get me one eventually, but I swear they're prolonging it as long as possible to stop me leaving. They need all the help they can get. Plus, you know. Trouble cutting the cord.'

It suddenly dawned on me I wasn't the only one with a parent trying to prevent me from escaping The Nowhere. I wasn't the only one being held captive to fulfil my duties on the farm. We were slaves to our own families. It didn't matter Jake's parents were friendly and New Age. They still needed to make a living.

'That sucks,' I said finally.

'It's all right. I'll think of something. We'll think of something.'

There was something about his assertive tone that put my mind at ease. Something that gave me hope for the future. It was a feeling I hadn't experienced in a long time. My eyes traced the hairs along Jake's arm. They were so even. So intricately positioned.

'Hey, in the meantime, I've got something I was gonna ask you,' he went on. 'My folks are heading back up to Byron for the weekend, my grandma's been rushed to hospital, and they wanna go see her before she carks it.'

I had to hold myself back from laughing at his dark humour. Only Jake could turn something so sad into a joke.

'I'm sorry to hear that,' I eventually mustered.

'It's all right, mate. We're not close. Anyway, they want me to stay here to look after the farm. You wanna stay over this weekend?'

The bats were back. Flapping against my rib cage with their elasticated wings. It was a mixture of excitement and fear. Would Dad allow me to stay over? It was unlikely, which was completely ridiculous. Six months short of officially being an adult, surely I could make my own decisions about staying over a friend's place for the night?

'All good if you're busy,' he said, half sarcastically.

I laughed. 'Sounds fun, let me just check with the old man. But should be fine.'

He nodded.

I liked that Jake didn't question my relationship with Dad. It would have been stupid for him to assume I could do what I wanted. But I hoped more than anything Dad would say yes.

'Cool, mate. Let me know.'

'I better get back, he'll be home soon.'

'I know. Same time tomorrow?'

'Sure. Same time tomorrow.'

*

I knew I'd have to find the right time to speak to Dad. I observed his moods closely, like a bird circling the water before swooping down to swipe a fish. The first part of the day was a write-off. He was in the sort of mood where he just wanted us to keep quiet and get on with our work. We managed to get through all our chores faster than usual, so I noticed his mood lift by the time he was lighting up a cigarette on the porch in the dull afternoon sun.

'Dad,' I began hopefully, 'can I ask you something?'

'Sure, Son. As long as it's not about a bloody car again.'

'No, it's not. I know I won't be getting one of those for a while.' Maybe playing the victim would help with my request.

'What are you after, Seb?'

I decided to just get it over with quickly. 'Oh, it's just Jake's family have invited me over for dinner on Saturday. And they've asked if I wanna crash.'

Surely a little white lie wouldn't hurt?

'We live five minutes away, Seb. Why would you need to stay over there?' Dad drew back on his cigarette. 'You're not planning on getting up to any mischief, are you?'

Goosebumps covered my body and the little hairs on the back of my neck stood up. Did Dad suspect something? Was it that obvious to everyone but myself? That would be stupid. Of course he didn't. He must have been talking about us drinking. After all, we were two teenage boys.

'Of course not,' I answered in a beat.

He started to laugh. 'Oh, calm down, Seb. I was young once too, you know.'

What was this? Was he trying to relate to me?

'Look, sure. As long as we get all our work done this week, you can crash at your mate's. Just make sure you both behave. We get on with these neighbours. We don't want to ruin that.'

Euphoria. Relief. Excitement. All at once. But I made sure I played it cool. I didn't want to mess anything up and make him go back on his word.

'Great. Cheers, Dad.'

'Now come on.' He stamped out his ciggie. 'In case you've forgotten, we've got work to do.'

I was particularly upbeat that night. I couldn't wait to tell Jake the good news. Why had he invited me to stay? Dad was right. We did only live five minutes away. Really, it wasn't necessary. Could Jake be feeling the same confusion I was about him? As if. Jake was obviously just excited to smoke a heap of his dad's tobacco and skull his mum's vodka with someone who would be happy to participate. I could have been anyone. Anyone that would have made him feel less alone in his self-destruction.

'You're quiet,' Jeremy said.

Scrubbing the remaining mashed potato and gravy off Dad's plate, I turned to look at my brother, who was obediently drying each piece of cutlery. I'd been so distant with him lately. Before Jake turned up, Jeremy and Scampi were all I had. It was easy to forget I was the only person my brother had, too. It wasn't exactly easy for him to make friends at school, what with Dad never letting him hang out with the other kids at their homes or at ours. It also reminded me how observant he was and how quickly he was growing up. I decided I'd make more time for him.

'Sorry, J.' I dried my hands on a tea towel. 'I'm just tired. We've been working heaps hard lately.'

'That's okay.' There was a brief pause before he spoke again. 'Can you help me with something?'

'Sure, dude. What with?'

'Come with me,' Jeremy pointed towards his bedroom. I followed quietly, making sure not to disturb Dad as he dozed in front of the television with the footy blaring.

What could Jeremy possibly need my help with? He occasionally asked me to help with his homework, but it was rare as he was a bright kid. Much brighter than I was at his age.

We walked into the dark room. Jeremy switched on the lamp on his bedside table.

'Here, look.' He pointed towards the window.

A huntsman was perched on the windowsill, the size of my outstretched hand. Even in the dull light, I could see the tiny hairs scattered all over the spider's spindly legs. It was a relief it was nothing more serious. Jeremy had always been scared of spiders. We used to get heaps of them back in Perth, mainly redbacks out in the garden shed. They didn't seem to lurk in The Nowhere as much. But this hairy fella had obviously lost its way from the bush and found itself in my brother's bedroom. Sitting on the bed, I patted the spot next to me, closer to the windowsill. Jeremy hesitated, before walking over and sitting down.

Seeing Jeremy's reaction to the spider reminded me how young and innocent he was. Sure, he was growing up fast. But he was still just a kid who happened to have been through a lot in his short life. That he'd approached me about the huntsman reminded me that he would always come to me instead of Dad for help, despite how distant I'd been with him. He'd always be my little brother, who would look up to me.

'J, there's nothing to be scared of. He's not going to hurt you.'

Jeremy sat in silence, staring at the huntsman.

'Here, look. This is a friendly spider, not a scary one. His name's Harry.'

'Harry?'

'Yeah, Harry,' I improvised. 'He's Harry the friendly huntsman and he's here to keep the flies away.'

'Really?' Jeremy asked, his eyes widening with curiosity.

'For sure. So you've got to learn to live with him. He's not going to hurt you, I promise.'

My brother continued to sit in silence. I softly turned his face towards mine with my thumb and index finger.

'Nothing's ever going to hurt you, all right? You have my word on that.'

Jeremy nodded obediently. I watched his head slowly turn back to the spider. 'Hello, Harry.'

I smiled. Leaning down, I gave Jeremy a gentle kiss on the head. 'Goodnight, J. And remember, you've got nothing to be scared of.'

He bobbed his head in agreement.

I left Jeremy with his newfound friend and went to bed.

How could I leave him here alone?

19ᵗʰ July 1997

Two cockatoos squawked as I approached Jake's house. I looked up at their brilliant yellow feathers as they soared through the clear sky. Even though the mid-winter chill cut right into the marrow of my bones, it was still a beautiful morning. The kind where the sun lightens the sky into a silver-blue. It was going to be a good day.

After standing on the porch just short of a minute, I finally summoned the courage to knock on the door. Compared to ours, which was sheathed in a thick layer of dust and covered in cracks, it was in perfect condition. Jake's family must have found a buyer for their maturing crops, as they were constantly improving the house. My mind had been so preoccupied on my walk over I hadn't even noticed how much the canola had grown since my last visit, nor that Rob and Alison's ute was absent. They must have already left for Byron.

Jake swung the door open. 'Hey, mate. You're just in time for brekkie. Have you eaten?'

I shook my head. My stomach had been churning and food had been the last thing on my mind.

'Perfect. I'm just about to make pancakes. Come in.'

As I followed Jake inside, I realised I'd never actually been any further than the front porch. It had that same idyllic feel it had the day I'd sat outside with Alison. But inside was a slightly different story. Tins of paint sat in the corners of every room, and countless colour swatches dotted the walls. Tack strips framed the untreated floorboards, and a stale smell of sawdust lingered.

'I know, it's a state in here. Mum keeps urging Dad and me to sort it out, but we just haven't got around to it yet. Besides, she can't seem to decide on a colour.'

'Don't apologise. You've seen my place – it's hardly a palace.'

'Yeah, but at least yours feels like a home.'

I would've described my house as many things, but not a home. It'd never felt like that, nor did I expect it to. It was the same with our house in Perth. It stopped feeling like home after Mum died.

'It doesn't feel like that to me,' I uttered as I followed him down the narrow hallway.

Walking into Jake's kitchen was refreshing. Even though the structure of the house mirrored ours, the kitchen walls had been painted sherbet lemon and new cabinets had been installed. The room felt big and bright.

'This isn't so bad,' I offered.

'Yeah, one of Mum's only conditions about moving out here was that she got her kitchen looking swish as soon as possible.'

So it'd been Rob's idea to come here, not Alison's. The scenario echoed that of my own parents. Sitting myself down at the kitchen table, I decided to dig a little deeper. 'It was your dad who made you all move out here?'

'Oh yeah.' Jake pulled a frying pan out the cupboard. 'He's always had this hippy dream to leave the city and live out in the sticks. I think he just talked Mum into it, to be honest. Me screwing up was just another reason to pick up and leave.'

As Jake opened the fridge to hunt for the eggs, I started to realise how many parallels there were between his life and mine. Although he was an only child, seeing inside Jake's home offered a glimpse of what my life could have been like if Mum hadn't passed away. She probably would have stopped fighting Dad about leaving Perth in the end and given life on the farm a try. I would have been so much happier to have her with me in The Nowhere. She would have found a way to make everything better. It was sad Jake would never get to meet her.

Jake cracked an egg open and dropped it into the flour.

'Need any help?'

'Nope, I've got it covered.' Jake moved around the kitchen quickly, seemingly knowing what he was doing.

'Okay, well just let me know if you do.' I couldn't help but smile as I watched on. I would have been just as happy with a slice of toast or bowl of cornflakes.

Jake flipped the final pancake and joined me at the table. We proceeded to cover them in freshly squeezed lemon juice and sugar.

'Go on then, mate. Tuck in.'

It didn't take much persuasion. All the confusion circling my head vanished at the thought of the fun weekend ahead. That's all that mattered. The future could wait.

'Well, at least we've lined our stomachs now,' Jake said with his customary rebellious grin.

I'd been right to assume there'd be booze involved, I just didn't realise it'd be making an appearance so soon. My expression must have given away my surprise.

'Don't look so scared. We don't need to have a drink until later. And no vodka this time, I promise. Let's just stick to beer.'

I smiled in agreement. I didn't want to ruin the weekend with my dumb insecurities.

'I was thinking we could go camping tonight,' Jake continued.

Another surprise. 'Camping? Where?'

'In the bush, idiot. Where else?'

'Do you even have a tent?' I realised how stupid my question was as soon as I'd asked it.

'Why would I ask if I didn't have a tent?' Jake raised an eyebrow then laughed. 'So what d'ya think? Are you in or are you out?'

I paused momentarily, weighing up my options. They were limited. Besides, camping outside with Jake with no worry about having to get home? It actually sounded pretty fun.

'I'm in.'

After we gave the kitchen a quick clean, we packed up our overnight bags and set off with Jake's camping equipment. I'd never even been camping before. Dad had suggested it several times for our annual summer holiday, but Mum decided she worked hard enough to deserve a swanky hotel by the beach once a year. This meant my experience in pitching a tent was limited.

'It's all good.' Jake began sorting out the poles, which clanked as he removed them from the bag. 'Watch and learn.'

We'd found the best spot in the scrub to set up our tent. It turned out Jake was a pro.

'My folks are hippies, what did you expect? All my holidays were in campgrounds.'

'I wish my parents had done this with Jeremy and me growing up.'

'Well, you're doing it now. Aren't you?' Jake flashed a dimple.

I smiled back and nodded. 'Sure am.'

The winter afternoon slipped into premature twilight, prompting Jake to reach into his bag and pull out a couple of tinnies.

'I think we're done,' he announced with a burst of achievement before cracking open two beers and handing me one. Cold foam dripped down and covered both our hands. 'Cheers, mate. To us!

Happiness fizzed through me as I knocked the can against his.

'To us.'

The moon glowed as darkness swathed The Nowhere. Deciding not to risk starting a campfire amongst the tinder-dry grass, we instead zipped ourselves up in the fluorescent green tent and began stuffing our faces with potato chips and Tim Tams Jake had taken from the pantry. Dad rarely bought junk food, so both were a novelty to me. It took me back to afternoons with Kylie after school when we spent all our pocket money at the 7-Eleven.

We smoked our way through an entire pack of Marlboro Lights, opening a small vent in the tent to allow the smoke to drift out. We dropped the stumps into a beer can. They hissed as they made contact with the small drop of grog we'd left.

'You wanna try something new?' Jake pulled out a small copper tin from his bag of supplies.

What road was he taking me down now? He'd already introduced me to smoking and drinking, so there was only one logical answer. Jake opened the tin to reveal exactly what I'd expected to see. Little green buds ground up to create the perfect consistency for smoking.

'Woah. Where'd you get that?'

'Come on, Seb. You know my dad's a hippy, right?' He flashed a toothy smile.

The thought hadn't even dawned on me that Jake's dad could be a stoner. Maybe because it was the last thing I could imagine my dad ever doing. Although he'd smoked my whole life, he had a strong stance on the use of illegal drugs. As did Mum. This was why I felt so uncertain about trying them myself. Was Jake dragging me into his world of risk and self-destruction?

You're letting him. You know you're letting him, faggot.

'I dunno. I'm not sure about this.'

Jake rolled his eyes. 'Oh, come on Seb. Don't be a pussy. It's no worse than knocking back vodka. People act far worse when they drink booze than when they smoke weed. It's scientifically proven. Let's face it, it's just a bloody plant.'

He had a point. It wasn't like he was handing me a fist full of ecstasy.

And if he did you'd probably do that too, wouldn't you? You'd do anything he tells you to, queer boy.

'All right, you win. Let's do it.'

Jake flashed that smile again. A sign he'd won, once again.

'Awesome. Let's get fucking high.'

Jake rolled the joint with skill and precision. It wasn't the first time he'd done it. Heaps of people tried weed in high school, but much like smoking cigarettes, it was something that was never on my radar. But if there were ever going to be a right time to try it, it would be in the tent with Jake.

'So when's the first time you tried this shit?'

Jake was quiet for a few moments as he tightened the joint. He inspected it with pride. I was certainly no expert, but I could see it was a well-made spliff.

'Would you believe me if I told you I was twelve?'

My face said it all.

A roar of laughter escaped his mouth. 'I know. It's pretty bad, right?'

'I'm not judging you.'

I was being honest. Who was I to judge Jake? Who knew what sort of childhood he'd had?

'I guess Dad openly smoking it at home makes it feel pretty normal. He'd smoked it around me heaps of times growing up, so I kinda was too. Passive smoking, y'know.'

Jake lit the joint and took a long drag. A smoke ring fled

his lips and headed straight towards the gap in the tent. The smoke seeped out into the rapidly cooling night air. 'I used to hang around with a couple of guys who were a few years older than me. I guess because I didn't have an older brother or anything, they kinda took on that role. They just happened to be complete stoners.'

He passed me the joint. I hesitated. He could sense my uncertainty. He tried a different approach. 'You know you don't have to do anything you don't want to, mate.'

I nodded. The reverse psychology worked. Or at least, I let Jake believe it did.

I lifted the joint to my lips and took a small toke. The sweet-but-stale scented smoke rushed down my oesophagus and into my lungs. Even though I'd already smoked half a dozen cigarettes, this gave me an instant head rush.

The moonlight beamed through the tent to create a green cast that illuminated the glint in Jake's eye. 'How you feeling, mate?'

I answered by taking a slightly bigger toke and holding my breath for a moment before exhaling.

'Here, try this,' Jake said. 'Open your mouth.'

I passed him the joint and he took another drag before leaning in towards my face. I felt dizzy. Was he about to kiss me? I had to be imagining it. Was this the effect of the weed kicking in already? My heart rate quickened. I resisted the urge to pull away.

Kiss him, fag. You know you want to.

Jake's soft lips touched mine as he blew the smoke directly into my mouth. I instantly coughed it all back out.

Jake laughed. 'Your first shotgun, mate.'

I must have looked confused, but I quickly pieced together what he meant.

You stupid queer boy. You actually thought he was going to kiss you. Not everyone's a poof like you.

'Thanks?'

'Don't worry. You'll learn.'

As Jake and I sat sharing the rest of the joint, the embarrassment of the near-kiss soon slipped away. Everything he said became increasingly funny with every toke. Before long, both of us had erupted into fits of laughter.

'Wanna go outside?' Jake asked as the laughter eased. 'Go and have a bit of an adventure?'

It was cold outside compared to the cosy warmth of our tent, but an adventure sounded like a fun idea.

'Sure.'

We climbed out the tent and lay on the dehydrated grass, staring at the indigo sky above. Countless stars freckled the skyscape. Were they burning brighter than normal, or was it the weed playing tricks on me?

'It blows your mind, doesn't it?' Jake said suddenly.

'The weed?'

He pointed towards the sky.

'No, dummy. Just how big it all is. And how small we are. How insignificant we are.'

'I guess we are, aren't we? It always gives me a bit of comfort looking up there though. Makes me feel less alone, you know?'

'I know. But you're not alone anymore, are you?'

Was it the beer or the weed talking? Either way, it made me happy to hear him say those words.

'I know. And I'm grateful for it.'

There was a long pause before Jake asked: 'Have you ever been with a girl?'

It took me completely by surprise. 'What?'

'You know, as in fucked one.' He unnecessarily spelt it out.

'Where did that come from?'

'Just wondered. It's okay. You don't have to answer.'

'Well, sure I have,' I lied.

Jake laughed. 'You don't sound very convincing. It's all right, mate. There's plenty of time.'

Where was this going? Embarrassment leached back into my bloodstream. There was something about his tone that made me feel so small. So inferior. Just because he had a bit more life experience didn't make him any better than me. He was only a couple of months older, and he hadn't been through the things I'd been through. He'd never lost a parent. He had no idea how that felt.

'Have you?' I found myself asking without thinking.

Jake sniggered. 'Yeah, a few. It's no big deal though.'

I didn't say anything. I wasn't sure if he was telling the truth or not, but I assumed he had no reason to lie. He was a good-looking guy with heaps of confidence. Why wouldn't he have been laid by now?

There's the proof for you, faggot. He's straight and you're not. You might as well just get over it and move on.

'Jesus, it's cold out here,' Jake continued. 'Shall we go

back in?'

'Sure.'

I followed him back inside the tent that smelt of weed, tobacco and potato chips.

My eyelids felt heavy. I could see Jake was feeling tired too as he pulled out a single sleeping bag and unzipped it.

'Sorry, mate. Only have one.'

'It's all right.' I pulled the collar of my jumper up over my neck. Even with the tent zipped up it was freezing cold. 'I'm warm enough.'

Jake suddenly pulled off his sweater and t-shirt at the same time. His skin was much paler than the last time I'd seen him with his top off. His scar stood out like a lake in the desert. I realised I was staring blankly at him, so I forced myself to look away.

'It's all right, dumbass. You're allowed to look. Here, have this. It'll keep you warm.' He threw the sweater and t-shirt at me.

'Thanks,' I said, trying to decipher his comment. Why did he tell me it was okay for me to look? Did he know how I was feeling? Was it that painfully obvious?

Course it is you fucking faggot. Obvious to everyone apart from you.

I could hear him unbuckling his belt and unzipping the fly of his jeans. This was followed by the sound of his crumpled denim being thrown to the side of the tent. I shut my eyes, wrapping myself up in Jake's sweater and t-shirt. They had his scent, mixed with weed and beer. I tried to convince myself I didn't like it.

We lay in silence for half an hour or so. It was hard to tell if Jake was sleeping, but I was now wide-awake, half strung out from the joint, half petrified by my feelings. It was so clear to me now. No matter how much I tried to push it away. I was attracted to him, and that attraction intensified every moment we spent together. What would Dad say? What would Mum have thought? What would Jake think? Would he disown me as a friend? Did he know? Was he fucking with me? I couldn't process all my thoughts. A knot formed in my stomach that physically hurt. I listened out for Jake's breathing, to see if he was asleep or not. Nothing. Silence. Was he doing the same to me? I realised I was shivering.

'Seb, mate. Get in.'

I froze. Was he for real? Was he really asking me to get in his sleeping bag with him? He only had undies on. Surely he was playing a prank on me. Or worse. Could he be testing me, only to beat me up when I fail? I wouldn't put it past him.

'Nah, you're all right, mate,' I said in the deepest voice I could manage.

'Seb... get in.'

This time I realised it wasn't a joke, but a command. I put down his sweater and t-shirt and slowly shifted over to where he was lying. He moved over to give me enough room to wiggle my way into the sleeping bag, but I kept my back turned to him. Jake wrapped his arms around my waist. His warm body pressed against me, his soft groin against my arse. My heart started beating rapidly. There's no way he couldn't feel it.

'Night, mate,' he said.

'Night… mate.'

Then silence. Just the steady rhythm of our breathing, which I managed to synchronise by taking deep breaths, in turn slowing my heartbeat.

Happiness and self-hatred slapped me simultaneously. What did this mean? I knew then that I was a fag. It all made sense now. But was Jake? He couldn't be a fag. It just didn't add up. He'd bragged about the girls he'd slept with. He'd heard me shivering, so he must have just been keeping me warm. Not to mention he was pretty bloody drunk and high.

In that moment, the aching longing to be somewhere else was finally gone. Somewhere that wasn't The Nowhere. Somewhere that wasn't my own skin. In the darkness, I was sure I could hear the night whispering to me. Telling me its secrets, now it knew mine.

21st July 2017

A burgundy film glazed Sandra's lips as she sipped her pinot noir. She studied my eyes carefully, making sure I'd finished talking. 'So that's when you realised?'

I downed what was left of my beer. 'I guess so, deep down. But it took me a lot longer to accept it. Want another one?'

Sandra shook her head. 'I'm all right for the moment. You go ahead though.'

Normally I wouldn't, but the extra drink felt necessary on this occasion. I was numb. It was the first time I'd spoken to someone about Jake. Ever. Not even in any of my half-hearted relationships had I even uttered his name. Nor had I spoken about the long, sad days in The Nowhere. How I'd wanted so badly to escape. How we both had. It made it all feel so real, and not just a distant memory that I'd blocked out for so long.

But beneath the numbness, there was another feeling, like the dull throb of a tooth extraction beneath the anaesthetic. Relief. Relief I was finally beginning to release what I'd been carrying inside me for so long. There was something about Sandra that put me at ease. At that moment I felt like I could tell her anything.

On my way back to the table I passed an old man tapping ferociously on a poker machine. He almost knocked into me as he fist pumped the air, releasing an ecstatic roar.

An overpowering smell of beer, smoke and body odour followed.

'Looks like someone won big.' I laughed as I sat down.

Sandra grinned. 'He sure did. This place is so daggy, right?'

'We can go somewhere else?'

'Oh no, it's fine. I'm just kidding. There's something charming about these old pubs, don't you think?'

'Yeah, I guess so.' I supped the liquid through the frothy head of my beer. 'Thank god Dad doesn't come to them anymore. He was quite addicted to pokies at one point when we were kids. Mum freaked out when he lost a few hundred dollars one night.'

'Ouch. I'm not surprised.' Sandra swept her hair back from her face. Her expression had changed. I knew she had a difficult question in store for me.

'What?'

'Nothing. Why?'

'I dunno, you just look… deep in thought. Like you want to ask me something.'

'You know me too well already, Seb.'

'Fire away.'

'I was going to ask–'

A growl from the man behind interrupted her momentarily.

'There go his winnings!' Sandra joked, possibly to lessen the blow of her question. Her eyes focused back on mine and she drew a short breath. 'I was going to ask you about your mum.'

I flinched. I knew this would be coming sooner or later.

'You obviously don't have to talk about it.'

'It's okay. It was a long time ago.'

'I'm sure it doesn't make talking about it any easier.'

I drank more of my beer. I was starting to feel more relaxed, which was why I didn't mind opening old wounds. It was probably why Sandra had suggested the pub. 'Breast cancer. Unfortunately, treatment wasn't anywhere near as advanced back then as it is now. It had already spread to her other organs by the time she was diagnosed.'

'I'm sorry, Seb.' Sandra reached out and squeezed my hand.

'It's okay. I do think about it a lot though. How different things would have been if she'd been around. On the farm. With Jake.'

'I'm sure she would be very proud of you.'

I necked the rest of my drink. I wasn't so sure.

26th January 1995

Dad led Jeremy and me down the stretching corridor towards Mum's ward. The sterile smell of antiseptic I'd come to know so well filled me with dread. Every nurse looked at us with the same sympathetic expression. The expression that said it all: *Your mother is dying.*

We entered the room and Dad left us to it. He'd be back soon enough to come get us. I knew we had to make the most of every second we had alone with Mum. Every moment. She looked so different now. I barely recognised her pale, gaunt face. Her skin was ghost white. All of her hair had fallen out from the chemotherapy. The dark circles under her eyes made them look hollow. It was as if she'd already left us. All that remained was her soft voice: 'Hello, boys.'

'Hi, Mum,' I said meekly.

'You look scary,' Jeremy added.

I winced. If only he was a bit older and could realise the enormity of the situation. If only both of us were older. It wasn't fair. Why us? Why Mum? Why was she being taken from us now? She would never see us grow up. Get jobs. Get married. Have kids of our own. Why was this happening to *us*?

Mum managed a little laugh. 'I know, Jeremy. But it's still me. It's still me, okay?'

Jeremy stared blankly until he finally managed a nod.

'And I don't want you to remember me like this. Okay,

Jeremy? You too, Sebastian. I want you to remember me the way I was.'

Mum had been beautiful. I suppose every child thinks the same about their mother, but mine really was. Dad always said he'd landed on his feet when he met her, and he was right. I would never forget the image I had of Mum before she got sick. That's how I'd remember her forever.

'You still look beautiful, Mum. Just as beautiful as you ever did.'

She smiled a tear and reached out to grasp my hand in hers. 'Now you boys have got to be strong, okay? You've got to be my brave boys. Can you do that for me?'

We must have looked terrified as we nodded back. Terrified of the responsibility.

'Sebastian, you have to look after your brother now,' she went on. 'And both of you look after your father. You have to be men now. Can you do that for me?'

'Yes, Mum.' I held back the tears.

'Jeremy?'

'Yes, Mummy.'

'Good boys. Now, come here and give me a big hug.'

We wrapped our arms around her emaciated frame, careful not to hurt her. I wanted nothing more than for her to squeeze back the way she used to. That strong embrace that made me feel so safe. But she couldn't.

'I love you both so, so much.' Her voice was a trembling whisper. 'Never forget that, okay?'

'We won't,' I said, wiping the tears from her eyes. 'We love you too. I love you too.'

'I love you too,' Jeremy copied.

I knew that would be the last time we saw her.

20th July 1997

With my eyes still closed, I fumbled around the empty space next to me. That's when I realised I was alone inside the sleeping bag. When I opened my eyes, it became clear I was also alone in the tent. Jake was gone.

I unzipped the tent. It was a misty morning, silent but for the cry of a lone crow perched somewhere in the canopy of silver gums surrounding us. Jake was sitting a few metres away with his back to me. He was dressed. He must have already gone back to the house and come back. Was he pissed off? Did he feel embarrassed about what happened? That must have been it. I couldn't stop myself calling out anyway: 'Jake, are you all right?'

Jake shrugged his shoulders. A lump appeared in my throat. I'd fucked it up. I shouldn't have got into his sleeping bag. I'd embarrassed him and now lost a friend. The only friend I had in The Nowhere.

What's wrong with you, queer boy? Why'd you have to screw it up? Couldn't you see he's not a poof like you?

'Okay. Well, I'll start taking down the tent.'

'Mum left a message. Grandma died,' Jake said.

I paused, before releasing a quiet sigh of relief. Even though he'd told me he wasn't close to his grandma, it clearly still had an impact. Maybe he felt guilty for not going with his parents. Maybe this was the first time he'd lost somebody.

'I'm sorry, Jake. Is there anything I can do?'

'Nah, don't worry about it. I think I just wanna be by myself for a while. Don't worry about taking down the tent. I'll sort that out.'

I got the hint. I was disappointed our weekend was being cut short so abruptly. Couldn't I have at least stayed the rest of the day? I wanted to be there for him.

'Okay, no worries. I'm sorry, again.'

'Not your fault,' he said flatly.

Was I being paranoid or was there hostility in his tone? Picking up my bag and throwing in a few items that were scattered around the tent, I set off home without stopping to look back.

Dad was already up and cooking breakfast for himself and Jeremy when I got back to the house. I'd forgotten it wasn't a church day.

'You're home early,' Dad sounded surprised.

'Yeah.'

'Well, I've only made enough brekkie for J and me. But I can fix you some up in a minute.'

'It's all right. I'm gonna take a shower and then I'll make something. Thanks, though.'

I turned the water up so hot it reddened my flesh. It was as if I was trying to burn away a layer of who I was. Shed a skin. Start again. Why was I such a fool? Only a fool would be attracted to his friend. His *male* friend.

Faggot. Faggot. Faggot.

But why would he ask me to get into the sleeping bag with him? Why would he wrap his arms around me? Did he know how I was feeling? If he did, why was he tormenting me?

Queer boy. Queer boy. Queer boy.

I turned up the water, the pressure pummelling my body. I was done with The Nowhere. Done with Jake. Done with myself.

Dad banged on the bathroom door.

'How long you gonna be in there, boy? You think we're made of money?'

I turned off the shower. 'Sorry, Dad.'

*

The frosty air embraced me as I stepped outside. I placed Scampi's bowl down on the porch. He launched forward and began eating. I sat down on the ground next to him. He stopped for a moment, looking up at me to see if I was in the mood to play, but resumed his dinner, probably noticing my odd, reflective mood. I stared up at the same velvet sky Jake and I had lay beneath last night. It was clear enough to see the purple and orange swirls of the Milky Way. The Southern Cross shone down in all its patriotic glory. I felt a pang of guilt.

As I glanced over to the silver crescent moon, which was half obscured by a crawling cloud, I heard my mother's voice for the first time in a long while: 'It's okay, Seb. I love you no matter who you are.' Her soothing tone seemed as real as it had the last time she'd spoken to me.

After she was gone there were to be no tears, no questions and no further discussion. We had a small funeral with close family and friends before Dad made the decision to leave Perth and head out to where the country meets the Outback. To an isolated farm in the outer reaches of the Wheatbelt region. To The Nowhere, where I would have to go from a boy to a man overnight. And I did.

Mum's voice faded. I prayed she would accept me. I prayed Dad would accept me. I prayed God would accept me, or at least forgive me. That was when I realised tears were streaming down my cheeks. Thick, salty rivers that burnt my face and stung my eyes. I never cried. I never allowed myself to. I'd never cried about losing Mum until now. Until this very moment, sat out on the porch of our old farmhouse with Scampi lying by my feet. The tears just kept coming until I was sobbing. Stuttering, sniffing. Snot dripped from my nose, and my face felt flushed from the emotions. I cried for Mum. I cried for Jake. I cried for being so fucked up I didn't know who or what I was. I cradled myself until the tears stopped and all I was left with was the throbbing, dry pain in my head.

'It's all going to be okay.' Mum's voice again. 'You just wait and see, Seb. It's all going to be okay.'

If only she was right.

22nd August 1997

The moment Dad's ute was out of sight I dialled Jake's number, which I'd memorised. I hadn't heard from him since his grandmother died and I'd decided it was best to give him some space. Two weeks slipped into three and three weeks fell into a month. The mornings were noticeably lighter and the bite in the air not as harsh. Spring was preparing for its return, and the dry heat of the summer wouldn't be far behind. It was time to break the silence.

The phone rang so long I almost hung up, before someone finally answered. 'Hello, Alison speaking?'

'Hey, Alison. It's Seb.'

'Oh, g'day, Seb. How're you going?'

'Good, thanks. I hope you're well too. I'm sorry to hear the news.'

'That's okay, sweetheart. Rob's mother had been sick for quite some time. She's out of her misery now.'

Alison's matter-of-fact response wasn't what I was expecting. It took a few moments to know what to say next. 'How's Jake doing?'

'He's okay. A little quiet, but he's getting on with things. He came to the funeral with us, which I think was healing for him. It was also good for him to catch up with some of his old mates back home.'

I was surprised to learn that Jake had been to Byron and back since I last saw him. It was as if I'd been completely wiped from his mind. If he genuinely had been affected by the loss of his grandmother, why couldn't I be there for him? Why couldn't I be the person he talked to, instead of his friends back home?

'That's good,' I said eventually.

'Jake's outside helping his father at the moment. Let me go get him for you.'

'Don't worry if he's busy.'

'Don't be silly. He'll be happy to hear from you. Hang on, darl. I won't be long.'

The line went quiet. Should I just hang up? It was clear he didn't want to hear from me. He would have been in touch otherwise. I stopped myself, realising how weird it would be for Jake to come back to nothing but a dial tone.

After an eternal wait, Jake came on the line.

'Hello.' His voice was lifeless, just as it had been when we first met.

'Hey, Jake. How's it going?'

'All right.'

A silence hung heavily in the air. I held on for a moment to see if he was going to ask how I was. Nothing.

'I'm sorry I haven't been in touch. I thought it'd be best to give you some time.'

'Don't worry about it.'

Was he pissed off I hadn't reached out? He was the one who said he wanted to be by himself for a while. Surely it was obvious I was waiting for him to come to me.

Stupid poof. You fucked up bad.

But *he* was the one asking me to get into his sleeping bag.

And *he* was the one who wrapped his arms around me. It's not like I asked him to.

'I gotta go,' Jake said vacantly. 'I'll see ya round.'

'Okay, see you round.'

The phone went dead. I placed it back on its holder and stood in silence. My heart fell to the pit of my gut. What had I done? Why was he suddenly being like this with me again? Was he just sad about his grandma, or was it about what happened in the tent? Was he angry with me, or angry with himself? Although I didn't have the answers to my questions, I was determined to find them out.

4ᵗʰ September 1997

'You all right, Seb?' Dad peered at me from under the brim of his hat as he rolled his cigarette.

It was just past midday, and the harsh sun was at full glare. The temperature was rising, so we stood huddled in the shade. A huge magpie circled overhead, cawing. Cicadas screeched in the distance.

'Yeah, why?' I wasn't in the mood for one of his lectures. I'd have to be careful with my words.

'You seem... distant. Like you're not doing so great.'

Had he noticed I'd lost weight? The fruitless phone call with Jake had suppressed my appetite. At first, it was subtle. I noticed I couldn't finish a full bowl of cornflakes. Then it became more obvious. I'd feed the most substantial part of my dinner to Scampi under the table, being careful not to let Dad notice. Stopping eating had an almost immediate effect on my health. I had quickly become thin. My face was noticeably gaunter, and my cheekbones more defined.

'You upset about Diana?'

Was he serious? How did a princess getting killed on the other side of the planet affect me? Maybe he was being sarcastic.

'What? No. I mean, yeah it's sad. But it's not that.'

'Everything all right with Jake?'

A spike of fear pierced my chest. Did he know? I should have pretended it was Diana. Could he sense what I was feeling? And if he did, why hadn't he already said something? Why hadn't he beaten me to a pulp and left me for dead? Surely me being a fag would be enough to awaken his violent side.

'Yeah, everything's fine.'

He paused for a moment as if contemplating what to say next.

'You know, maybe it'd be good for you to spend some time with another friend. It's not healthy to spend all your time with one person.'

I didn't get it. What other option did I have? Surely he wasn't talking about Jeremy. There was only so much I could talk to a seven-year-old about.

'Summer's coming, Seb. Why don't you give one of your mates from Perth a call? See if they want to come and help us on the farm. I'd pay them, of course. And it'd give you a chance to catch up.'

I suddenly met my Dad's gaze, which I'd been avoiding. Was he really suggesting I invite someone to the farm? It was strange behaviour for him.

'Thanks, Dad. I'll think about it.' The only person who came to mind was Kylie, although I wasn't immediately taken with the idea. But why not? It would be great to have a friend in The Nowhere with me. It would be great to have the distraction from Jake's coldness. Was it because he was the one and only person I wanted to spend my time with? That had to be it. Why else would I not jump at the chance to invite Kylie to the farm?

Dad blew a definitive plume of smoke and stamped out

his cigarette. It was time to get back to work.

As the rest of the afternoon passed, I couldn't stop thinking about Kylie visiting the farm. I could picture her freckles and big watery eyes. It was an uplifting image. Seeing a familiar face would connect me to my past, back to a time when things were simpler. When the coast was close. When Mum was alive. It had to be a good idea for Kylie to come and spend time with me over summer. That's if she'd even want to. The way we'd left things was hardly ideal, and she'd probably have her own exciting plans for the hot months ahead. Far better than coming to The Nowhere. She probably had a boyfriend she'd be spending it with. But what did I have to lose by asking her? It wasn't like Jake was making an effort to hang out anymore.

Once Jeremy was in bed and Dad asleep on the couch, I finally decided to reach out to Kylie. I kept a notebook in a box underneath my bed that had the phone numbers and addresses of the few friends I had back in Perth. Kylie's was right at the top. I dialled her number. Would she even live in the same house? Her mum had struggled financially ever since her dad left so I wouldn't be surprised.

'Hello?'

I could tell by the voice that it was Kylie's sister. Nicole was three years older and had started training to be a hairdresser as soon as she left school.

'Oh, hey, Nicole. It's Seb.'

'Seb? Oh my god… Seb. How the hell are you? It's been such a long time.'

It really had. The last time I saw her had been so rushed, I didn't even get a chance to say a proper goodbye. It was a shame because Nicole had always been kind. I always thought we'd probably have been friends if I'd been a bit older. She was similar to her sister, but maybe even more extroverted. She'd been one of the most popular girls in school and definitely the most attractive. She always had a different boyfriend over whenever I visited. Kylie would tell me they were never good enough for her sister. None of them could fill the space in her life left by their dad.

'I'm… good, thanks. It has been way too long.'

'How's life on the farm?' Nicole sounded like she genuinely wanted to know. For a second I considered being brutally honest but decided I'd save it for Kylie if she decided to visit. The last thing I wanted was for it to get back to Kylie and put her off coming.

'It's great, thanks. Very different from Perth, obviously.'

'I bet it is. Sometimes I'd just like to pack up and leave. Go somewhere random like that.'

Nicole wouldn't have lasted very long in The Nowhere. She'd have gone mad. No boys to flirt with. No girls to paint her nails with. No shops. No cinema. No anything. Just dry dirt and scorched grass.

'Is Kylie around?'

'Not at the moment, I'm afraid. She's staying at a friend's place tonight. She'll be back tomorrow after work. I'll tell her to give you a call.'

A friend's place. Could that be a boyfriend?

'Great. Thanks, Nicole.'

I gave her our number and said goodbye. The connection with my old world gave me a glimmer of hope, but I wasn't allowing myself to get too excited. Given the state in which my friendship with Kylie had been left, would she even bother returning my call?

5th September 1997

'How's Harry?' I passed the last plate to Jeremy to dry.

'He's good.' A Cheshire cat grin formed across his face.

'Yeah? That's great news.'

'I've been feeding him flies.'

I chuckled at the notion of Jeremy going from being terrified of the spider to bringing it meals.

'So you're not scared anymore?'

Jeremy shook his head. 'Nope. There's nothing to be scared of. He's just hairy Harry.'

I laughed. 'Come on, J. It's time for bed.'

Just as I finished feeding Scampi, the phone rang. Finally. I'd been waiting all day for this.

'I'll get it,' I called out, despite Dad being fast asleep on the couch. 'Hello?'

'Hi, Seb.' Kylie sounded just as I remembered her. That silky tone. Sugary sweet.

'Kylie, hi.' Was my awkwardness going to kick in? 'Thanks for calling back.'

'Sure. It's so good to hear from you.'

'It's good to hear from you too.'

'What's up? Is everything okay?'

'Oh yeah, everything's fine. I just wanted to see how you are. And... whether you wanted to catch up.'

'Catch up? Are you coming back to Perth?'

'No, I mean... I wanted to see if you wanted to come

hang out here? At the farm. For the summer. Dad said he'd pay you to help out.'

It must have seemed like a strange idea. We hadn't spoken in two years, and I suddenly wanted to see whether she wanted to come out to the middle of nowhere and spend the summer with me? Had I lost my mind?

The line went silent. What was she thinking? It didn't matter. I knew her answer already. I might as well have just hung up to save her from having to formulate an awkward response.

'Wow, Seb. That was unexpected.'

'Sorry, yeah. I realise that now. I shouldn't have called…'

'No, no. I'm glad you did. I mean… I've missed you. A lot. I didn't think you wanted to be my friend anymore.'

She didn't think I wanted to be friends with *her* anymore? Had I really been so caught up in my own problems since leaving Perth that I hadn't realised I'd pushed her away too? Perhaps I wasn't the only one who'd lost a friend when we'd moved to The Nowhere.

'Of course I want to be your friend, Kylie. I'm… sorry I haven't called. It's been pretty busy out here.'

Why hadn't I called? Sure, the days were busy. But I'd had plenty of time, so many lonely nights and weekends before Jake entered my life. And since he'd left it again. There had been no excuse not to call her apart from being afraid. I couldn't be afraid anymore.

'It's okay, I understand. I'm sorry I haven't called either.'

'So… what do you think?'

'You know what… a change of scenery could be just

what I need right now. I've been working weekends in a café in the city, so I've saved up some money I could use to get there. My contract's about to come to an end, but I need to keep saving money for uni. I'm planning to study in Melbourne, and I need the cash to get set up there. If your dad's happy to pay me to work, and I get to hang out with you at the same time, that would be perfect. Thanks so much for the invitation!'

Melbourne. Uni. It was all happening for her. A twang of envy tried to surface, but I managed to suppress it. I was happy for my old friend. She was talented, and Melbourne would be perfect for her. I'd never had any doubt she'd go far in life. And I was the one that should have been thanking her. I'd forgotten how much I'd missed Kylie before Jake came into my life. Would she really come to The Nowhere? Dad didn't give me these sorts of opportunities very often. I couldn't take no for an answer.

'So… is that a yes?'

'It's a yes. Just let me speak to Mum and figure out when I can come.'

'Fantastic! It's going to be amazing.'

'I'm sure it will. See ya, Seb. I'll give you a call when I know more.'

'Great, see ya.'

Was this really happening? Kylie was coming to The Nowhere! But as excited as I was, all I could think about was telling one person the news. My heart ached just thinking about him. Maybe this was what I needed to forget about Jake for good. A summer spent with one of my oldest and closest friends. It didn't matter he wasn't calling me. It didn't matter he'd gone cold. I'd be spending my days with someone who genuinely gave a shit about how I felt. He'd be the one alone. I wouldn't waste another second thinking about the boy on the farm beyond the scrub at the end of our property.

If only it were that simple.

12th February 1995

We rolled into the driveway and Dad abruptly hit the brakes of his brand new ute.

'I won't come in, Seb. You're not gonna be long, are you?'

I shook my head. 'It won't take long.'

I hated goodbyes. As if saying goodbye to Mum hadn't been enough. Now I had to say goodbye to Kylie? It just didn't seem fair.

'Hurry, Seb!' Jeremy called out from the back window as I walked towards Kylie's front door.

If only he realised what awaited us.

Nicole answered the door. She wore a light dress and had her hair tied back in a relaxed ponytail. It was strange seeing her without her usual makeup. 'Seb, how are you? I can't believe you're really moving to the Outback. Are you excited?'

'I guess.'

'If you meet any hot cowboys, make sure to give them my number, okay?'

I wasn't in the mood for her humour. 'Sure.'

She started laughing. 'Come in. Kylie's waiting for you. She's really sad you're going. We both are.'

Not as sad as I was.

I knew the way to Kylie's bedroom with my eyes closed. Letting myself in, the sweet scent of coconut and patchouli greeted me like it always did. Loud rock music blasted from her stereo.

'Hey.'

'Hey.' Kylie's red locks hung limply, partly obscuring her face, and a strange expression. Was she upset or tired? It was hard to tell.

'Who's this?' I pointed to the stereo.

'Pearl Jam. Haven't you heard this yet, Seb? It's been out for months.'

'You know what I'm like. Always out of the loop.'

Kylie nodded. 'Yep.' She still had the same odd expression.

She wasn't herself. She was evidently still pissed off about the night at the skate ramp.

'I can't stay long; Dad's in the car. I just wanted to come and… well, you know.'

'Say goodbye?'

It sounded so final. 'Say see you soon.'

'But you won't.'

Why was she making it so much harder? Didn't she realise how much pain I was in already?

'Kylie, you know I don't want to go.'

'Then don't. Why don't you stay here? Mum and Nicole love you. You know that.'

She made it sound so easy.

'Kylie, you know I'd love that. But it's complicated. I can't just leave J. I can't just leave Dad.'

'He treats you like shit, Seb. Do you really think that's going to get better when you move to the middle of nowhere?'

Dad honked the horn. It was as if he'd heard her.

'I'm sorry, Kylie. I've got to go.'

'There's nothing there for you, Seb. Nothing there for your future. You haven't even finished school yet.'

She was right. Could everyone see it but Dad? Maybe he just chose not to.

'I know, but I can get a private tutor.'

She looked at me blankly, obviously not satisfied with my response.

'Goodbye, Kylie. I'll see you soon.'

As I started to walk away, she called out: 'Well, aren't you going to at least hug me goodbye?'

I turned around and caught her misty eyes with my own. A lump formed in my throat, but I wouldn't give in. I wouldn't allow myself to cry. I had to be strong. I had to be a man. Just like Mum had said.

We embraced before Dad honked the horn again. I pictured the vehicle waiting for me outside – the back piled high with our belongings strapped down under bright blue tarpaulin.

'Bye, Seb. Have fun in The Nowhere.'

I grinned wryly at the name she'd given my soon-to-be new home. 'Bye, Kylie.'

It wasn't until I'd run out the house and jumped back in the ute that I realised I hadn't even said goodbye to Nicole.

'Finally, Seb. The traffic's going to be terrible now. I hope you don't mind sitting in it for the next few hours.'

I didn't. In fact, I'd cherish it. Every last second of civilisation.

Dad reversed out the driveway and put his foot on the

pedal. My old life disappeared through the rear-view mirror. Kylie's street. Her suburb. Our high school. Mum's grave-yard. All gone in an instant.

*

As we motored further through the Wheatbelt region the earth turned redder and the crops more sporadic. Westonia's welcome sign stated its population as two hundred as if it were a badge of honour. I couldn't have thought of anything worse than living in a town of that size. But once we got to The Nowhere, which was another forty-minute drive to-wards the Goldfields-Esperance region, Westonia suddenly felt like a metropolis. The ute began to shake as it pulled up to the farm and turned onto the uneven gravel of the drive-way. Jeremy's eyes met mine for a moment, but he quickly turned away. He looked worried. The ute, along with my heartbeat, ground to a halt.

'Well, what are you waiting for?' Dad said, slamming the door of the ute. 'Get out and take a look at your new home, boys.'

We obeyed our orders. I jumped out first, followed by Jer-emy seconds later.

'Don't just stand there gawping. Tell me what you think.'

It was hard to know what to think. It's not that it wasn't picturesque. It was just hard to comprehend the dry, desert-ed cattle station in front of us as our new home. This was where we were going to be living. Permanently.

Under a pallid sky, littered with a few scattered clouds, stood an aged farmhouse with a steel wire fence wrapped around it. The house was small but stretched back, made mostly from wood except for its grey tin roof, which had patches of burnt orange rust all over it. The grass was dry, sun-scorched amber. To the left, multiple paddocks spread out as far as I could see. While to the right of the property was bushland, which brought me an element of comfort. At least there would be somewhere to hide.

But it was the windmill that stood out the most. Towering beside the house, the steel structure was the same shade as the roof, but even rustier. It stood motionless – not even the lightest of breezes to turn the decayed blades. In that moment, I felt just like the windmill. Frozen in time, with parts of me rusting away – my past, my memories, and my hopes for the future. All had turned to steel, and I longed for a gust of wind to push me back to life.

'Sebastian.' Dad was serious now.

I swallowed. 'It's definitely different… from what we're used to.'

He rolled his eyes. 'Course it's bloody different, Seb. Is that all you've got to say?'

He started unbuckling the straps on the back of the ute and pulling off the tarp. 'You worry me, Son. Now c'mon, give me a hand. You too Jeremy. The cattle's arriving Tuesday morning and we've got heaps to do before then.'

'Yes, Dad,' we said in unison.

15th January 2005

He was attracted to me. Or at least, he was keen. Through the crowds of people dancing and the strobe lights flickering, I could see him staring directly at me, fiddling with the straw in his drink. He gave me a small smile – as if I needed any more reassurance. I smiled back and paced over to where he was standing, pushing past the well-built shirtless men, varnished with sweat as they gyrated against one another. I moved to the pulse of the booming bass. He waited until I was only a few steps away, and walked towards me. Gulping down the last of his drink, he whispered in my ear: 'I'll have a double gin and tonic, handsome.'

The stranger was very attractive. High cheekbones. Ashy hair, long on top and cropped at the sides. Piercing grey eyes. Huge biceps on show through his tight grey t-shirt. I was going home with him tonight. Or he was coming home with me.

'Sure thing.' I moved towards the nearest bar and sensed him following me.

Sweet dreams are made of this, crooned the vocals against the pulsing electronic beat. I recognised the lyrics through the distorted remix. They summed up exactly how I felt. I got to the bar and ordered two double gin and tonics. I grabbed one straw for the stranger. He pinched my arse.

I suddenly realised I'd completely abandoned Matt. We'd only been loosely seeing each other anyway, and it wasn't going anywhere. He knew that too. He must have picked someone else up by now anyway. I hoped he had.

Turning back around, I passed the striking stranger his drink. 'What's your name?'

'Adam. Yours?'

'Sebastian.'

'Cute name. And cute accent. I love Aussies.'

The Brits always loved my accent. I loved theirs too.

'You wanna dance?'

'Sure.'

We moved towards the dance floor clutching our drinks. Adam took my hand and took the lead. Manoeuvring through the maze of gorgeous men I realised I was being led to the podium. I was too old for that.

'I'm okay down here.'

'Come on, don't be boring.' He wasn't taking no for an answer.

I hated the podium. The podium was for attention-seeking queens. The podium was for twenty-year-old boys and their fag hags. The podium was for chiselled pretty boys with bodies created from lifetimes spent at the gym. The podium wasn't for me. But Adam wasn't taking no for an answer. I downed my drink in two large gulps and followed him up.

*

We stepped out into the night air. I still wasn't used to the peak of London's winter, and the blustery wind pierced my flesh like shards of ice. I instantly began sobering up. I dug my hands into the depths of my coat pockets and buried my chin into the collar. A faint white cloud billowed from Adam's mouth. He was crazy not to have a jacket on. We climbed into the nearest black cab and sped off into the night.

'Nice place.' Adam eyed the Victorian facade of the town-house as we walked up the stairs that led to the front door. 'The Aussie boy's done well.'

'Thanks. Come on in.'

The warmth greeted us as we walked into the flat. I knew I'd thank myself for scheduling the heating to come on at midnight.

'I'll pour us a drink. Gin again?'

'Sounds perfect.' Adam sank into the leather couch.

By the time I returned to the living room he was racking up two lines of coke on the coffee table.

'What do we have here then?' I pretended to be naive.

'Do you want some? No worries if not, all the more for me.'

'Yeah, I want some.'

I placed our drinks on the coffee table and sat down next to Adam. He rolled up a twenty-pound note and snorted back his fat white line. He pointed his head upwards and drew back. I could hear him clearing his throat.

'So what brought you to London?' He passed me the dusty note.

I tightened it, snorted the entire line, leant my head back and shut my eyes.

What *had* brought me to London? As much as I'd longed to leave The Nowhere and make it to a city, I hadn't even considered moving somewhere overseas. But the novelty of living in Perth wore off over time, and I started to consider different options. I thought about moving to Melbourne or Sydney but decided a complete change was what I needed.

My first day in London was one I'd never forget. I'd taken a taxi from Heathrow airport towards Clapham where a friend from Perth was staying. She'd decided to take a gap year and allowed me to crash on her couch while I set up. I'd been warned summers in England weren't even the equivalent to spring in Perth, but the day I arrived, it was pushing thirty degrees and the hoodie I was wearing caused me to build up a sweat. It was more of a sticky heat compared to the dry summers of my home city.

Everything looked so different. The trees and bushes were a darker, richer green than the silver gums I was used to. The buildings were old – *really* old. Everything had so much charm and character. Straight away it was clear it was going to be somewhere I'd enjoy. And I did.

The three years I spent in London were fun, crazy and chaotic. They'd gone fast and they'd been anything but dull. My time in The Nowhere seemed like a distant dream. For the first time in my life, I barely thought about those days at all.

'I needed a change,' I replied simply. The effects of the cocaine were already kicking in. Adam appeared to feel the same thing as he downed the gin and tonic.

'I've never been to Oz. I'd love to one day. All those beautiful beaches covered with hot guys. Do you miss it?'

Of course I missed it. I missed it more than anything else.

I missed the long, hot summers. I missed the sandy beaches. I missed the smiley, friendly faces and the laid-back way of life. I missed the sweet scent of eucalyptus in the air and how much better the fruit tasted. But I didn't miss the familiarity. The routine. I didn't miss my father.

'Sometimes, a bit.' I wasn't in the mood for this conversation. Even with the rush of the coke hitting my brain, the last thing I wanted was to be reminded of Australia. Of my past life. I wanted to continue being anonymous. I wanted to sleep with the man in front of me and I didn't want to think about tomorrow. I took a sip of my drink before leaning in and kissing him. He tasted like a bitter mix of gin and cocaine.

16ᵗʰ January 2005

It was at least midday when the light broke through the gap in the curtains. Opening my eyes slowly I stared at the naked torso in front of me. A faded tattoo of a dragon glared back. It took me a few moments to process who he was. Adam had a beautiful back. Should I have reached out and held him? I stopped myself. There was no point.

Quietly getting out of bed and slipping on the same undies from the night before, I chucked on a holey sweater and some trackies before grabbing the first two socks from my top drawer. It didn't matter they didn't match. All that mattered was that I needed coffee.

I drifted towards the kitchen without saying a word to Adam. Looking outside at the slate-grey sky, I quickly made the decision I wouldn't be stepping out there today. My jog could wait. I clicked on the heating and the kettle. What time did we get in last night? What time did I get to sleep? Did we get through all that coke? After I filled a mug with black coffee, I sat down at the kitchen table. The bottle of gin was empty. We'd clearly got through all of that too.

'That smells amazing,' Adam said, walking into the kitchen.

'Hang on. I'll pour you one.'

'No, it's okay. I better get going.'

He was fully clothed and ready to go.

'Aren't you going to be cold?'

'It's all right. There's a tube stop just around the corner, right?'

'That's right.'

He walked over to me. Was he deciding whether to give me a hug or kiss? Perhaps neither.

'I had fun last night.'

'So did I.' It was the truth, from what I could remember.

'I've got your number, right?'

'Yeah, you've got it.' I had no idea whether he did. Or whether I had his.

'So we'll see each other again, right?'

I nodded. 'Sure.'

I knew we wouldn't.

Adam stepped out, allowing a blast of glacial air to enter the house before he shut the door behind him.

How had it come to this?

21ˢᵗ October 1997

Sun drenched the arid landscape as a drop of sweat fell into my eye, stinging like hell. Dad rode in front of me, which was why he spotted our neighbours' ute in the distance first, rolling down the road towards our farm. Was Jake finally going to break the silence?

I could sense Dad's frustration as he swerved his bike in the direction of our unexpected guests. We were behind on our chores already and really didn't need any distractions. Scampi seemed thrown by the sudden change of course, but happily adjusted.

By the time we reached the ute, it was parked in our driveway. Rob and Alison climbed out, but there was no sign of Jake. How did I think it would be that simple? He obviously wasn't just mourning. He felt awkward about what happened and didn't want to see me. Why did I get into the bloody sleeping bag?

You stupid fag. You got what you deserved.

'G'day, guys.' Rob tipped his hat. 'It's been a while.'

'It sure has, mate.' Dad emulated his greeting. 'How's the farm?'

Business as usual. No surprises there.

'The crops are doing well,' Alison interjected. 'Although we'd welcome a bit of rain.'

Dad's smug face made me squirm. He'd been right. He was always bloody right.

'The storms will be here before you know it.' His arrogant expression turned into one of sympathy.

'How've you guys been?' Rob seemingly ignored Dad's false compassion.

'All good here, thanks. We're gonna have an extra pair of hands on the farm for the summer, which will be great. Won't it, Son?'

I nodded.

'Oh yeah? Who will that be then?' Rob probed.

'A friend from Perth's coming to stay.' As I spoke, I could feel Alison's eyes on me.

'That will be lovely for you. Have you heard from Jake much, Seb?'

How could she not know we hadn't been spending time together? It was pretty damn obvious. Even Dad knew Jake and I weren't hanging out anymore.

'Not lately.' I chose my words carefully. 'We've both been busy.'

Alison remained quiet for a few moments. Once again, it was as if she was searching for something in my eyes.

'Well, it's his birthday this weekend, and we're planning to have a little barbie,' she continued, panning her vision to my dad. 'We'd love for you all to come over.'

Was this coming from Jake or his parents? It was doubtful he would have sent them over to invite us. Not with the way he'd been avoiding me. Regardless, I hoped Dad would say yes.

'This weekend? That shouldn't be a problem.' Dad scratched his nose. 'It would be good to catch up. So yeah, count us in. What time and what should we bring? I can't promise homemade lemonade.'

Alison laughed, creases forming around her eyes. 'Just bring your lovely selves. Any time around midday on Saturday will be perfect.'

'Great,' Dad confirmed. 'We'll see you then.'

'See you then,' I echoed.

25th October 1997

Dad knocked twice on the front door with a curled index finger. For a moment I wondered if he'd been loud enough, but the door soon swung open to reveal a cheerful Alison and a waft of perfume. It made a change to see her dressed up, instead of in her usual work gear.

'G'day, boys. Great to see you. Come on in.' She glided through the house and into the backyard, the loose fabric of her dress billowed obediently behind.

The yard had been decorated with silver balloons, the number eighteen stamped on each of them. Jake was officially an adult now. Soon I would be too. The feeling of freedom I hungered for was more in my grasp than ever before. Just three more months. Just three more bloody months.

Would Jake have been given a car for his birthday? There hadn't been one in the driveway. Maybe his dad had told him he'd drive him to the nearest place to buy one, wherever that might be, so that he could pick it out for himself. That was something Dad would never do. I'd get what I was given.

There he was, standing next to Rob, who was firing up the barbie. It was the first time I'd seen him wearing a shirt. The top three buttons were undone revealing a chest that was much more tanned than the last time I saw it. His hair was lighter too.

You fucking queer boy. You're so disgusting you're going to make your dad sick. You're going to make Jake sick. You'd make your mother sick, you fucking queer boy.

Jake nodded at me and offered a half-smile. It was like we were back at day one. As if I had to win his approval all over again. Did I even have the energy?

'G'day, fellas.' Rob pushed his long unkempt hair back behind his ears. It had started to dreadlock. 'You're just in time. The snags have just gone on.'

I took a seat and avoided eye contact with Jake. Just like the last barbie, he'd have to come to me. The ball was in his court.

Dad kicked off the charcoal-versus-gas debate with Rob as he turned the spitting sausages. Alison emerged from the kitchen clutching an oversized burl walnut salad bowl full to the brim with succulent green lettuce. Jeremy sat crossed-legged on the frail grass, shyly flicking bits of dirt that had crumbled away from the cracked earth.

Jake finally took a seat next to me. 'Hey, Seb. Long time no see.'

As if that had been my fault. 'Hey, Jake. Happy birthday. And yeah... it's been a while.'

There was a bloated pause before he spoke again: 'I'm sorry I haven't been hanging out. I guess it hit me harder than I thought it would. Grandma dying, I mean.'

Was that really the issue? It wasn't that I wanted to make light of his grief, but there was something off about his explanation. My instinct told me not to believe him. But at least he was acknowledging he'd been out of touch.

'That's okay, I understand.'

'So how've you been?'

'Good, thanks. Just busy on the farm. Oh, I do have one bit of news though.'

'Yeah? What's that?' His eyes lit up, suggesting he thought it had something to do with a car. Hopefully he wouldn't be too disappointed. 'Actually, lemme go grab a couple of beers first.'

As he bounded off to the kitchen, I drew a deep breath and composed myself. What was with me when I spoke to him? I wasn't myself. It was like I'd left my body and was hovering above, staring down. But I looked like a stranger. I sounded like a stranger. Fuck. I hated myself around him.

My thoughts ground to a halt with Jake's return. Thick foam frothed down each bottle in his hands.

'There you go, mate. Cheers.'

'Cheers.'

Our bottles clinked as they collided. I'd missed that sound.

'So what were you gonna tell me?'

'Oh yeah. My friend Kylie's coming to visit. From back home.'

He looked surprised as he took a swig of his beer. 'Really? Sweet! Is she your girlfriend?'

Now I knew he was fucking with me. Jake knew very well I didn't have a girlfriend. He knew I'd never even slept with a girl. I decided to play along. 'Nah, but hopefully she will be.'

I'd caught him off guard. 'Do you like her, mate?'

What was it to him? 'Yeah, she's nice. I mean, she's pretty hot.'

'Even better.'

That mischievous smirk. Man, it was good to see it again.

Tiny crystals scattered across the infinite darkness overhead as Rob simultaneously poked the small campfire he'd created and swigged a bottle of beer. Even though it was the middle of spring, the evenings still felt brisk. The erratic flames danced and twisted around one another while the embers beneath made gratifying crackling sounds. Jeremy stared at the flares with wonder. Jake and I sat near each other, close, but not too close.

Alison, who now had a thick knit wrapped around her, held her palms towards the fire. 'This is lovely, isn't it? It reminds me of our camping trips. Don't you think, Jake?'

Jake grunted at his mother, making it clear he didn't want to reminisce about old times.

'Those trips were so special.' She was quieter this time. I wasn't sure whether anyone but me had even heard her.

Jake stood up and turned to look at me. 'I'm getting another beer. You want one?'

'Sure, thanks.'

When he returned, he took a seat by the windmill.

'I think he's had enough of us oldies.' Alison pointed towards her son before burrowing her hands back into her knit. 'Go ahead, darl.'

It didn't take much convincing. I got up and ambled towards Jake, like a lamb to the slaughter.

'Sorry, mate.' He passed me my beer. 'I've had enough of 'em for one day. I reckon Mum was about five minutes away from getting the baby photos out.'

'That would have been funny.'

'Shut up, dick. It's messed up though, right? I'm eighteen today. We should be out partying, not singing bloody Kumbaya round the fire.'

'I take it you're not getting a car for your birthday, then?'

'Nah, it doesn't look like it, mate. They want me to stick around for at least another year. Help them get properly set up.'

I swallowed my shock. His answer was so definite. Were his parents really that selfish? I expected it from Dad, but not from Alison and Rob.

'But you're legally an adult now. They can't actually stop you.'

'Well, if I haven't got wheels… then yeah. They kinda can.'

He had a point. Without a car, it didn't matter how old Jake and I were. We wouldn't be going anywhere. We were trapped. Would we be here forever?

'This is why it's over to you now, mate.'

I knew this was coming. With my eighteenth birthday only a few months away, it's a possibility I could be getting a car of my own. I'd got close to it since my last birthday, so this could be the time. Dad had a nasty streak, but he wasn't all bad. Surely, eventually, he would meet me halfway. He had to. He was now the person who could turn the dream of running away with Jake into a reality.

'I'll do my best.'

'You have to. I mean, there's no point me even asking for a car for Chrissy now. That's obviously outta the question.

But you've got two chances, mate. Christmas and your birthday.'

A sudden twinge of resentment towards Jake raced through me. He'd blocked me out for weeks, possibly hanging on to the hope he'd be getting a car so he could drive off without giving me a single thought. But now his plan had fallen apart, and he was back to being my friend under the condition I'd be able to get my hands on some wheels to help him escape. Was he using me? Could I be that much of a fool?

'Yeah, well... I'm not sure there's much hope in me getting one either.'

Jake looked stunned. 'What d'ya mean?'

His mesmerising eyes did what they always did. They made me feel joy and emptiness at the same time. I was trying my best to keep my walls up, the barriers I'd built not to let him back in. His friendship was toxic. Especially now I realised I was just an accessory to his getaway plan.

'I mean, it's highly likely my dad won't buy me a car either. He's already said he won't heaps of times. I can't see it changing anytime soon.'

Jake's top lip curled. 'So what, we're just stuck here? We're just gonna stay here in this shithole forever?'

His whole demeanour changed with his tone. I felt the frustration. The anger. The longing. I got it. I got every damn bit of it. I felt every fucking ounce of it in my skin. In my organs. In my bones. But what could we do? Perhaps this was our destiny. To remain in The Nowhere, slaves to our families, slaves to our farms. Would it be possible for us to learn to accept this? Could we make the best of a bad situation and enjoy each other's company? Maybe it *was* for the best. If we left and moved to the city, the likelihood of us remaining friends was slim. And with the city could come all sorts of complications. Perhaps our parents were protecting us from the world? From reality?

Jake didn't see it that way. 'Well, I'm getting outta here. With or without you.'

There was a long silence, awkward and bordering on eerie. I had to break it. I had to fill the void. Fill it with some sort of hope.

'I'll see what I can do. I mean, I'll do my best. You know I will.'

Jake looked up and gave me the half-smile I longed for. 'Thanks, Seb. You won't regret it.' He placed his hand on my thigh. '*We* won't regret it.'

I froze, hoping more than anything I wouldn't.

15th September 2017

It was only when the soft glow of dusk settled in that it occurred to me how long Sandra and I had been talking. Or at least, how long I'd been talking at her. The park had emptied out a while back but was now filling up again. Couples walked off their dinner. A teenager ran around the large stretch of green with his dog. A little old lady sat on a bench near us, staring vacantly at the sky.

That numb feeling I'd felt in the pub was back. We'd seen each other since, but when the topic turned to those days, it still unnerved me.

'Are you okay, Seb?'

'Yeah. I'm fine.'

'I can tell it's… difficult for you talking about that time in your life.'

She'd started to sound like a therapist. Not that I minded – perhaps that was exactly what I needed. I'd debated going to a professional many times over the years but had always decided against it. Although they'd be there to listen and help me, I knew I'd always be conscious they were just doing their job, and that no matter what they would say, they would be judging me, discussing me. We talked about patients all the time at work, why would it be any different? But that's not how it felt with Sandra. There was no judgement. Or if there was, she did a good job at disguising it. She made me feel cared for. She made me feel heard.

'Yeah, it's just weird. Talking about this stuff out loud, you know?'

Sandra nodded. This is what she was so good at. Knowing when and when not to talk. She never pushed me. She gave me all the room I needed. Which was a lot.

'Anyway,' I continued, 'it's getting late. I guess we should get going.'

'Yeah, I guess we should.' Sandra folded her arms, her tone a degree colder. She could obviously sense the shutters had been pulled back down. The door was firmly closed.

'What are you up to in the morning? I know a cute café that's just opened up in the city if you want to meet for a coffee? Perhaps you could tell me a bit more of your story.' There was a pause before she continued. 'Maybe you could tell me about when Kylie came to stay.'

Her words dug into me. Did I still carry the same pain and resentment towards Kylie? Even after all these years? When would I be a big enough person to let it go? I'd been in such a rush to grow up and leave The Nowhere that I must have forgotten the part where I was actually supposed to grow up. Supposed to mature. Surely part of maturity was being able to let things go? To forgive. To forget. But was I ready to progress to that chapter with Sandra? Onto Kylie's chapter, when Jake and I were no longer just Jake and I. We were a triangle. Jake, Seb and Kylie. The start of where it all went wrong.

You can't keep it secret forever. The truth always comes out eventually.

'Yeah, maybe. I'll check if I'm free and let you know later.'

I regretted being so abrupt as soon as I spoke the words, but I knew Sandra would understand. She seemed to be able to connect with me in a way no one had before. Perhaps it was empathy. Maybe it was simply sympathy. But I was grateful all the same.

'Sounds good, Seb. Let me know.'

Moments later, we went our separate ways. A sliver of magenta moon peeked out from behind the scattered grey clouds that were forming in the darkness. By the time I reached the car, I already knew I'd be texting Sandra when I got home, asking if she was still up for that coffee. Why not? I'd only be spending another weekend cooped up at home with Dad. But how far could I go? Was I ready to tell her the whole story? Time, as always, would hold the answers.

4th November 1997

Her auburn ringlets were instantly recognisable, even from a distance. The window wound down, Kylie leaned out to get her first look at her new home for the summer. The taxi rolled along the bumpy road, its sleek, silver body contrasted the rugged terrain. Had her mum forked out what would've surely been an extortionate fare? It seemed unlikely. She found it hard enough to pay the bills. Kylie must have used her own savings she'd been squirrelling away in her summer job. Either way, it didn't matter. What mattered was she was here. She'd found a way, just like she always did. That's one of the many things I admired about her and was one of the reasons I was enraptured as I watched her draw closer and closer. It was as if I was waiting for the Queen of England to arrive. She might as well have been. It was as if her presence could be felt miles away. Whenever I was with her, it felt like little bolts of electricity were crackling in the air. I smiled a combination of joy and relief that she was finally here. She would break up the loneliness. She would bring much-needed energy to The Nowhere. But how would she get on with Alison? With Rob? With Jake?

The sound of screeching cockatoos was deafening, their resonating cries signalling the brewing of a storm. It was a bit early for the stormy season, but we'd welcome the rain. We'd had so little of it the previous summer. Perhaps this was a stroke of luck Kylie had already brought with her.

The blood red sky was coated in finger-painted swirls as she climbed out of the cab. She hadn't aged at all in the last couple of years. Her face still held that youthful innocence it had when we first met. Those large eyes were still filled with a mix of wonder, naivety and an undercurrent of anxiety.

'Seb!' she called out – as if she'd only just spotted me through the dust thrown up by the retreating taxi. I knew her better than that. She'd seen me as far back as I'd seen her.

'Kylie... I can't believe you're really here.'

'I said I'd come,' she declared in her best I-told-you-so tone as she threw her arms around me.

It felt good to be hugged. A proper hug. That closeness to someone I longed for. That connection I craved. Her scent had changed. She was using a different fragrance. Less sweet, more sophisticated. Feminine instead of girly. Perhaps this was her way of showing me she was a woman now.

'Well, what do you think?' My words echoed those of my father when we first arrived on the farm. I shuddered at the thought of mirroring him.

'It's so cool.' Kylie's eyes widened as she looked towards a herd of cows gathering under a tree in a nearby paddock.

Her reaction was so different to what mine had been. But why wouldn't it be? For her, it was just a change of scenery. A novelty, not an indefinite place of residence. But how would she feel after spending a few days here? Or a few weeks?

'It's not so bad, I guess. I'm just... I'm glad you're here.'

Kylie stopped for a second to hold my focus. It was like she'd only just really seen me since climbing out the taxi. She was studying my face, like an astronomer searching for answers in the night sky.

'You look… different.'

'What do you mean?'

'I don't know. I can't work it out yet, but something about you has changed.'

I opened my mouth to reply but was interrupted by Scampi barking and the sound of the front door swinging open. Dad strode over to us.

'G'day, sweetheart. It's been a long time.'

I hated it when he called Kylie *sweetheart*. It felt condescending and slightly creepy. She didn't seem to mind though.

'Stu, hi. It's been far too long.'

Kylie glided over to Dad and gave him a quick hug. She knew him. She knew what he was capable of. But she also had a kind soul that was able to overlook certain things better than I could. She'd experienced enough of her own family drama to know nothing was ever black and white. She knew how losing my mother would have affected him. She almost seemed to have a soft spot for him, which was something I found close to impossible to tap into. But I appreciated the sentiment. The last thing we wanted was a summer of awkwardness and fights. I hoped Dad would put in the same effort to keep the peace. I didn't want him to come between us. It was one of the only friendships I had – if I could still call what I had with Kylie a friendship. I wondered what it would look like in a post-Jake world?

All I knew was she'd made the effort to travel halfway across the state to be with me in The Nowhere. Whether that was to help me on the farm or to keep me company when I was at my loneliest, it didn't matter. I had to take the shattered fragments of our friendship and rebuild it. Make us like we once were.

Dad looked up at the sky closing in. 'Come on inside, guys. Storm's brewing.'

He was right. The moisture was swelling in the air. Seconds later, thunder and lightning rippled through the steaming grey sky.

*

The smell of onions frying found its way into my room, despite the door being tightly shut. I kept expecting Dad to call out for my help, but he knew Kylie and I had a lot of catching up to do. It was good of him to respect that. But if he were hoping we'd be fooling around, he'd be disappointed.

Kylie gave me an edited overview of her last couple of years, from troubles at home to trying to figure out what she wanted to do with her life. I told her what it was like first moving to The Nowhere, and how isolated I'd felt. It felt good to converse so naturally. With Jake, I could never completely be myself. Never fully relax. It was as if I had my guard up with him, worried about looking cool enough, or something like that. I never had that concern with Kylie. Despite how she looked, she was a dag, like me.

'I'm sorry I haven't come sooner, Seb. I really am. It kills me to know how lonely you've been here.'

There was a part of me that resented Kylie for not making an effort to keep in touch. That hurt, but I figured it was down to what had happened on the skate ramp. I understood why she would have phased me out of her life, especially with me living so far away. But it was her friendship I missed the most. The connection.

'It's okay. You're here now.'

'Yes, I am. And we've got a whole summer to look forward to.'

There was a knock at the door, interrupting our conversation.

'Seb,' Jeremy called. 'Dinner's ready.'

I was just about to start telling Kylie about Jake, but it would have to wait. I was starving and she must have been too. I said a silent prayer that nothing would go wrong at the dinner table. At least not on her first night.

Dad had pulled out our best tablecloth. Royal blue, without a single food stain. He really was going the extra mile. The table was set neatly, and he was serving up beef casserole as we walked in the room. 'Quick, guys. Don't let it get cold.'

This was the side of Dad I liked. The warmer side I wished he'd show more often. The side before the eruptions arrived.

'Wow, this looks amazing.' Kylie pushed a few ringlets behind her ear as she sat down. 'And it smells amazing too.'

'Well, I hope it tastes just as good. That's the important part. Right, sweetheart?'

He was enjoying the compliments. It was also clear he was just as happy to have a visitor as I was. Maybe having Kylie with us was exactly what we all needed. Perhaps she needed it too. There was something different about her as well. Had she been through more than she'd let on over the past couple of years? I was sure I'd learn about that in time. A lot can happen in a teenager's life in two years. Unless they're living in The Nowhere.

Kylie looked to Dad. 'This place is so cool!' she exclaimed. 'You must love it here.'

The rain crashed against our thin windows, causing them to rattle.

'Yeah, we do.' Dad spat a gristly piece of chewed up beef out onto his plate. 'Well, I think Seb gets the shits now and then. Don't you, Son?'

'Yeah, something like that.'

'Well, you're not missing anything back in Perth, that's for sure.'

Dad liked Kylie's response. It would have given him satisfaction knowing I'd heard that. But she didn't know how lucky she was, living in civilisation. If she'd lived in The Nowhere as long as I had, she wouldn't still have that youthful, hopeful expression. She would be different, the same way she pointed out I was.

'Hear that, Seb? You're not missing anything. What do I keep telling you?'

I ignored Dad's comment. Kylie filled the silence, which I was grateful for.

'I won't be there much longer anyway,' she said. 'I'm hoping to move to Melbourne next year for uni. Can't wait.'

Envy overcame me. It was only Kylie's first day in The Nowhere, and she already had a destination beyond it to look forward to. No wonder she liked it. It was just some-where she was passing through. She wasn't trapped, like me.

Dad's expression changed. He must have seen the jeal-ousy on my face. At least it'd wiped the smug look off his. 'Melbourne, brrr. Rug up.'

Would Kylie take offence to that? If she did, she didn't bite. She probably didn't care what Dad thought. Why would she? She had an exciting path ahead of her, which was more than could be said for him or me.

'I will.' She flashed a smile. 'Already got my knits ready.'

Kylie offered to wash up after dinner, so I dried, relieving Jeremy of the chore. Dad had already fallen asleep in front of the television, so Jeremy had taken the opportunity to slip *Toy Story* into the VHS player. Kylie and I went to our rooms. I'd offered her my bedroom as the spare room was about half the size, but she politely declined. She sat on the floor unzipping her suitcase as I lay on the bed. It squeaked with my every movement. Outside, the rain continued to pum-mel the earth in between flashes of lightning and rumbles of thunder.

'It's so weird that it's raining.' I propped myself up and peered out the window. 'It never rains here.'

'Maybe I brought some good luck with me.' Kylie began folding her clothes and neatly putting them away in the chest of drawers. It was surprising how much she'd brought with her, like she'd packed for a trip to New York, not to work on a sweaty cattle station in the Outback. But seeing her pull out each brightly-coloured top and printed dress was like feeling a cool breeze on a hot day. It brought about a sense of joy, making me smile.

She pulled open another drawer with a creak and a sneeze of dust. 'You really must be so alone out here, Seb.'

Even though I'd already told her of my loneliness, it was like it'd only just sunk in. Was it really that difficult to understand? Of course I'd been bloody lonely. Banished to the end of the earth with only my father and brother for company. Although that wasn't completely true, as of late. It was time to tell her about Jake.

'I am. I mean... I was. I actually made a friend this year, so I haven't been completely alone.'

Kylie raised her eyebrow a fraction. 'Who? An imaginary friend?'

'No, I'm not that lame!' I laughed. 'We had a family move in at the beginning of the year. They live in the next farm down. A nice couple called Rob and Alison and their son, Jake.'

Kylie was intrigued. 'I had no idea there'd be anyone else living out here. It's so far from anything.'

The memory of being cocooned with Jake in the sleeping bag returned. Feeling his warm body on my back. And then how cold he'd been with me in the weeks that followed.

'Well, Jake and I kinda drifted apart for a little while. But it's all good now – we're mates again. I'd love for you to meet him.'

Once again, it was apparent Kylie was trying to figure me out. Trying to read my thoughts. I thought back to her comment: *Something about you has changed.*

Did she know? Had she figured me out already, ever since that kiss on the skate ramp? The notion troubled me.

'That's awesome! I'm so glad you've found a friend out here. I can't wait to meet him.'

Surely she couldn't know. I was just bloody paranoid, spending too much time on my own.

'Anyway, we should get some sleep. It'll be a tiring day tomorrow. Your first day on the farm.'

'Can't wait!' Kylie's teeth gleamed as she smiled. How long would that smile last?

Stepping over Kylie's now empty suitcase, I headed for the door.

'Don't I get one more hug?' She sounded just like she did when I'd said goodbye to her in Perth.

When I turned back around, Kylie was already on her feet. She squeezed me even tighter than when she'd arrived.

'I really am so happy to be here, Seb. Happy to be with you.'

'I'm happy you're here too, Kylie. Night.'

'Good night, Seb.'

I closed the door behind me. The rain continued to thrash against the windows, like demons trying to get in.

5th November 1997

The sun crept through the crack in the curtains and burnt my eyes, signalling the storm had passed. I immediately remembered Kylie was asleep in the room next to me. I pushed off my thin sheet and clambered out of bed. Normally I'd put off getting up for as long as I could, usually until Dad yelled at me to get my lazy arse up and out to work. But now I had a reason to wake up early. My anticipation grew by the second. Would she be up yet? Would she really be able to cope with working on the farm? It didn't matter. She was here now. Surely she wouldn't just turn back around at the first sign of hard work.

I quickly got dressed and made my way out into the hallway. Simultaneously, Kylie emerged from her room with a burgundy towel wrapped around her.

'Morning, Seb. Sorry, I meant to wake up earlier than I did. Still tired from the journey, I guess.'

'No worries. You get dressed and I'll help Dad with brekkie.'

The image of Kylie with only a towel wrapped around her stayed in my mind as I walked down the hallway that led to the kitchen. I thought about the smooth curves of her body, her delicate skin. What would it feel like? Soft, like butter. When Jake held me in the sleeping bag, his flesh felt rough. The hair on his arms was as coarse as the dried grass outside.

The smell of slightly burnt bacon wafted towards me as I walked into the kitchen.

'Morning, Son.' Dad turned around and gave me a quick nod. 'Can you set the table?'

I was glad to see him putting in the effort for Kylie's first breakfast on the farm, so I didn't comment on the smoke.

'Is Kylie up?'

'Yeah, she's just in the shower.'

As I walked back to the table with a carton of orange juice in hand, Dad gave me a brief smirk and a wink. I knew exactly what he was thinking, but was glad he didn't give voice to those thoughts. Dad had never put any pressure on me when it came to girls. He hadn't even had 'the talk' with me. I'd figured out what sex was quite young when I'd heard a group of guys talking about it in the playground. They were older than me but were happy to let me eavesdrop on their whispered discussion. One of them had managed to get their hands on their dad's porno mag and between us all, we'd joined the dots.

Back in Perth, Dad had asked me a couple of times whether Kylie was my girlfriend. I'd told him no and was glad he let up on the questioning. Another time, he asked me plainly: 'You're not a fag, are you, Son? You've never had a girlfriend, what's the deal?' To which I'd spat back at him: 'No bloody way. I'm not a bloody fag', before stalking away, part angry, part worried. Although I hadn't addressed it consciously at the time, I was obviously anxious about anything close to the truth being revealed.

Dad's questions had made me even more certain that

talking to him about anything relating to sex or sexuality was off the table. I was happy for it to remain that way. I ignored Dad's wink and set the table with a mishmash of cutlery from the kitchen drawer.

'Morning, boys,' Kylie said, entering the room. 'It smells wonderful.'

'Morning, sweetheart,' Dad replied, scooping the slightly over-fried bacon and eggs onto the toast he'd lined up on each plate. 'Dig in, guys.' He looked at Kylie and smiled. 'You'll need all the energy you can get for work out here.'

He wasn't wrong there.

After we'd finished eating, Dad took off in the ute with Jeremy. I fed Scampi, before leading Kylie outside to where the quad bikes stood waiting.

'Now, are you sure you're good to do this without any practice? You said you've never ridden one before.'

'Yeah, I'll be fine. How hard can it be? After all, I can drive now.'

Kylie's words hung in the air. They dangled in front of me, taunting me. She could drive now? Jake could drive too. It was only me who bloody couldn't.

'You drive now?'

'Yeah, I passed last summer. I've even got a little car back at home.'

'Really? Why didn't you drive it here? Surely that would have been better than forking out for the taxi?'

'Are you crazy? I can drive from home to work and back again. I'm not driving all the way across WA!' She surveyed the quad bike. 'Hmm, maybe I'll just jump on the back of yours today. Just to make sure I definitely know what I'm doing.'

My eye was suddenly caught by a figure approaching. The bright white tee and pale blue denim shorts were instantly recognisable. Jake. He was walking towards us quickly.

'Is that your friend?'

'Yeah. That's him.'

'Hey, mate!' Jake shouted as he got closer. It was nice of him to make the effort to come and meet Kylie.

'Hey, Jake. This is Kylie.'

Jake nodded. 'Hey, Kylie. Nice to meet you.'

'Nice to meet you too.' Her eyes locked with his as she confidently held out her hand.

Jake ignored the gesture and reached out to give her a hug instead. Kylie accommodated him with a brief embrace. That was more than I got when I'd first met him. My hug was weeks of silent treatment.

'So what are you kids up to today? You actually working?'

I didn't like being called a kid by Jake. I didn't like him calling Kylie a kid either. What made him so high and mighty?

'Yeah, we're working. Gotta fix a fence in one of the paddocks.' My tone bordered on defensive.

'Well, that's a shame.'

'Maybe we could hang out on the weekend?' Kylie offered.

'That'd be good,' Jake replied. 'Reckon your dad would be okay with that, Seb?'

I shrugged. I wasn't hopeful. 'I can find out.'

What was he doing? He knew my dad would probably have an issue with us all hanging out. Was he purposefully trying to belittle me? Make me look small in front of Kylie? Surely I was imagining it. That had to be it.

'Great, well let me know,' Jake said, pushing his thick fringe out of his eyes. 'I better head back anyway before your old man gets back. Just wanted to come and meet the lovely lady.'

Lovely lady? What game was he playing? I'd told him I had feelings for Kylie. Why wouldn't he respect that and leave her alone? Maybe this was just the way he was around girls.

'See ya,' I said.

'Bye, Jake.' Kylie twirled a ringlet.

'Bye, kids.' Jake turned around and made his way back towards his farm.

He was acting. I didn't like it. I didn't like it at all. For once, I was disappointed that Jake had stopped by.

'He seems nice.'

'Yeah, he's all right. Come on. Hop on my bike and we'll go get that fence fixed.'

12th March 2005

'Red or white?'

'Red.'

'We'll have a bottle of the merlot, please.'

The waiter was kind of cute. He was eyeing Adam up. Would he reciprocate? I scanned his eyes for signs, but there was nothing. Either he wasn't interested in the waiter, or he was good at acting.

'Are you ready to order?'

'Can you give us another five minutes?'

I loved Adam's accent. The night we'd met, I hadn't really noticed how well spoken he was. I'd been too obliterated to care. He pronounced each word with such precision that it made me feel like a total bogan. I noticed myself articulating my words when I was around him. Dad would never let me live it down if I returned to Australia with a British twang.

Adam interrupted my thoughts. 'What are you going to have?'

I hadn't even looked at the menu. I'd have the same thing I always did at an Italian restaurant. Spaghetti bolognese. And he'd have a pizza. Did I know him that well already? It'd only been a couple of months.

'Let me guess, the bolognese?'

'You got it.'

Sitting back in my chair, I took a few moments to marvel at Adam's features. The high cheekbones. The ashy hair.

The grey eyes. Why couldn't they be sea blue? Then he'd be perfect.

Then he'd be Jake.

I couldn't lie to myself. I couldn't pretend that I hadn't been looking for Jake in every man I'd met since. But as much I tried, the guys I got to know would never be him. They couldn't even come close. Despite this, I knew it was time to break the cycle. What had it been, almost a bloody decade? It had to change, starting now. With Adam.

The waiter returned with our wine and filled up our glasses as he took our order. This time I caught him smiling directly at Adam. What a prick. Not that I could blame him. Adam *was* the hottest guy in the restaurant. The waiter was the second hottest. I questioned why Adam was there with me. I took a large gulp of the merlot and waited for the numbness to follow.

Shiraz would have been better. An Australian shiraz. I missed the full-bodied taste. It was a wine just as delicious on a hot summer's day as when winter's chill crept in. I could have killed for a glass of Aussie shiraz. I could have killed to be in Australia. Just thinking about how warm it would be Down Under made me long for home. I missed it. I missed the way the sun's harsh rays penetrated my skin. The way the foamy waves splashed against my thighs. The way the gum-trees peeled their red and grey bark – as if shedding skin.

I loved London. I loved everything about it. The way it hummed with movement, whether it was day or night. The way the neon lights could shine brighter than an entire galaxy. The way I could get lost in a sea of faces and feel myself drown in anonymity. That's what had brought me here in the first place. I longed to be anonymous. I longed to get lost within its shadows. And I did. And it was healing, for a while. But something was beckoning me, pulling me to return to the southern hemisphere. Waiting for me to return to all I'd left behind.

You can't keep it secret forever. The truth always comes out eventually.

But not yet. Not now. I'd always said, five years, and it had only been three. What was there for me to return to anyway? At least in London I'd met someone. Someone who seemed to genuinely like me. This was clear because the pretty boy waiter was smiling at him and he wasn't smiling back. He wasn't even giving him a second look. He was staring straight ahead. Staring directly at me.

I'd never imagined seeing Adam again after our drunken first encounter. He was just a lay, like all the others. But this was different. I didn't know how I knew, I just did. It was the way he listened to the things I was saying. Really listened. He'd hang off my sentences, and then bring things up much later I'd completely forgotten I'd even mentioned. I hadn't given away too much about my past, kept it to the basics. Lost my mother when I was young. Had a turbulent relationship with my father. The usual. But there were certain things I couldn't bring myself to tell him. Not yet, anyway.

'You're distant tonight.'

'Sorry, I'm just tired. How's your week been?'

'Pretty stressful. Working on a case that's driving me crazy. I think I'm going to lose it.'

'I'm sorry.' I never pressed Adam to tell me about the legal cases he was working on. I figured he'd tell me if he wanted to. I was well-versed in holding things back, so the people around me tended not to open up much either.

'It's all right. How's yours been? How's the hospital?'

'Yeah, it's okay. Sometimes I feel like quitting and doing something completely different. I guess I moved over here for a change – for an adventure. I probably shouldn't be doing the same thing I did back home.'

'Then why don't you try something different? Go for a complete change? Shake things up a bit.'

I sighed. 'I don't even know what else I would do. That's the thing. I'd probably just work in a bar or café or something. I know, token Aussie overseas. At least it wouldn't be as stressful, and I'd meet different people.'

'Well, why don't you just do it? I know loads of people who work at bars and cafés, I'm sure I could set something up.'

He had an answer for everything. I appreciated how he always took an interest in my ideas, even if they were stupid.

'Yeah, I dunno. I guess I should keep my skills sharp – it'll be easier to get back into the game when I'm back home.'

Adam's face dropped. He was bad at hiding his emotions. Even though it'd only been a couple of months, he always looked disappointed when I said that I'd most likely return to Australia one day. I quickly changed the subject.

'What do you think you would have been if you hadn't been a lawyer?'

'God knows. I never knew what I wanted to be. I just

woke up one day and decided I would study law.'

It hadn't been like that for me. I knew exactly what drew me towards becoming a nurse. It was the least I could do.

'How about you?' he asked. 'Did you ever have a backup plan?'

'Not really. I always knew I wanted to… help people.'

Adam reached over and squeezed my hand. Self-consciousness swept over me. Times were changing, but I still wasn't ready to express public displays of affection with another man outside the four sweaty walls of a gay club. Even in another city in a country on the other side of the world. I pulled my hand away slightly, but Adam didn't take offence. He knew my insecurities and didn't appear to have an issue with them. I liked that about him too. He was more progressive than I was. The fact he'd been raised by parents that were completely accepting of his sexuality helped. I was endlessly envious of that.

The waiter returned with our food. This time I gave him a look that said: 'Yes, he's mine. So you can keep your dirty hands off.'

He got the message. Avoiding any eye contact with Adam, he quickly disappeared. Adam had noticed my sideways glance, but he didn't react. He smiled and proceeded to tuck into his pizza.

The cold air was visible on our breath as we made our way towards the tube station. Surely it would start to warm up soon? It felt like winter had hung around forever.

'Thanks for tonight.' Adam sunk deeper into his Burberry

scarf. 'I had a great time.'

'So did I.'

Our stroll went from leisurely to static as Adam ground to a halt.

'What's up?' I asked him. 'Why're you stopping?'

Adam looked at me intently. 'Seb... I think I love you.'

There it was. The words we wait our whole lives to hear. I definitely had. It was the first time someone had actually told me they loved me in that way, aside from a random night with a guy who was coming up from so much speed that he told the bus driver he loved him in the next breath.

The question was: did I feel the same?

Adam shrugged. 'It's all right, you don't have to say anything. I just wanted you to know.'

He could tell I was shocked. I wanted more than anything to say it back. To complete what should have been a perfect moment, just like in the movies. But instead, I said nothing. I just waited for people to push past us and jolt life back into motion.

'Come on.' Adam grabbed my hand. 'It's freezing. Let's go.'

23ʳᵈ April 2005

The second time I got close to telling Adam I loved him was after a footy match he'd dragged me along to. I'd made it clear to him I hated sports, which he said made me a fake Aussie. I tried explaining to him that not every Australian was obsessed with sport, but he was having none of it. Every Aussie he'd met up until me was a footy fanatic.

'I'm going to come with you to Oz one day so you can prove to me you're not the only one,' he once said.

I eventually agreed to go with him to see Fulham, his favourite team, play against Chelsea. I actually enjoyed the game more than I thought I would, probably due to the five pints of beer I knocked back. And because I got to watch a bunch of hot men run around a field with their muscly calves on show. I was certain that's why Adam loved it too, even though he assured me it wasn't:

'It takes me back to my childhood. My dad used to take me to see Fulham play all the time.'

As we walked out the stadium amidst a noisy crowd of drunken footy fans, it didn't matter that Adam's favourite team had lost. It didn't matter that pissed Chelsea fans were singing victory chants at us walking along in our black and white striped Fulham scarves. All that mattered was I'd had an amazing afternoon, I'd had five pints and I was ready to tell my boyfriend I loved him too. Once we got away from the homophobic meatheads, of course.

We drifted away from the deafening crowds and made our way back into the busy backstreets of London. This would be my chance. I'd catch him off guard, just as he had with me the month before. We twisted through the scattered crowds, this time minus the hooligans. It was now or never.

'Adam, I ...'. My sentence was cut off by the sound of a siren as a police car sped past. I leapt out my skin.

This was always my reaction when I heard a siren, particularly when I knew it was the police. It'd been this way since I left The Nowhere. I carried the fear with me wherever I went. Fear of getting caught. Fear of getting found out. Fear. Siren. Fear. Siren. Fear.

'Seb, it's okay.' Adam threw an arm around me. He'd seen me freak out many times at the sound of sirens over the past few months we'd known each other. Sirens were as common as rain in London, so it was something he'd already got used to, even if I hadn't. I must have looked visibly shaken because Adam sat me down on the pavement, which felt cold against the seat of my jeans. He told me to breathe.

'In, out. In, out. In, out.'

I followed Adam's instructions. Slowly, the world came back into focus. I'd prevented the panic attack from rearing its ugly face again. This time.

'Are you okay?'

'Yeah, I'm fine.'

'What were you going to say?'

'Oh, nothing. Don't worry about it.'

The moment was gone. The words would have to wait.

18th May 2005

The third time I got close to telling Adam I loved him, I told him. Half asleep in a twist of sex-sodden bed sheets and sweaty flesh, I climbed on top of his naked body and whispered the words into his ear. I meant it. At least in that moment.

'I love you too.'

5th June 2005

I woke to the sound of rain battering the windows. Adam rolled over so we were no longer back to back. He scooped me up in his arms. He loved spooning me, which I could tolerate for about five minutes. After that, I just started to feel claustrophobic.

We hadn't made a habit of saying 'I love you', for which I was grateful. I was pretty sure that's exactly what you're not meant to do if you don't want the magic to wear off. The trouble was, ever since I'd spoken the words to Adam, I'd begun to doubt them. Sure, I was attracted to him. I cared about him. But something was missing and I couldn't put my finger on it. Maybe things were just moving too quickly. Either way, I was sure I had the capacity to fall in love with him. I would just take it one day at a time. One breath at a time. In, out. In, out. In, out.

'Morning, baby,' he whispered in my ear.

'Morning.'

'You want coffee?'

'That's a stupid question.'

It had taken Adam a few attempts to make my coffee the way I liked it. His version of the beverage was instant with two sugars, which didn't sit well with an Aussie. Each time he made me one in the plunger he made it a little stronger. He was a quick learner.

Adam climbed out of bed, kissed me on the head and

made his way towards the kitchen. Although he hadn't officially moved in with me, he might as well have. He was at my place all the time. I didn't have any housemates, so it made sense, but I wasn't sure whether it was a bit soon for that level of commitment. Telling him I loved him was a big enough deal.

Adam was pouring the coffee into two matching mugs when the home phone rang. It caught me off guard, as I rarely received any calls. The fact it was so early made it even stranger. My eyes darted towards the kitchen clock as I reached out to pick up the phone. Seven-thirty on a Sunday morning. It had to be a wrong number.

'Hello?'

'Hello, is that Mr. Johns?' A woman's voice with an Australian accent.

'Yeah, it's me. Who's calling?'

'My name's Tina Matthews, I'm calling from Royal Perth Hospital.'

Where I'd trained to become a nurse. Must be chasing up some paperwork or something.

'I'm sorry to inform you that your father has suffered a heart attack. He's currently unconscious and on life-support.'

The nurse's final words trailed off as static white noise filled my ears. My vision blurred and the colour drained away, leaving everything motionless and monochrome. A heart attack. It was hard to process. I suddenly felt awful. Knowing how far away I was made it feel that much worse. He could have died. He could be dead and I wouldn't have been there. Yes, he could be a bastard, and I hated him sometimes. But he could be dead, and I wouldn't have been there. The thought made me feel physically sick. As if I didn't carry enough guilt around with me.

You can't keep it secret forever. The truth always comes out eventually.

'Seb? Seb is everything okay?' Adam's words made their way through my thoughts like bullets cutting through a thick fog. I realised Tina was still on the line waiting for my response.

'Mr. Johns? Mr. Johns, are you still there?'

'Yeah. Yeah, I'm still here.'

'I understand this must be a huge shock. Your father is in an induced coma, but he's going to be fine. He's in generally good health and still has youth on his side.'

Why was she lying to me? He didn't have youth on his side. Neither did I.

I thanked Tina and wrote down her details, before hanging up. Even before I'd talked to Adam, it was clear what I had to do. I'd been thinking about it for some time now, and the news had just made the decision for me. Maybe it was happening for a reason. Perhaps that's why I wasn't allowing myself to fall fully in love with Adam.

'Are you okay?'

'No.'

'Did something happen? Back home? Did something happen to your dad?'

The worry was written all over Adam's face. Under any other circumstance, I would have found it endearing. But not today. Today, I just needed to get moving. I was wasting time already by just sitting there.

'Yes. I have to go.'

'Go? As in… back to Australia? Is he okay?'

'Yeah. Well, no. He had a heart attack.'

'Oh, baby. I'm so sorry.' Adam reached to hug me.

I pulled away. 'I'm sorry, Adam. I have to go.' I walked into the hallway and pulled my suitcase out from the cupboard.

'What, so you're just going to up and leave? You're just going to fuck off back to the other side of the world without even considering me?' He had raised his voice to an incredulous yell.

There it was. The side of him he'd been hiding. Every guy I'd met seemed to have this demonic side. Most were just good at keeping it locked away. Adam had hidden it well until this time of crisis. When I needed him to not freak out the most.

'Yes, I'm going to fuck off back to the other side of the world. Because it's my home. And because my dad is back there lying in a hospital bed. Lucky to be alive. If he even pulls through.'

'But you hate your dad.'

I didn't need this. I didn't need this, and I didn't want him here anymore. I knew I didn't love him. I knew it wasn't possible to feel the same way for anyone as I had for Jake. Why was I even wasting my time?

'Goodbye, Adam.'

Our two cooling coffees sat untouched.

*

Standing hypnotised by the flickering LCD board, I watched each city and country melt into one another. People rushed past, hitting into me with their backpacks and scuffing my ankles with their luggage. I hated Heathrow, but tonight I didn't care about its chaos. It paled in comparison to the chaos within, and to the chaos that awaited me back home.

The last ten hours had also been chaos. Part of me felt guilty for not just jumping in a cab and onto the first flight when I heard the news. But I knew he was in good hands and he was a fighter. I also knew I wouldn't be coming back to London, so I needed to pack up any shit that was coming back with me and let my landlord know I was leaving without notice. That had gone better than I'd expected, purely because he'd lost his own father in the last year. Not that it stopped him from keeping my deposit and making me pay the remaining month's rent.

Brussels. Amsterdam. Barcelona. Paris.

The names started to shapeshift and blend into one another.

Tokyo. Hong Kong. Dubai. Singapore.

There it was. The destination I'd be stopping in to refuel. How much longer did I have to wait?

Go to gate, the lights commanded.

It was time.

As I walked quickly down the moving walkway, I peered out the long windows that ran alongside it, and out at the tarmac. The night sky was peppered with clouds, and there wasn't a star in sight. That wasn't unusual – you could never really see stars in London. The city lights obscured them, just as I obscured my own feelings. Until now. I imagined the world I was going back to. Would it have changed? I pictured the eucalyptus trees. I imagined the dry heat and the blistering sun. I imagined the sounds of all the different birds. Sounds that would be so exotic to someone travelling from London for the first time. But they were so familiar to me. They were the sounds that would signal my homecoming.

It was a relief I'd landed a window seat. I planned to get my hands on a mini bottle of red as soon as the flight attendants came around, and knock back a Valium with it. That way I'd be out cold for the next few hours. That way I'd block out everything I was leaving behind, and everything I was returning to.

The distant sound of upper-middle-class Brits conversing grew louder and louder until they reached the seats next to me. The guy had long, light hair that hadn't seen a brush in a few months, while the girl took it one step further with dusty dreadlocks. From their conversation, it sounded like they were just starting a round-the-world trip, but looked like they'd been round it a few times already.

'Hey, man,' the guy started. 'Where're you travelling to?'

'Perth.' My reply was blunt, but enough for them to detect my accent.

'Are you going home?' the girl asked, pulling a neck pillow out of her backpack.

'Yeah. I'm going home.' I didn't know whether to laugh or cry.

The lights finally dimmed as the plane taxied across the tarmac. The safety presentation was just a distant blur as I closed my eyes and sunk back into my chair. When the wheels finally lost contact with the runway, I felt a jolt. Like a cord being cut. I was no longer a Londoner. I no longer belonged to that world. I no longer belonged to Adam. I opened my eyes and peered down through the oval window. The arteries of my former home glistened, indicating life would go on without me. Closing my eyes once more, I pictured home. I pictured Dad. I pictured Jake.

You can't keep it secret forever. You can't keep it secret forever. You can't keep it secret forever.

14th November 1997

When Kylie stood directly in the sunlight, I noticed her milky skin had started to bronze, and a constellation of freckles had broken out across her face.

'I just fed Scampi.' Her eyes squinted in the sun. 'I thought you'd have the bikes out by now.'

'Oh, thanks Kylie. You're too quick, beat me to it.'

It had surprised me how easily Kylie had acclimatised to life on the farm. Any preconceptions I'd had of her struggling to adapt from city life were soon dispelled. From day one she'd tied her hair back, ditched her make-up, rolled up her sleeves and got stuck in. If only I'd adjusted to life in The Nowhere so easily.

The day passed quickly as we rode our bikes with Scampi running along beside us. It made me so much happier having Kylie around. Her positive energy radiated into me like starved lungs filling with air. Her wide smile, teeth gleaming. Laughter. Genuine laughter every day was something I'd longed for. Having her there seemed to make things better with Dad too. He was mostly on his best behaviour with Kylie around. He'd stopped starting pointless fights over nothing. And he'd give us space. Even when we were working, he'd ride his quad bike ahead or behind us, for which I was thankful. We'd still stop and stand under a tree for shade during breaks to keep him company while he smoked.

It was clear Dad loved having a woman around, and I often wondered if it made him miss Mum even more. But I could also tell he was happy that I was happy and getting on with my chores without complaints. That's ultimately all that mattered to him.

'It's been so much more fun since you turned up.' I dropped a cassette into the player Kylie had brought me as a gift when she arrived. It was Pearl Jam's *Vitalogy*, the album she'd been playing when I went over to say goodbye.

'I'm enjoying it too.'

'Really? Are you sure?' Could she really be enjoying life in The Nowhere?

'Really. It's great to catch up with you, and it's refreshing to be away from everything back in Perth. And your dad and Jeremy are so nice.'

Now I knew she was sugar-coating reality. There were many ways to describe Dad, but *nice* wasn't top of the list.

'I guess Dad's been on his best behaviour.'

'So, it's Saturday tomorrow,' Kylie continued. 'What do you wanna do?'

Making plans for the weekend had never been a priority before she showed up. Although I tried my best to hang out with Jake as much as I could, it was often hard work convincing Dad to let me do what I wanted. He usually wanted me to play with Jeremy. This had also changed with Kylie's arrival, with Dad pretty much giving us free reign on the weekends. This naturally meant most weekends included hanging out with Jake.

'I dunno. What do you wanna do?' I knew the answer already.

'I guess we could see what Jake's up to?'

I sensed it right away, as soon as I introduced them. Kylie was that easy to read. The way she looked at him was exactly how I wished he'd look at me. What wasn't so easy to figure out was whether her feelings were reciprocated. Jake remained forever the enigma.

'Yeah, cool. Sounds good. I'll give him a call now.'

As if I'd turn down an excuse to hear Jake's voice.

15th November 1997

As we pushed our way through the scrub, the morning light shining through the trees, part of me wished Jake had said he didn't want to meet us. Part of me wished he hadn't even answered the phone. As much as I wanted to see him, Jake acted differently around Kylie. It was like he was putting on a show. Whether it was to impress her or impress me remained a mystery. But it wasn't the Jake I'd come to know. The thought of anything happening between the two of them made my skin crawl. Was it because I was jealous of Jake, jealous of Kylie or jealous of them both? All I knew for certain was that I was jealous. And I hated it.

We pushed our way through the shedding eucalyptus and followed the faint path that had started to form from all our travails back and forth between the farms. We were dressed lightly to combat the morning heat. The scent of summer was in the air. It wasn't even ten o'clock and sweat glossed my brow. Kylie's cheeks were rosy – as if she'd just been caught in the act.

He was already there waiting at the edge of the scrub, which was unlike him. He welcomed us with his signature mischievous grin. I hated myself for feeling that same mix of happiness and excitement when I saw him. The feeling that no matter what we'd be doing, we'd be having a good time.

'Hey, kids. It's gonna be a scorcher. I brought a picnic.'

We decided to stay in the bush for the day to escape the

heat. Jake pulled out a metal flask from the basket. It didn't take a genius to work out it didn't contain water or lemonade.

'Who wants the first swig?' That smile again.

'I will.' Kylie matched his with her own mischievous smirk. I always knew she had a rebellious side to her. Despite being well behaved at school and always coming out with top grades, it was as if there was a defiant soul hiding beneath, waiting to break free. Jake was the perfect person to bring that side of her out, the same way he had with me.

Kylie took a swig from the bottle before shutting her eyes tight and pursing her lips. 'Shit, what's in there, Jake?'

Jake had already begun rolling three cigarettes. 'A little concoction of whatever I could find in Mum's liquor cabinet.'

He passed us both a cigarette before lighting his own.

'You guys are pretty ballsy smoking in here. It'd be so easy to have the whole place up in flames.' Kylie took the cigarette and allowed Jake to light it for her.

I thought about saying no, but I needed to smoke. I needed to feel that nicotine hit and subsequent head rush. I took the lighter from Jake's hand and lit up. The smoke from all three cigarettes curled into one thick pool that floated towards the sky.

'Your turn.'

Kylie passed me the bottle of mixed spirits as if it were a challenge. It was obvious Jake liked that. He sensed she was as drawn to danger as he was. I felt outnumbered. Deep down I longed for order. For colouring within the lines. For following the rules and keeping safe. But I couldn't let this show. I wouldn't.

They know you're a fucking faggot. You might as well just be honest about it.

I took a huge swig from the metallic bottle. It was like drinking petrol. The inside of my cheeks and throat burnt like hell. But the rush that followed felt fantastic.

'Thanks.' I passed the flask to Jake. 'Your turn.'

It didn't take much temptation. Jake swigged down a couple of mouthfuls as if to show how much harder he was than me. This didn't stop him from erupting into a closed-mouth coughing fit.

'That'll put hairs on our chests.' He gulped, before spitting out the residual taste over his left shoulder.

'I don't want hairs on my chest.' Kylie laughed, cupping her breasts. It was so obvious what she was doing. Jake's eyes followed her movement, exactly the way she'd planned. Taking a longer drag from the cigarette, I found myself wishing she wasn't there. Why couldn't it be back to how it was? Just Jake and me. Hanging out, drinking. Getting high. Why did I have to go and complicate things by bringing a girl into the picture? It was my own doing. It was my own fault.

'That's true.' Jake laughed, passing the bottle back to her. 'But it'll make you feel pretty good all the same.'

We spent the next hour talking, smoking and passing the bottle around until it was empty. I'd lost track of time, and realised we'd have to head home for dinner soon, so would need to sober up before then. The last thing we needed was to rock up at home legless. Dad would slaughter us. At least, he'd slaughter me and get Kylie the next taxi home. Maybe that's how I'd get Kylie out the picture, so I'd have Jake all to myself again.

You fucking fag. He doesn't want you. He wants her. Why don't you just let them fuck and get it over with?

The joy of having Kylie back in my life was quickly disintegrating. I had to stop thinking about trying to get rid of her. It had to be the alcohol. It was Jake I had to thank for fucking things up. Not Kylie. Why was I such a pushover? Why couldn't I just say no to smoking and drinking and letting him walk all over me? Was it that important for me to look bloody cool in front of him? In front of Kylie?

You're pathetic. Weak and pathetic.

'Seb… are you all right, mate?'

Jake's voice. I realised I'd gone into a bit of a trance. 'Yeah, I'm fine. Just thinking.'

'Thinking about what?' Kylie asked as she rolled over and took Jake's cigarette out his hand. She took a long drag.

'I can roll you another one, babe.'

I hated that he'd started calling her that. The word made my blood boil.

I decided the best thing was to change the subject entirely. 'Just about… how we're gonna escape this bloody place.'

Jake took the cigarette back off of Kylie and inhaled. 'Fair enough, mate. I've been thinking about that a lot lately too.'

'You guys really hate this place, don't you?' Kylie asked.

My vision was starting to soften, and it was clear Kylie's eyes were losing their focus too.

'Yep,' Jake responded swiftly.

Something about his answer made me feel relieved. I was worried that now Kylie was around meant he wasn't in such a rush to leave. Turns out not even a pretty girl could stand between Jake and his surfing dreams.

'Well, why don't you both just come with me when I leave? You're technically adults now. Well, you will be soon enough, Seb. So when summer's over, and I call my taxi to take me back to Perth, you guys should just jump in with me. I'll be paying for it anyway.'

She made it sound so simple. But why couldn't it be? The idea of jumping in a taxi with Kylie had never occurred to me. Jake was an adult now and I wasn't far behind him. But what about Scampi? What about Jeremy? What about Dad? What about the fact we had no money?

'You serious?' Jake's eyes lit up. 'You reckon we could do that?'

'Sure, why not? I'm sure you guys could crash at my place until you get set up. My mum loves you already, Seb.'

I'd always been fond of Kylie's mum. She'd been like a second mother to me, especially after Mum died. But I still felt a bit uneasy about just turning up on her doorstep with Jake, announcing we were moving in. I wouldn't have wanted to put her in that position. Not to mention it would be the first place Dad would come looking for me. I'd always liked the thought of driving off somewhere he'd have no idea where to find me.

'Yeah, sure,' Kylie said.

She was drunk now. I could hear it in her voice. Perhaps

the subject had started to sober me up, making her lack of sobriety more apparent.

'That sounds awesome!' Jake exclaimed. 'What d'ya reckon, Seb?'

'It's definitely an idea.'

'An idea? What the hell are you talking about, mate? This could be our ticket outta this hellhole once and for all. I thought you'd be over the moon.'

It was all so easy for him. Just come up with a spontaneous idea and that's it. Ride off into the sunset and live happily ever after. He had nothing to think about. No one to worry about. No thoughts about the consequences. How would we afford food? Would he just expect Kylie's family to look after him? I was starting to figure out how selfish he really was. The world revolved around him, and everyone else purely existed to help him achieve his goals.

'You're right,' I said, drawing a deep breath. 'There could be something in that idea.'

Jake obviously wasn't satisfied with my answer. He was giving me a look of bewilderment, but we were distracted when Kylie suddenly jumped up.

'Let's not worry about tomorrow yet. Let's focus on right now. Bet you can't catch me.'

She sprinted in the direction of Jake's farm. She was the same girl I'd known years ago, free-spirited and spontaneous. Running with the wind whipping her hair, without a care in the world.

'Hey, wait!' Jake began to run after her.

He was obviously worried she'd turn up to his place

drunk and get him in trouble with his parents. I smirked to myself. Not so cool now. Realising I'd been left behind, I ran after the pair.

It felt good to run. Even though I spent so much of my time outside, I rarely walked or ran anywhere. I just sat on the quad bike all day. I imagined we were running away from The Nowhere. Further and further with every step. Maybe Kylie's idea wasn't so bad. Perhaps we could just jump in the taxi with her and head back to Perth. Would Dad really come looking for me? Surely he'd accept that I had made my own decision as an adult and that if I really wanted to stay, I would. Surely Jeremy would understand. At least, he would when he got older. Maybe he'd be different from me anyway. Maybe he'd enjoy living in The Nowhere. It was pretty much all he knew. As the years would go by, he'd forget life before the farm more and more. It would be easier for him. It would never be easy for me. I'd never forget life before the farm. I'd never forget.

As we approached the bush clearing that marked the neighbouring property, I felt the sun burn my skin. Jake had nearly caught up to Kylie, and dived suddenly towards her, sending them both crashing to the ground. Running right behind them both, I tried to stop but ended up tripping over the root of a tree and on top of them both. We were a huddle of limbs and laughter.

'I was going to stop, you idiot.' Kylie snorted between laughs.

'No you weren't!' Jake yelled playfully. 'You'd have got us all killed.'

In that moment, lying there tangled up in the bodies of my two closest friends, I felt happier than I ever had. It suddenly didn't matter about not being in Perth. It didn't matter that we were in The Nowhere. I was just happy to be with Jake and Kylie and wished the moment would never end. I wished we could remain lying there, tied up in each other, for eternity. Surely I deserved that much? Surely I'd suffered enough for the universe to give me that? I closed my eyes and held onto the moment for as long as I could. I held onto the moment until it decided to let me go. Until our breathing had slowed down to a unified rhythm and all that was left was darkness.

*

I woke first. My eyes blinked a few times before jolting upright. The sun was setting now and the heat had dropped substantially. What time was it? Why hadn't I remembered to wear my watch? Jake and Kylie were still lying passed out beneath me. The image of Dad's angry face shot into my mind.

'Kylie...Kylie, wake up!' I began to shake her.

'Jesus Christ, Seb.' Kylie rubbed her eyes as she climbed upright. 'I'm awake, okay?'

'We gotta get home.'

'Hang on.' Jake pulled himself up. 'Drink some of this.' Jake reached into his backpack and pulled out a different flask.

'I think we've had enough.' I was grateful that my vision was no longer blurry, but I had no idea how long we'd been out. We must have slept it off.

'No, dickhead. It's just water.' He passed it to Kylie.

'Here you go, babe.'

That word again. But at least he had water, and at least Kylie was gulping it down. We needed to be completely sober by the time we got home.

'Thanks, Jake.' Kylie smiled sweetly at him as she passed the flask to me. She was such a fucking flirt.

After we'd polished off the bottle of warm water, Kylie and I headed back to the farm. Jake didn't have the same worries with his parents as I had with Dad. At least, that's how it appeared. Maybe it was a different story behind closed doors.

We walked in to the smell of oven pizza and hot chips. It couldn't have been as late as I'd thought.

'There you guys are,' Dad said. 'I wondered where you'd got to.'

His voice was friendly. He was in a good mood. The relief was immense.

'Hey, yeah. Sorry, Dad. We lost track of time.'

'All good, Son. There's still time to set the table.'

Sprawled out on the carpet with a cushion perched under her head, Kylie fell asleep in front of the television not long after dinner. Dad, who as always was stretched out on the couch, was happy to have the company before he also passed out with the cricket results blasting. Once I'd finished washing up and had fed Scampi, I tucked Jeremy up in bed. I decided to hang out with him a little longer that evening.

Perhaps it was guilt that drove me; I'd hardly spent any time with him since Kylie arrived. Or because Kylie, Jake and I had seriously talked about running away, forcing me to think more and more about what it would mean to leave him behind. Whatever it was, it was as if I'd somehow not noticed he was getting older. He might have only been seven, but he'd soon be a young man with his own hopes and dreams. How could I neglect him?

I sat down next to him on his Spiderman bed sheets. 'Aren't you getting a little old for Spiderman?'

'No. I'll never be too old for Spiderman.'

'That's true.' I chuckled. 'Speaking of spiders, no more visits from your little mate?'

'Nah, Harry went away.' There was a brief pause before he said: 'You smell like Dad.'

'What do you mean?' Could he smell the grog and cigarettes on my breath? I hoped not.

'I dunno. You just smell funny.' He'd already shut his eyes and turned away.

'Go to sleep, you little turd.'

Another pause.

'I love you.'

But he was already asleep.

24th November 1997

Scampi scoffed down the sloppy chunks of meat as soon as I'd finished pouring them into his bowl. I was grateful he didn't hang around. With the heat rising each day, the stench of uneaten dog food would be unbearable, and the flies wouldn't take long to start circling. They were already out in full force, signalling the start of summer. Kylie waved vigorously to shoo away a large fly that had taken a liking to her. It was so big you could make out the tiny hairs on its body as it landed on her face.

'Fuck's sake, they're relentless.'

'I told you,' I said, darting inside to grab some insect repellent from the kitchen drawer. 'Here, put this on.'

Kylie began applying the spray generously all over her exposed skin. It didn't always do much, but it was worth a try.

'Thanks.' She pressed her mouth into a line and closed her eyes as she sprayed her face.

Was she getting tired of the farm? In the weeks since we'd passed out in the bush with Jake, we'd pretty much had our heads down in our chores each day. Worried that Dad's good mood could be short-lived, I didn't want to push my luck. If Jeremy had smelt booze or cigarettes on my breath, it was only a matter of time before Dad would notice too.

'How are you going, Kylie?'

She paused as if trying to assess my words. 'Fine… why?'

'Oh, no reason. I just know work's been a bit tough lately and it's heating up a bit now. I just wanted to make sure you're doing okay.'

'I'm doing fine,' she said, smiling. 'You worry too much.'

I could hear the phone ringing faintly inside. Jake. It had to be. I ran in to answer it.

'Hey, mate.'

I was right.

'Hey, Jake. How's it going?'

'It's going good. I'll keep this quick – I know your dad will be home soon. My folks are heading off to Byron again this weekend if you guys wanna stay over?'

Excitement and fear surged through me simultaneously. What was I afraid of?

'Seb?'

'Oh, awesome. I mean, that should be fine. You know... if my dad's cool with it.'

'Yeah, I know. Fingers crossed. Anyway, let me know when you can.'

'Sure, I will.'

The phone went dead.

'Was that Jake?' Kylie had been standing in the kitchen doorway. I hadn't even noticed she'd been listening in.

'Yeah.'

'What did he want?' She tilted her head a degree.

'Something about staying over his place this weekend.'

'Sounds fun. You up for it?'

She obviously was. Why wasn't I surprised?

'Yeah, I guess. If Dad's cool with it.'

'Awesome. We could have a little party.'

'Yeah. A party would be fun. Anyway, we better get on with our work. Dad will be pissed if we get home and haven't even started on our bikes. I promised him we'd check the water troughs. He's paranoid the cows are gonna get dehydrated in this heat.'

'You know, I don't think your dad is half as bad as you make him out to be.'

Was she trying to make me angry? She knew Dad better than that. She just wanted to have a bloody party. She just wanted Jake.

Our conversation was cut short by the sound of Dad's ute pulling into the driveway. Party plans would have to wait.

29th November 1997

The shriek of a red-tailed black cockatoo echoed through the scrub as we made our way towards Jake's farm. Kylie's freckles had spread across her arms and legs now as the weight of summer had really started to set in. She pulled her defiant ringlets back into a ponytail to stop them sticking to her forehead.

'Does Jake's place have air con?'

'I'm afraid not. But it always feels a bit cooler than my place for some reason. It's a bit darker.'

'Good.'

She sounded agitated. She should have been grateful we were going to Jake's place. I hadn't really wanted to. Normally I would have jumped at the chance, but it was different now. I knew he didn't really care about me being there. He just wanted an excuse to hang out with *her*. It was surprising Dad had even allowed us to go. Maybe Kylie was right. Maybe he wasn't that bad.

The moment we broke out from the bush into the open air, our eyes were greeted with an ocean of fluorescent yellow. The canola was out in full force now, like a halo surrounding the farmhouse. The sight sent an instant rush of joy through me. It was clear Kylie felt the same.

'Wow.' Her eyes scanned the luscious fields ahead. 'It's beautiful.'

I nodded but played it cool. 'Yeah, it's pretty neat.'

The sky was clear and the sun's location signalled it was lunchtime. Jake had told us not to eat beforehand, as he'd be cooking something. My stomach growled. It had better be good. We reached the house and knocked on the door. Jake quickly answered and the waft of something sweet greeted us immediately.

'Hey, kids. You're just in time. Lunch is ready.'

The kitchen was a complete mess. Almost every inch was covered in a layer of flour, and cracked eggshells littered the counter. A mountain of dirty dishes waited in the sink.

'Jeez, Jake,' Kylie said. 'You've only had the place to yourself a few hours.'

Jake laughed. 'I know, I know. I'm pretty bad at cleaning up after myself. But I promise it'll be worth it. You guys head out back, I've set up some shade.'

We wandered out into the backyard and were met with a sun umbrella that had been hoisted upright to shade three deck chairs and a small table. On top was a bottle of champagne accompanied by three wine glasses.

'Is that from your mum's cabinet?' I called back inside.

Jake followed us outside carrying a large plate of steaming brownies. 'Nah, they gave that to us for looking after the place while they're away.'

'You're doing a brilliant job so far, aren't you?' Kylie laughed as she picked up one of the wine glasses. 'Hasn't your mum got any flutes?'

'Huh?' Jake placed the brownies on the table.

'Never mind. Oh wow, these look amazing!'

'Not exactly a very nutritional lunch.' I realised how

ungrateful I sounded as soon as the words were out. It was actually pretty endearing how much of an effort Jake was making. But it was clearly all for Kylie.

'Oh, they're nutritional all right,' Jake said with a cheeky grin as he sat down.

'Oh my god…' Kylie began. 'You didn't.'

Jake nodded as his grin broke into a devilish laugh. I should have known there would be more to the kind gesture.

'Here, let's get this party started.' Jake popped open the bottle, sending the cork flying into the canola. The fizzy liquid foamed as he poured it into the three glasses before he went on: 'I want to celebrate our exciting new plans. Here… to us.'

Kylie and I picked up the glasses he handed to us. For a moment I wondered if Kylie even remembered what he was talking about, as she'd been tipsy by that point. But if she didn't, she did a good job of covering it up.

'To us. And you boys getting the hell out of The Nowhere!'

Our three glasses clinked, sending golden foam gushing down the sides.

'You remember the nickname?' I asked.

'Of course I do, I came up with it, didn't I?' she replied.

'What nickname?' Jake's eyebrow arched as he picked up a brownie.

I smirked. He didn't like not being included in something. 'Oh, that's the name Kylie gave this dump just before I moved here. It's stuck with me ever since.'

Taking a bite from the brownie, Jake lifted his glass again

and echoed Kylie's words with his mouth full: 'To gettin' the hell outta The Nowhere!'

It didn't take us long to finish the weed brownies, as well as polish off the champagne and another couple of bottles of wine Jake procured from somewhere after that. Despite the umbrella over our heads, the punishing heat was enough to coat us all in a thick layer of sweat.

'How do you guys deal with the heat out here?' Kylie asked, swiping a fly that had landed on her brow. 'It's unbearable.'

'Well, it's my first full summer here too, remember,' Jake said. 'Seb, tell us the secret.'

There really wasn't one. I couldn't even tell them you get used to it because that would be a lie. They'd discover that for themselves soon enough.

'Fuck knows. Heaps of showers.'

The mischievous smile was back. 'That's not a bad idea, mate. Come on, let's get wet.'

Jake grabbed the half-drunk bottle of wine and headed back into the house.

'I guess he wants us to follow?' Kylie laughed.

I hated her in that moment. He wanted her to follow, not me. She knew that.

Kylie jumped up and followed Jake inside. Blindly following, I turned the hatred onto myself.

Why don't you just leave them to it, fag? You know they don't want you there.

When we reached the bathroom, Jake had already stripped down to his undies and turned the shower on. The sight of water dripping down his toned, tanned torso made my body tingle. My eyes were drawn to his wet, grey undies. It was the first time I'd seen him with less than shorts on since the night we'd camped out. The memory made me shudder.

'What are you waiting for, kids? Jump in.'

Laughing hysterically, Kylie tore off her clothes, so she was down to her bra and undies. There was no doubt she looked gorgeous. I took in her smooth skin and slim frame, the curves that hadn't been there when we were growing up.

Kylie jumped in the shower with Jake. 'What are you waiting for, Seb? Get in. It's cooled me down already.'

I thought about turning around and leaving them to it, but the weed and alcohol had started to kick in, and I was horny as hell. After stripping down to my undies, I joined them both in the shower. The cold water felt heavenly against my hot skin. I lifted my face up towards it and let it pour down on my face and refresh me. That was when someone pinched my arse.

'Hey,' I said, opening my eyes. 'Who was that?'

'Who was what?' Kylie asked.

Jake laughed. 'Sorry, mate. I thought it was Kylie.'

The pair broke out into laughter. But I didn't feel like laughing. I climbed out the shower and picked up the nearest towel.

'Hey, where you going?' Jake asked.

'I've cooled down now. I'm gonna go get another drink.'

'I've got it right here,' he said, taking a swig from the bottle of wine.

I grabbed my clothes and left the room. I'd had enough

of his games. Why was he doing this to me? Did he enjoy fucking with my head? I strolled through the hallway dripping water across the timber floorboards. They could do what they wanted. I was going to get myself another drink and ignore them both. I began pulling on my jeans but fell onto the floor. I burst into laughter. What the hell was I doing? I was stoned.

'Didn't get very far, did ya?' Jake threw himself down on top of me.

I pushed him off. 'Ouch! Get off, dickhead!' Each word was punctuated with a fit of laughter.

Jake slumped onto the floor, also laughing his head off.

'Come on, losers.' Kylie walked past us, dripping with water. 'We've got lots more drinking to do.'

We sat beneath the crimson sky, feasting on an assortment of snacks Jake had brought out for us. The munchies had well and truly kicked in. Cheezels, Tim Tams, fruit. Bread, cake, leftover pasta. We washed it down with yet another bottle of wine, this time an expensive-looking French merlot that made me even more dehydrated. The contents of Jake's mum's cabinet were slowly but surely being depleted.

'What are you gonna do when we get away from this place, Seb?' Jake asked.

The question hovered around my head for a few moments, partly because the weed and grog were making my thoughts cloudy, but also because I had no idea. It was different for Jake. He had a dream. He had ambition. He'd be amazing at surfing and it would take him wherever he wanted to go. That made me envious. Why couldn't I have had something I was good at? Something I wanted to do or be?

'I dunno. I haven't really thought about it yet. Guess I'll just decide when we get there.'

'There must be something you want to do,' Kylie said as she sipped the wine. 'Why don't you come to uni with me?'

It was easy for Kylie too. She had brains and talent. She'd go far with her studies. Land a high-paid job as soon as she graduated. But what would I even do there, at uni? I barely scraped by with my final high school exams, and that was only because I'd had private tuition.

'I don't think so. I reckon I'll just get a job. Any job, I don't care what. I just wanna make money. I just wanna be independent.'

It was as if they weren't my words, but someone else's. They were flowing from my mouth but came from somewhere else. Is that what I really wanted? Just to take any old job? Jake would be a professional surfer. Kylie would be an academic. And there'd be me. I might as well just stay in The Nowhere. At least I was good on my quad bike. Good at my chores. Maybe I should just let them leave without me. I'd probably just get in the way.

'You'll figure it out,' Jake said softly.

It was the first time since Kylie had arrived that I felt like Jake was being himself. I missed that Jake. I hoped he was back for good.

The sky turned pale lavender as the sun was pulled below the horizon. Soon, the darkness arrived and stars appeared.

We sat wrapped in blankets as the temperature dipped. The merlot had run out.

'Hey,' Kylie began with the mischievous smile she seemed to have caught from Jake. 'Wanna play spin the bottle?'

My heart sank. That bloody game.

'That's a great idea.' Jake suddenly sat upright.

Was he being serious? Couldn't they just make out and get it over with? Why drag me into it?

'We're a bit limited on players, don't you think?' I was proud of myself for not pandering to them both. I'd done enough of that already.

'That doesn't matter,' Kylie said, grabbing the bottle. 'Here, I'll start.'

She placed the bottle on the cracked, red earth and sent it spinning. It landed somewhere between us.

'Well, I can't kiss myself.'

Before I'd had time to process what was happening, Kylie leant in and kissed me. First softly on the lips, then with her mouth open. I remembered our first kiss, at the party years ago, also during a game of spin the bottle. But this was so much better. Maybe because I had a better idea what I was doing this time. Maybe because I was high. Either way, Kylie kissed me and I kissed her back. Her lips were soft and tasted like Cheezels and merlot. Kylie kissed me and I kissed her back and it felt pretty bloody good.

A wolf whistle broke up our pash. 'All right, lovebirds. I'm feeling a bit left out here.'

'Your turn,' Kylie said, smiling at me.

I twisted the bottle around so hard that it kept spinning

in circles. Round and round. Round and round. Until it finally stopped. And it stopped directly in front of Jake.

'Your turn,' Kylie repeated.

I expected Jake to tell me to spin again. He wanted to kiss Kylie, not me. But before I had the chance, he reached across and pressed his lips on mine. It started like Kylie's kiss. First, softly on the lips, next, he opened his mouth and our tongues met.

That's when I knew. That's when it all made sense. I'd kissed Kylie and it felt good, but it was nothing compared to this. His thick lips. His stubbly chin. His warm breath. The hairs stood up across my body. My cock started to go hard. My heart began to race and my skin perspired. It was love. I was in love with a bloody guy. With Jake.

You fucking faggot. If only your mum could see you now. If only your dad could see you now.

I pulled away abruptly, my stomach churning.

'That was hot!' Kylie shouted. 'You boys are hot.'

I stood up suddenly. 'I don't feel so good.'

'Was it that bad?' Jake said, laughing.

'I think I've had too much. I need to lie down.'

'That's cool, mate. You're just stoned.'

He had no idea what he was doing to me. Or maybe he did. Either way, I couldn't be near him right now. I couldn't be near her, either.

I walked quickly into the house and headed straight for the bathroom. I made it just in time to get down on my knees and vomit into the toilet bowl. A foul mixture of red-stained chunks and acidic bile came pouring out as I clung on to the bowl and gagged. Was I coughing up blood? It dawned on me it was the wine. I could make out the faint vinegary smell from the chewed-up pasta shells.

Once the vomit had transformed from solids to liquid and eventually stopped, I flushed and washed my face and chest. I wanted to get up. I wanted to go back outside and see what was happening. But my head was pounding and I felt physically exhausted. I grabbed the bath mat and folded it a couple of times to create a makeshift pillow. I lay down on the cold hard tiles in a crumpled ball, waiting to pass out. Waiting for my head to stop talking.

You fucking mess. You fucking mess. You fucking mess.

30th November 1997

A shard of amber light flooded the bathroom, forcing my eyes open with its unapologetic glare. Sunrise. How had I slept through the night? Physically I felt better, but a feeling of dread weighed down my body. What had I missed? Slowly pulling myself up onto my feet, I walked into the hallway and found my clothes in a crumpled heap next to the bathroom door. After I slipped them on, I headed outside and was met with an array of empty bottles and cigarette butts. The smell of smoke and wine was still strong, making me want to throw up again. I quickly went back inside. Where were they?

Wandering through the house, it suddenly dawned on me where I'd have to check next. The last place in the world I wanted to look. Jake's bedroom. I moved so fast, the thought didn't have a chance to mature in my mind. My stomach churned again. Dread. Jake's room was directly in front of me. Jealousy. The door was shut. Hate. Should I open it? Love. It had to be opened. Lust. My hand reached forward to push down the handle. Longing. Quietly, I opened the door.

Jake and Kylie lay tangled with a thin, white sheet barely covering them; the scent of sweat simmered in the air. There was an ashtray at the edge of the bed. Another empty bottle of wine. Kylie's bra on the carpet. An open condom wrapper. The dread surged through me again. Slamming the door shut, I ran outside and into the yard.

The whole world had turned cold. Stripped of its colour, stripped of its sound. I couldn't hear the birds chirping their morning song. I couldn't hear my own breath. I couldn't see straight. Crouching down I tried to focus on my feet. Barefoot and bruised. A little cut with fresh blood on my ankle. Stains of dirt and vomit.

You fucking mess. They don't want you here. They don't want you around.

He wasn't meant to be with her. He was meant to be with me. That should have been me lying in that bed with him. That should have been me tangled up in his arms and legs, breathing his sweat. That should have been me. I hated him. I hated her. I hated myself.

Why had I introduced them to each other? Why had I even bothered asking her to come here? This wasn't meant to happen. She was meant to be here for *me*. To distract *me* from *him*. But it didn't work. It fucked up. I fucked it up. She wasn't here for me now – she was here for him. She wanted him and he wanted her. I was just in the way. In the middle. It'd be better if I just left them alone. Let them run away together. He could leave with her the way she'd planned, and I could stay in The Nowhere forever. Where I belonged. Dad might've been aggressive sometimes, but at least he loved me. At least he was loyal. At least he never let me down. Here, with Jeremy and Scampi. The only things in the world that mattered.

The door creaked open and Kylie soon appeared beside me. 'Sebastian, are you all right?'

'I'm fine,' I lied.

'You don't look fine. Are you feeling okay? Are you hung-over?'

Still crouched down, my head was between my knees. I slowly got up and turned around to face her. It was only then I realised my eyes were full of tears.

'Sebastian?' Kylie was wearing a white t-shirt and her undies. *His* white t-shirt. Bitch.

'Seb, I'm so sorry.' Her face dropped with realisation.

Had it really taken her that long? Wasn't it obvious?

My silence must have confirmed what she was thinking.

'I didn't realise you have feelings for me.'

Was she serious? Was she that self-centred she thought it was all about her? I sighed with disbelief.

Through gritted teeth, I finally spoke. 'You don't get it, do you? This isn't about *you.*'

Silence. Shock. Disgust. Now she'd realise. Now she'd understand. But I didn't want her to understand. I didn't want her to understand, and I didn't want her pity. I just wanted to run away. Run home and not have to face either of them ever again.

'I think I better go,' she said flatly.

She'd better go? Go where? Back to the farm?

Kylie disappeared back inside, leaving me standing in pieces. Fragments of me were scattered all over the dry grass and maroon earth. Couldn't the ground just splinter open and suck me in? I'd rather face burning flames than stand here any longer, waiting for what would come next.

I strolled slowly over to a nearby deck chair and sat

down, putting my head in my hands. Numb. Should I just go? Should I go back inside? Should I just get over it? What did it have to do with me anyway? He wasn't into me. He was into her. It was time to let it go. It was time to let them both go.

Kylie emerged fully clothed with her bag and started to walk in the direction of the bushland.

'Kylie, where are you going?'

'Back to Perth, Seb. You need to sort your shit out.'

I needed to sort my shit out? What was that supposed to mean? I had to go after her. What would Dad say when he got home? What would she say to him? That I'd shouted at her for sleeping with Jake because I liked him? I couldn't let that happen. I began to follow her when a hand grabbed my shoulder.

'Oi, what did you do?'

Swerving around, I faced Jake, who stood wearing only his undies.

'What do you mean *what did I do?*'

'What did you say? To make her run off like that?'

Anger suddenly rushed through me. Anger at Jake for being so dumb. Why couldn't he see? Why couldn't he see what was right in front of him? Or maybe he did and he just wanted to torture me. I turned back around and began walking away.

'Don't turn your bloody back on me.' Jake grabbed me again.

'Don't touch me.' I pushed his hand away with force.

'What the hell is your problem, Seb?'

'You. You're my problem, Jake.'

'Why? What have I done?'

'Are you that stupid? Haven't you worked it out?'

It was then he hit me. A forceful blow from his fist to my face, sending me flying backwards. I fell to the ground. I didn't even feel the pain. I couldn't feel anything. I'd blocked it all out. I wouldn't let him hurt me. Not my face. Not my heart. He could sleep with my best friend in front of me. He could punch my face, break my jaw. But it wouldn't hurt me. Nothing would. I would block it all for as long as I needed to. I'd block it out forever if it came to it.

You fucking poof. You brought it upon yourself. You deserved it. You deserved the pain. He should hit you again, finish you off.

I slowly pulled myself up. The blood began to drip down the side of my face. I could taste it in the corner of my mouth.

'You should go, Seb. I don't think we should hang out anymore.' Jake turned around and made his way back into the house.

I wanted to stay there. Crumpled up on the ground, bleeding. Maybe I could get it over with and bleed to death. But I knew that wouldn't happen. And Kylie would be home now, packing her stuff and telling Dad what a bloody poof I was. That would be worse than bleeding to death.

Once I pulled myself up, I started to pace through the bushes. The twisted branches reached out to grab me as my run became a sprint. The blood dripped down my face, which was beginning to swell. The guy I loved had just hit me.

I wanted to smash his delicate face in. Ruin those perfect features. Then, I wanted to rip my own face off. Shed my skin and climb out of my body. Start again. Start over. Be someone else. Anyone else. Anywhere else.

Not me. Not with him. Not in The Nowhere.

It took a lifetime to reach the house, even using all my strength to sprint through the bush. I tripped over loose branches, the blood dripping down the side of my lip. The throb in the side of my face pulsated like a heartbeat. I knew the pain would really kick in in a few hours. Right now, I was in shock. Not from the punch, but by what I'd walked in on. That hurt more than the punch. The punch would fade away. My heart would never heal.

When I finally reached the farm, I entered through the back door and raced towards Kylie's room. A wave of relief overcame me that I hadn't seen Dad, but I feared he'd be in there, trying to talk her out of her decision to leave. She'd have told him by now that his son was a dirty faggot and I would see it on his face. The disappointment. The disgust. The disgrace. I was ready to walk straight back out of the house. Back out of the farm and onto the road. I'd follow it until I'd reach Westonia and I'd lie down and wait for a car to hit me. That would be a better fate than remaining in The Nowhere. Remaining a disgrace to my father and Jeremy.

Bursting through the door of the spare room, I found Kylie sitting next to her half-packed bag in tears. No sign of Dad. It dawned on me what day it was. The last Sunday of the month. A church day. That's where he would be. Maybe there really was a God. Maybe He really was watching over me.

My feeling of relief was quickly replaced by guilt. Even though she'd fucked him, I couldn't be angry with her. She wasn't to know how I felt. Somehow she had been naive enough to think I was hung up on her. Somehow she hadn't sensed how I felt. Maybe I was better at hiding my feelings than I thought.

'Go away, Seb,' Kylie said through sobs. 'I'd rather you just left me alone.'

'At least let me explain.' My lip was starting to swell now, coupled with the throbbing pain of a hangover.

Kylie looked up. 'What happened to your face?'

'Nothing, I'm fine.'

'You don't look fine. But it's hard to feel sorry for you. You deserve it.'

That hurt. Why was she doing this to me? Why did she feel this way? I'd opened my heart up for them both to see, and Jake had hit me, and Kylie told me I deserved to be hit. But then again, she was right. I did deserve it.

Of course you deserved it, you fucking fag. He should have finished you off.

'You're right. I did deserve it. I'm disgusting.'

Kylie looked up, wiping her tears on her sleeve. 'You're not disgusting, Seb.'

The room fell silent, broken only by the occasional sob or sniff.

'It's okay. I know I'm disgusting.'

'You're not disgusting, Seb. What's disgusting is that you

felt like you couldn't talk to me. That you lied to me.'

That wasn't fair. I hadn't lied to her. I'd lied to myself. I'd been lying to myself from the moment I met Jake. I just couldn't do it anymore.

'I'm sorry,' I said finally.

'It's okay. I can't imagine how hard it must be for you. But you've got to talk to him, Seb. You've got to tell him how you feel. I know it's hard. It'll be awkward. But you can't keep lying to him. You can't keep lying to yourself.'

Should I have told her about the night in the tent? How Jake had told me to climb into his sleeping bag? How he'd scooped me up into his arms and held me until we both fell asleep? Maybe then she'd see he was just as confused as me. But was I just kidding myself? Maybe that night hadn't meant half of what it meant to me to Jake. Perhaps it hadn't meant anything to him at all. She probably wouldn't even believe me if I told her anyway. I was a liar. A dirty fucking faggot liar.

'I better finish packing.' Kylie tucked a loose curl behind her ear, her eyes puffy. 'My taxi will be here soon.'

'You've already called a taxi?'

She was actually leaving? Dad and Jeremy would be back from church any minute, and she might already be gone. Then what would I say? How would I explain all this? How would I explain my swollen face, which felt worse by the second?

'Please, Kylie. Please don't go. Stay.'

'I'm sorry, Seb. I have to. I don't feel comfortable here anymore. It's not about that. I don't care what or who you're into. It's just going to be awkward now. Awkward for us all.'

'But it doesn't have to be.'

'But it will be. I know it. Come on, Seb. We can't both like Jake.'

Another punch. Much harder than the last one. This one went straight into my gut. Winded me. Took away my breath. Made my skin crawl. Sent shivers down my spine. Nauseated me. Made me want to put my own fist through the bloody wall.

'You… like Jake?'

Why couldn't I believe it? After all, she'd just slept with the guy. But this hurt more. This hurt so much more.

Kylie nodded. 'Yeah, Seb. I like him a lot. I liked him since I got here. Now do you see why I can't be here? You're my best friend, Seb. It's just not right. It's not fair.'

I shook my head. Partly out of agreement, partly out of disbelief. Maybe it was best she left. How could she hang around now? How would I be able to look her in the eye each day? How would the triangle of friendship that had formed between the three of us continue? It just couldn't. I wouldn't let it. No, she would have to leave now. And Jake would have to go with her.

'Why don't you go tell Jake you're leaving? I'm sure he'll be happy to sail off with you into the sunset.'

It was anger. I was speaking from anger and pain. I hurt so I wanted Kylie to hurt too. And she knew that.

'You're an arsehole, Seb. You know that? You made me come all the way out here to the middle of bloody nowhere, just to distract you from your stupid little boy crush. Well, looks like it didn't work, did it? And now your face is swelling up like a watermelon.' She rolled her eyes and continued to pack.

She was right. I could feel the skin on my cheek stretching. I needed to get ice on it quick, but I didn't care. I was too angry. I was too upset. I didn't care that Dad would walk in any minute and see me like this. I didn't care that he'd see Kylie packing up and leaving because she liked the same guy I did. *He* wanted to move here. *He* got us into this whole bloody mess. It was his fault. It was all his fault.

'You better put some ice on it,' Kylie said without looking at me. She zipped up her suitcase and wheeled it towards the door.

I nodded. Kylie leaving was out of my hands now, but stopping my face from swelling any further wasn't. My panic started to reside, and my rationality began to return. I'd accepted I couldn't make Kylie stay. Now I just needed to work out how the hell I was going to deal with Dad.

A vehicle pulled into the driveway outside. Was it the taxi or Dad? My heart dropped. I needed it to be the taxi. I needed Kylie to just leave quickly, so it would be left to me alone to explain what happened. At least I could think up a story, something to shield Dad from the truth.

'You're in luck,' Kylie said. 'It's my ride.'

'You don't have to do this, Kylie. You're my best friend.'

'And you're my best friend too.' She pulled the suitcase behind her. Her hair bounced as she paced towards the front door. 'But you need to figure out who you are before you can truly be a friend to anyone.' She looked back and held my gaze for a second before opening the door.

'At least let me carry your suitcase.'

'It's fine, Seb. I can manage. Go put some ice on your face before it swells up even more.'

A second vehicle pulled into the driveway. Fuck. I didn't need this. I didn't need it at all.

I wanted to hug Kylie to say goodbye, but there was no point. I'd seen her get into a mood like this only a few times in the whole time I'd known her, but it was never worth trying to snap her out of it. It would probably pass about halfway on her journey back to Perth, but I still wouldn't hear from her for a while. She could be stubborn like that.

The thought of following Kylie outside just as Dad and Jeremy had arrived was also too much to comprehend. Instead, I took Kylie's advice and dashed towards the kitchen to grab a handful of ice from the freezer. After wiping the blood away, I wrapped a tea towel around the ice cubes and pressed the cold lump against my face. It would soothe the pain for a few moments, at least until the next round began.

The door slammed.

'Sebastian.'

I knew that tone. This wasn't good.

I quietly made my way along the hallway from the kitchen to greet Dad and Jeremy. I kept the tea towel pressed to my face, the ice quickly melting, the water running down my arm.

'Sebastian? What happened to you? And where's Kylie gone?' The confusion was written across my father's face.

'We uh… we had a bit of a fight. Jake and I, I mean.'

Dad's face quickly transformed from perplexed to stern. 'Jeremy, go to your room.'

My brother, who'd been wide-eyed in shock at first sight of my face, quickly realised the situation was going to escalate and scampered to his bedroom. If only I could have done the same.

'Come in here and sit down, Son. You need to tell me what happened.' Dad's tone had softened slightly, but I didn't fully trust him. How would he react once I'd told him my story? It would have to be a story. Or at least, a deviation from the truth.

As I sat down on the worn-out couch in our living room, Dad fetched me some fresh ice. Wrapping the soaked tea towel around the cold cubes, I began my story: 'It was a stupid idea. Inviting Kylie to stay here, I mean. You'd probably guessed already, but I've always had feelings for her. Turns out, Jake developed feelings for her too. So we ended up getting into a fight over it. I got punched, Kylie decided to go home.'

Silence filled the room. It was like sitting by a perfectly still lake the moment before a pebble hits the surface. I waited for the void to be filled with Dad's response, watching him watch me. Trying to get behind my eyes. Trying to see what I was really thinking.

'There's more to it than that,' Dad said simply.

'What do you mean? That's what happened.'

'I don't doubt that's what happened. But I wasn't born yesterday, Son. A girl wouldn't just up and leave like that because two boys are fighting over her. What else happened?'

My heart sank. Was it that obvious? Was Dad really able to see through my fabricated depiction of events? Did he know who I really was?

Course he does, you fucking fag. Everyone knows. Jake, Kylie, your brother. Even your mother knew. You might as well come clean.

He couldn't know. My story just didn't fully add up. It was a rushed job anyway. I'd have to come up with something else quickly. Perhaps a little more of the truth. It was a price I'd have to pay.

'Let me guess, Son.'

Shit. This was it. He knew. He'd always known.

'Kylie likes Jake too.'

Relief. The sweet sensation of relief, zipping through my veins.

'Yeah.' I looked down at my lap.

'And you lost it at Jake and he hit you.'

I nodded. It didn't matter what the rest of the story was now. I was safe. I was safe from being exposed for what I really was.

'Well, Son. You know you've messed up. You've potentially lost two good friends here.'

Not the response I was expecting. Was Dad giving me fatherly advice? Better than another punch to the face.

'I know I've messed up. But I hope I haven't lost them.'

'Well, Kylie's just left and I doubt she'll be coming back anytime soon. Bit overdramatic if you ask me, but less money for me to fork out I suppose. And Jake, well you know I'll have to ban you from seeing him now.'

Worse than another punch.

'What do you mean?'

'What do you think, Seb? Not that he'll want to see you now by the looks of things anyway, but I don't feel comfortable with having you hanging around with a bloke who throws his fists around. Sorry, mate. You're on your own now.'

A lump in my throat blocked out the pain on my face. Screwing up my nose, tears welled in my eyes, obscuring my vision. I couldn't help it. Was I really going to let him see me cry?

Go on, you fucking faggot. Show him what a fucking sissy you are and cry your eyes out like a little baby girl.

'But, Dad... Jake's the only friend I've got out here. He's all I've got.' My voice was cracking. There's no way he wouldn't have heard it too. I was defeated, but I still managed to hold back the tears.

'That's not true and you know it. You've got your brother who is growing up fast and needs you now more than ever. I've been feeling for a while now you've been hanging round too much with that kid, so it's time you took a break from seeing each other. How long for I'm not sure yet.'

A break. That was better than a ban. A ban sounded like forever. So infinite. A break I could manage. And it was probably for the best. Dad was right. Jake probably wouldn't want to see me now anyway. What would he even think of me? Did he think I liked Kylie? The way she'd also assumed? Or had he worked out the truth? Did he know how I really felt about him?

'Now go to your room, Seb. You're also grounded. Don't

think you're getting away from this scot-free.'

As if being grounded made any difference to me. That's how I lived my whole life.

'Okay, Dad. I'm sorry.'

Dad shook his head. 'You worry me, Son. You really do.'

The water trickled down the side of my cheek as another ice cube melted. That would do for now. The swelling was subsiding, and the pain had eased to a dull throb. I replayed what had just happened again and again in my mind. It was a nightmare I prayed I'd wake up from. I wanted to wake up back at Jake's house and find that nothing had happened between him and Kylie. Then she wouldn't have got upset and left. He wouldn't have got mad and punched me. And Dad wouldn't have been disappointed with me and grounded me.

But I didn't wake up. It wasn't a nightmare. It was real life. And I had to face it.

A light rattle on my bedroom door. 'Seb, can I come in?'

Jeremy. He'd want to know what happened.

'Not now, J. I'm too tired.'

'Dad said to tell you dinner will be ready in ten minutes.'

His voice was tinged with sadness. Was I wrong to ignore him? Dad was right – Jeremy was growing up fast. And he did need me. It was time for me to stop acting so selfish and be there for my little brother.

'J... you can come in if you want.'

A brief pause before Jeremy slowly opened the door and slipped into the room. He closed the door behind him, twisting the knob so not to make a sound. Dad obviously didn't want him coming in.

'What happened to your face? Dad says you're grounded.'

Nothing like the unfiltered honesty of a child.

'I fell over.'

'Liar.'

Turns out I couldn't even pull the wool over a seven-year-old's eyes.

'You got punched... didn't you?' Jeremy's eyes were as wide as saucers.

'Yeah. I got punched.'

'By Jake?'

'Yep.'

'But I thought you were friends?' My brother's innocence slayed me.

'Yeah, we are. Well, I think we still are anyway.'

'Did he say sorry?'

'No, not yet. I mean, it's my fault anyway.'

'How come? Did you punch him first?'

'No. Look, it doesn't matter, J. Just leave it, okay?'

'Okay.'

Silence.

'Why did Kylie leave?'

'She just had to, all right? Now quit it with the questions.'

Jeremy nodded. He knew he was overstepping the line. I could tell he didn't like seeing me hurt. Despite how much he could drive me up the wall, my brother cared about me very much. That was more than I could say for Jake and Kylie. Maybe blood really was thicker than water.

'Hey, Jeremy. I know I've been a bit... distant lately. But

I just wanted to let you know that I'm going to be around more often.'

'Course you are. You're grounded.'

I chuckled. The little bugger had a point.

'Yeah, I know. But aside from that. I'm going to be around more often for *you*. I'm your big brother, never forget that.'

'You're acting weird. Must be because you got punched and it scrambled up your brain.'

This time I let out a full laugh. 'You're right. It must be. Come on, J. Let's go eat.'

The mood was light over dinner, despite the visible lump on the side of my face, the fact I was grounded, and that we were one person less at the dinner table. Jeremy and I joked and laughed over our meals for the first time in a long time. Dad was pleased to see this. Perhaps even more pleased this was a result of what he'd said.

'You boys are in a good mood. It's good to see.'

'Course we are.' Jeremy smiled. 'He's my big brother.'

It was a cheesy-as-hell moment. But it made Dad happy. That made me happy – or at least relieved. Despite all the dramatic events of the day, I felt genuinely content. And I wasn't going to let anyone or anything stand in the way.

17th December 2017

The ginger glow of streetlamps spread across the pavement as we strolled back to the car. Sandra had her hair wrapped in a tight topknot, highlighting her features. It was the first time I'd seen her wear lipstick, a deep rose that exuded elegance. As I walked alongside her, it hit me how beautiful she looked, in such an effortless way. In another life, she probably would have been the right person for me. But not in this one.

'Thanks for today, Sandra. I had fun.'

'Me too. I think it was good for you to get your mind off things. You don't have to talk about it all the time though, sometimes I feel like I'm prying. Just let me know if it's ever too much.'

'No, I know you're not prying.' I reassured her with a smile. 'It does help. Even if it is painful.'

There was a comfortable silence as I started the car and began weaving my way through the quiet streets towards Sandra's house. Driving through suburbia on a Sunday was a breeze.

It didn't take long for Sandra to meander back onto the subject of my story. 'So, did you ever hear from Kylie again?'

She seemed particularly intrigued by Kylie, but I couldn't quite work out why. It didn't matter. It was refreshing for someone to be so interested in what I had to say. She had a way of breathing new life into me. A way of healing those old wounds.

'I did, yeah. Once. I think it was about 2009 or something. She found me on Facebook before I'd worked out how to make my profile private. I don't even know why I had an account. It's not like I had enough friends to make it worthwhile. But Kylie had managed to find me and work out I was living in Perth. She sent me a message and a friend request, saying how long it had been and how she'd love to catch up. She was living in Melbourne but was willing to travel to see me. Just like she had that summer, I suppose.'

Peering at Sandra out of the corner of my eye, I could see she was surprised.

'And?'

'And what?'

'And... did you respond?'

'Oh, no. No, I didn't. I declined the request and worked out how to make my profile private. I wasn't ready to face her then.'

Another brief silence. I could sense Sandra was processing each word carefully, working out what she was going to say next. Perhaps being cautious not to overstep the line.

'What about now?'

'What *about* now?' I repeated.

'Well, are you ready? To face her, I mean?'

Why was she even asking me? Why would I need to be ready to face her? There was no reason to speak to Kylie then and no reason to speak to her now.

'I don't know. I guess so. But I have no reason to. It'd be a waste of time.'

'Would you see Jake again if you had the chance?'

A swollen silence. Did she sense something? 'That's different.'

'Is it? To me, it's the same thing. It's about *closure.*'

She put extra emphasis on the word. Closure. I liked that word, but I was also intimidated by it. It was so final. Definitive. Nothing in my life had ever felt like it had proper closure. Starting with losing my mother.

'I'll think about it.'

As I reversed out from Sandra's house and made my journey home, I replayed her words. Why had it mattered so much to her that I reach out to Kylie? Was closure of that friendship really so important? It was so long ago, buried deep in the depths of my past. Why dig it back up? Besides, surely I'd made my feelings clear enough when I declined her friend request all those years ago.

I pulled into the driveway and could see the familiar blue glow of the television through the blinds. Taking a deep breath, I closed my eyes and readied myself for another evening with Dad. The awkward silences. The complaints. The television shows I had no interest in watching with the volume cranked so high they were impossible to ignore. I exhaled, reminding myself it was all for the better good. I was doing the right thing. I wasn't a bad person.

You know the truth. You know exactly what sort of person you are.

Climbing out the car, I was immediately greeted by the scent of lavender. Dad grew it out the front and back of the house, and the smell somehow managed to overpower the strong scent of the surrounding eucalyptus. No matter how I was feeling, it simultaneously comforted and calmed me. It took me right back to my childhood, before the days of the farm, back when we lived in Perth and Mum had been alive. Dad had always grown his own veggies and he'd always grown lavender. It was as if that plant was somehow the only connection we had to our past. To happier, simpler days.

As soon as I let myself into the house, that brief moment of serenity vanished in an instant. Dad was lying in a crumpled heap by the television, which continued to blast noise out into the living room.

'Dad?'

As I ran over to him, a feeling of nausea overcame me. His skin was a drained grey. I pushed my fingers gently into the side of his neck to feel a pulse. Thank god. He was breathing. He was alive. Grabbing my phone out of my pocket, I managed to dial 000. My hands were uncontrollably shaking.

'Stay with me, Dad. Please stay with me…'

*

'It was another heart attack,' Dan said frankly. 'Quite a severe one. He's lucky to still be alive right now. He's not in a good way.'

Although it was painful to hear, I was grateful for Dan's honesty. We'd worked together closely on several occasions, but I understood it was his job to remain professional.

'Thanks, Dan. Do you have any idea how long ago it might have happened? I feel so awful for not getting home sooner.'

'It's hard to tell. But you can't beat yourself up about that, Seb. You weren't to know, okay?'

'I know. I still can't help but feel terrible.'

'That's understandable. Once he's out, he'll be wearing a safety button around his neck. If anything like this were to happen again, he can push it and alert an ambulance right away.'

As if Dad wasn't paranoid enough about getting older.

'Thanks, Dan. So he's definitely getting out, right?' I just wanted to know. I just wanted to know what I was dealing with.

'Look, I'm not going to lie to you. It's not great. But your old man's relatively young still. So he's got that on his side.'

Not to mention he's a stubborn old bastard. So I was pretty sure he was going to be just fine.

'Seb.' Sandra's voice came from behind me.

She was in the same outfit she'd been wearing when I'd left her a couple of hours ago, clutching an enormous bouquet of flowers, lavender amongst the petals. She was so observant.

'I came as quickly as I could. How is he?'

'He's stable,' Dan answered for me. 'But still unconscious.'

Sandra's expression bore deep sympathy. She really was so caring.

'He's going to be fine, okay?' she said, rubbing my arm. 'He's going to be just fine.'

'I know. He's a tough cookie. Thanks for coming.'

I suddenly felt so grateful to have Sandra in my life. And to have Dad's care in Dan's hands. It was enough to keep me from losing all hope.

'Can I see him yet?' I asked.

'Not yet. We just need to keep monitoring him. But hopefully in the next hour or so. Why don't you guys go get a coffee or something? Don't worry; he's in good hands.'

'I know… thank you. A coffee actually sounds pretty amazing right now.'

My vision focused on the faded rose-coloured stain on Sandra's polystyrene cup. It was all that was left of the lipstick that'd made her look so beautiful just hours ago. Now she looked exhausted. Strung out. Her bloodshot eyes a reminder of her genuine care. I swigged the remainder of my tepid black coffee. It tasted terrible.

'He's going to be okay, Seb. You know that, right?'

'I do. I think.'

Was he? This wasn't the first time it had happened.

'You must find it weird,' I continued. 'How this is affecting me, I mean. Considering my story.'

Sandra shook her head. 'Of course not. He's your father. He'll always be your father. No matter what happened. And no matter what happens.'

She spoke with such conviction, as if from experience. We'd never really spoken about her family. What was her relationship like with her own parents? Were they even alive?

'Sandra, I'm so sorry. I've been such a selfish friend. It's been all about me. I hardly know anything about you. About your family.'

'Oh, there's nothing much to tell. My parents divorced when I was a teenager. Dad left with another woman and cut all contact with my brother and me. Mum and I have a pretty good relationship. She lives further down the coast. I try to see her once every couple of months.'

It struck me how similar Sandra's story was to Kylie's. A disappointing father. A weak father. A father who walked out and never came back. My dad was far from perfect, but he never walked out. He stuck it out through thick and thin.

'I'm sorry, Sandra.'

'Oh, please don't be. He's been absent most of my life, so I don't miss him at all.'

An interesting concept. Mum had been gone most of my life, but I still missed her every day. But I did have her, once upon a time. And I would never forget that.

'It's a weird thought though,' I started. 'If he doesn't pull through, I mean.'

'What do you mean?'

'Well... my whole life is still pretty much centred on Dad. He's the only real reason I'm still here in Perth, you know? I realised what I'd just said. 'Well, aside from my friendship with you.'

'You're sweet.' Sandra smiled. 'Don't worry, I'm not offended. I just feel bad for you, if that's how you feel.'

Was it how I felt? I wasn't even sure.

Sandra placed her hand on my arm. 'Don't worry, Seb.

You'll figure it out.'

The circles under her eyes seemed to darken by the second.

'Sandra, you should go home. We've got to be back here tomorrow morning for work. You need to rest.'

'How about you? You should take tomorrow off.'

'Well, I'm going to be here all night. So I guess I'll see how I feel.'

There was no way I'd be working tomorrow. I knew that already. But I was thankful Sandra would be able to come and check up on us.

'Okay. I better get going. You try to get some rest though, okay?'

'I will. Thanks, Sandra. You being here means more to me than you know.'

She smiled. 'I know.' She took one last swig of her now-cold coffee before giving me a momentary hug and disappearing through the sliding doors into the night.

A gentle nudge brought me back into consciousness. Dan stood over me, dressed in his surgeon's scrubs. My face was attached to the crumpled polystyrene cup. I'd fallen asleep where Sandra had left me. Wiping the wrinkled foam from my face, I squinted my tired eyes.

'Is he awake?'

'Not yet, I'm afraid. But you can see him now.'

That was something. It was a start.

'Great. Thanks, Dan.'

He helped me to my feet, and I followed him back

towards the ward. The corridor was ghostly quiet except for one man's unnerving moaning. They obviously needed to top up his morphine. I could have done with some too.

7th June 2005

Racing down the bright white corridor, I tried my best to dodge a nurse pushing a hunched over patient in a wheel-chair. My speed almost caused the old man's drip to fall from its stand. To my left, a surgeon checked his notes en route to theatre without acknowledging my frantic pace. Fluorescent lights beamed down on me. How long had I been awake? I couldn't let the jetlag kick in. Adrenaline was the only thing keeping me going as I pushed past a small group of student nurses who stopped talking quietly amongst themselves as they witnessed my mad dash.

Finally, I reached the ward. I was greeted by a tired-look-ing woman at reception.

'Name?'

'Sebastian Johns. I'm here for my father, Stuart Johns.'

'Ah yes, he's been in here for a little while now. We've been expecting you.'

Did she realise how far I'd had to travel? Over twenty hours spent in a flying coffin hurtling through the sky. A sud-den end to the life I'd worked so hard to build for myself on the other side of the planet.

It's your fault, anyway. You should have been back at home with your dad.

It had been my one chance at starting over. At escaping my past and actually having a shot at being happy.

You're selfish, Seb. You always were and always will be.

'How's he doing?'

'He's doing well. He was in intensive care for a while, but he's been in this ward for a couple of hours now. He's recovering well. He's got luck on his side. You're lucky.'

She looked at me with an odd expression. I couldn't work her out. Was she torturing me for taking so long to arrive? She had no idea about my life or situation. She had no idea about my relationship with my father.

Approaching Dad's lonely little corner of the ward, I instantly noticed there was no window. The room across the hallway had heaps of light, so why had he been given this one? It wasn't the time to complain. The main thing was that he was alive and recovering well and I was home. All I'd been able to think about on the flight was that he might die. He might die and I would have no idea until my plane landed, finding out from a voicemail at Singapore airport thirteen hours later, and then again only after arriving back in Perth. Anything could have happened during that time. He might have died, and I would be too late and never able to forgive myself.

The nurse pulled the navy curtain away, revealing Dad lying on his back with countless wires and cords connecting him to the machines around him. His skin was pale and seemed thin like parchment paper. His heart monitor beeped steadily. Each beep gave reassurance.

'I'll leave you to it.'

'Will he be able to hear me?'

'Maybe. But probably not at this stage. But don't worry. We're expecting him to regain consciousness in the next few hours. He's doing well.'

The nurse disappeared behind the curtain, and all was quiet except the sharp, metallic beep of the heart monitor. That, and the sound of my thoughts. Growing louder by the second.

I could never leave him again. I could never leave him again. I could never leave him again.

18ᵗʰ December 2017

Stepping into Dad's ward, the memory of his first heart attack flickered through my mind. Those long days and even longer nights spent sat beside his narrow bed, wondering when he would open his eyes. If he even would. Is that what it was going to be like again? I prayed not. At least this time his ward was completely different. There were wide windows all the way along the walls, allowing heaps of light to flood in. There's no way Dan would have let my father stay in another windowless room. Not that there should have been any special treatment because I worked there.

Dan and I walked over to Dad's bed. It felt so different being a visitor. Those same navy curtains. We really needed to update those. The hospital was generally beginning to look tired. Not to mention, it was getting busier. As staff, we were overworked, under-resourced and underpaid. But none of that mattered right now. All that mattered was seeing Dad.

Dan peeled back the curtain to expose my father lying on the bed, once again connected to a morphine drip, heart machine and catheter.

'I'll leave you both to it.' Dan's words echoed those of the nurse who'd left me with Dad the last time.

'Thanks, Dan.'

Making my way to the side of the bed, I took a seat next to my father. He looked even more frail than he had after his first attack. He also looked paler. Weaker. And this time I wasn't looking at him through the eyes of a naive twenty-five-year-old boy. I was a thirty-seven-year-old man. A thirty-seven-year-old nurse with years of experience looking after people just like my dad. But it felt so similar. I'd come full circle but felt just as helpless as back then. And I still didn't have the words. I still couldn't bring myself to explain everything. I still didn't have the strength to tell my truth. My side of the story. To release the monsters I'd been hauling around with me my entire sorry excuse of a life. Even with Dad in an unconscious state.

You're pathetic, Seb. Weak and pathetic.

Beep.

The dull, cold sound of the heart monitor. The sound that had haunted me for the last decade was back again. And with each beep, it was as if it was speaking to me.

Beep.

You can't keep it secret forever.

Beep.

The truth always comes out eventually.

Beep.

*

A nudge. Harder than before. I must have been in an even deeper sleep. Opening my eyes slowly, Dan greeted me once again. This time he looked tired too.

'You should get home and get some rest, Seb. Your Dad will be fine.'

I looked around at Dad who was still lying in the same

position. I'd fallen asleep in my chair.

'I should stay.'

'Honestly, Seb. You should go home and get some sleep. Don't worry about working tomorrow – I'll let your team leader know. Come in and spend the day with him if you want. It doesn't matter about the visiting times. Just don't forget you need to look after your own health too.'

I knew he was right, even if it was a stock answer we gave all visiting family members. 'I'll go home and come back first thing in the morning. Thanks, Dan.'

'No need to thank me.' That warm smile. 'Goodnight, Seb.'

Cruising down the highway towards home, only one thought circled my mind. I had to get in touch with Kylie. To finally have *closure*. As I drove, I imagined the past as an infinite cycle. A loop that can't be broken. But a loop from which I could escape.

11ᵗʰ June 2005

It was my fourth black coffee in a row. I needed to slow down. Otherwise it'd be me having a heart attack next. Shuddering at the thought, I gulped down the bitter liquid. It had been so long since I'd tasted Australian coffee, but this was not how I remembered it. The past few days had been torturous. In a constant state of anxiety, thoughts of every kind had relentlessly pummelled my brain as I waited by Dad's side.

Making my way back to his ward, I looked out the window where slices of bright blue sky taunted me, peering out from beyond the city's buildings. It was a stark reminder of the world outside the claustrophobic walls of the hospital. Why couldn't he at least have a window next to his bed? Perhaps that little blast of sunshine would have been enough to wake him. I'd suggest it to the nurse. What did I have to lose? It'd been her that had wrongly said Dad would wake days ago. How could she have made such an assumption?

Once I'd downed the last drops of coffee, I entered the ward. I instantly knew he was awake. I could see it in the nurse's eyes. Darting straight to where the curtain had been pulled back, the surgeon stood speaking to my father.

'Dad.'

'Sebastian?'

Did he not even know I was there? Had they not told him?

'Your father's a little confused at the moment,' the

surgeon began. 'But he's doing well. He's going to be just fine.'

My loud sigh an announcement of my relief.

'I'll leave you both to catch up. Just, don't overdo it, Mr. Johns. You still need to take it easy. The more you rest, the quicker you'll heal.'

Easier said than done. This was my father he was talking to.

The surgeon pulled the curtain shut behind us as he walked away.

'Hey, Dad.'

'G'day, Son. It's good to see you.' His words were soft. Like honey in warm milk. 'But you shouldn't have come back. I'll be fine. There's still life in this old ticker yet.'

There he was, back to normal and sure of himself.

'It's okay, Dad. I was ready to come back anyway.'

'What do you mean?' He sounded shocked.

'I mean, I'm done with the UK. I'm ready to be back in Perth.'

I hadn't even realised that was what I wanted until I'd said the words out loud. Did I know what I was getting myself into?

'Why the hell would you wanna come back *here*?'

I was perplexed. Why didn't he want me to come back? He was the most patriotic man on earth – he loved Australia and had always wondered why I wanted to live in the cold and perpetually rainy motherland. He didn't know much about my life there, either, whether I was struggling or living the high life. For all he knew, I could have been living in a gutter.

'Why wouldn't I? This is… this is home.'

There it was. How I really felt. How I really felt about Perth. About Australia. Despite spending so long trying to run away. From my past. From The Nowhere. From that fateful summer. It had all caught up with me, sitting there by my father's hospital bed.

Dad smiled. For a second I thought he would offer his hand or a hug. But instead, his smile quickly melted away. 'Well, you better let me get some rest. I'm lucky to be alive right now, and I deserve a kip.'

It was far from a Hallmark moment. But it was something. It was enough. And he was right. He was lucky to be alive.

And I was lucky to be home.

15th December 1997

Catching a glimpse of my reflection in the shiny red bauble, it dawned on me how much weight I'd lost. My cheekbones were sharper than they'd ever been, and I was visibly thinner. It was no surprise Dad had noticed and kept on at me about it:

'You need to eat more, Seb.'

'You're not leaving the dinner table until you've finished your plate.'

'You worry me, Son. You really do.'

But it wasn't intentional. I wanted to eat. I didn't want to look sinewy and gaunt. I'd just completely lost my appetite since Kylie left. Since I stopped seeing Jake. Since everything was plunged into darkness.

'Are you gonna put it on then or just stare at it?' Jeremy's cheeky impatience made me smile.

I reached up and hung the last bauble on the tree. To the highest point where my brother couldn't reach. Despite how the year had ended, the show had to go on. And we had our Christmas tradition, which was important to my brother. Ever since Mum died, we'd always put in the extra effort to keep the spirit of Christmas alive. I couldn't let that die just because *I* was dying inside.

'There you go, smartass. All done.'

Jeremy beamed back at me.

Dad entered the room. 'Good job, boys. You've outdone

yourselves this year.'

The tree did look great. We kept the colours basic and festive – red, green and gold. There was no tinsel, just some white fairy lights and a little star on the top of the tree we dedicated to Mum. The only thing missing was the scent of pine. We always used to buy a real tree when Mum was alive. Then there had been no tree at all the first Christmas without her as none of us felt like celebrating. Not even Jeremy, who loved Christmas more than all of us. The following year Dad bought us an artificial tree, and we'd been using it ever since.

'Now, you boys understand that there won't be many presents this year, don't you? Money's tight as work has been slow. One pressie each, okay?'

We nodded in sync. Dad knew there was only one present I wanted, despite everything that had happened and how much had changed. Getting a car and learning to drive so I could finally escape The Nowhere was the only piece of hope worth clinging onto.

'Now come on, both of you. Set the table.'

We obeyed.

Once the last piece of chicken had been scraped off the plate, I rinsed it clean and handed it to Jeremy.

'I'm going to feed Scampi now, J. You okay finishing that?'

He nodded as he began to wipe the plate with a holey tea towel that was now soaking wet.

I quickly glanced into the living room where a game

show presenter obnoxiously shouted out questions in his thick Melbournian accent. Dad was already asleep with half his beer left untouched.

Outside, the warm air enfolded me and the crickets chirped at full volume. Scampi wagged his tail vigorously as I scooped the smelly chunks of meat into his bowl. Crouching down onto the dry earth next to him, I looked up at the stars, shining beyond the purple clouds that swooped across the sky, obscuring the moon entirely. The sadness I'd been carrying around for months still crippled me when I was alone. At least during the day I was busy with my chores, and there was no time to let the thoughts in. Night-time was the worst. My mind always caught up and suffocated me, like a pillow being pressed against my face.

'You okay, Seb?' Jeremy's voice accompanied the metallic creak of the flyscreen door. It was unusual for him to join me outside.

'I'm fine, J. Don't worry about me. But thanks for asking.'

'You seem... different. You've been acting strange ever since Kylie left.'

Was I really that bad at hiding my sadness? Or was my brother just particularly observant?

'You liked her, didn't you? Like Dad liked Mum?'

I smiled at the sentiment. 'I do like Kylie, J. A lot. But not how Dad liked Mum.'

A fleeting silence.

'Is it Jake then?'

'What do you mean? Is what Jake?'

'You don't see him anymore. Is that why you're sad?'

My brother's question floored me. 'I do miss Jake a bit I guess, yeah. We were good mates.'

'Do you like him the way Dad liked Mum?'

A volcano erupted inside my stomach. 'What? Of course not. What are you talking about, J? You do realise that's wrong, don't you?'

It worried me that the concept had even entered my brother's mind. What could have given him that idea? Did I give off those signals? Was it something Dad had said? I felt sick at the thought of it.

Everyone knows, faggot. Your brother. Your father. Even your mother knew.

'Then, why are you so sad? And why aren't you eating enough? You're too thin. You look creepy.'

My fear and shock were replaced with gratitude. We might have fought at times, as all brothers do, but we had each other's backs.

'I'm fine, J. I'll be okay. I've just felt a bit off lately. But I'm getting better. And Christmas is coming. You know what that means, don't you?'

'What?'

'Heaps of food. Turkey and gravy. Roasted veggies and pavlova. I'll be fatter than Santa before you know it.'

Jeremy giggled. It was good to hear him laugh. There hadn't been enough laughter in the house recently. If there was one thing I was going to make sure of this Christmas, it's that there would be heaps and heaps of laughter.

'Now get inside. It's getting late, time for bed.'

Jeremy followed my orders.

I decided to give myself another five minutes outside in the warm summer air with Scampi. I felt less alone at the thought of all the stars surrounding me, now standing out more and more as the clouds cleared and the sky darkened. Less alone at the thought of my mother. At the thought of Kylie. At the thought of Jake.

When would I see him again?

19th December 1997

The engine of Dad's bike stuttered and then ground to an abrupt halt. Time for a break. We'd parked up close to the tree that provided the most shade from the baking December sun. We were already both caked with sweat, so the shade didn't do much heat-wise, but it would stop us from getting burnt. As I applied more sunblock, Dad lit up his cigarette and took a long, deep drag. Scampi collapsed in a tired heap next to my bike.

'Don't forget to give him more water, Seb.' A fly landed on Dad's cheek, which he instinctively flicked away.

'I won't,' I muttered quietly as I liberally applied the sunblock to my neck, ears and nose. Passing it to Dad, I reached into my backpack and pulled out a warm bottle of water. I took a quick swig, before pouring it into my cupped hand so Scampi could sup it. Dad started to run the sunblock over his face and arms while finishing off his cigarette. It was ironic, watching him smoke while protecting his skin from the sun. But at least he was cautious in some ways.

'How are you doing, Seb?'

It was the same question he'd asked me so many times in that same spot. As always, I'd search my mind to try and find the perfect answer. Something to avoid an argument.

'I'm doing okay thanks, Dad.' It was the best I could do.

'I'm not going to go on about you not eating. I know you're trying. And it'll take time. To rebuild yourself I mean.'

What was this? Vulnerability? I had the sudden memory of Dad losing weight when Mum died. It hadn't taken long for him to build himself up again. Perhaps he did it for Jeremy and me.

'Thanks, Dad.'

'Have you heard from Kylie at all?' His eyes narrowed as he drew back more smoke.

'No, not yet.' An uneasiness came over me. Surely he wasn't going to try and pry into my private life?

'She'll come round. They always do. What about Jake? You heard from him?'

Why was he bringing Jake up? He was the one who'd banned me from seeing him. Why would he even entertain the thought of us working things out? Maybe it was a trick. Testing me to see if I'd been in contact with Jake.

'Nope, nothing. That's what you wanted, right?' I couldn't help myself.

'What I wanted was for that boy to think about his actions. There's no good in swinging your fists around.' That was rich, coming from him. 'But I'm sure he's missing his mate as much as you're missing yours.'

I doubted it. If Jake missed me half as much as I missed him, he would have at least tried to reach out to me by now. But nothing. Not a peep. I was dead to him. I was dead to me, too.

'Yeah, maybe.'

'Look, Seb. I don't want to punish you forever. Let's just have a nice Christmas, and you can start hanging out with Jake again in the new year if you want. Providing he never hits you again.'

Christmas had come early.

'Serious?'

'Serious. Now come on, let's get back to it. If we don't start making some money, there won't be a Christmas at all.'

I could already feel my appetite returning.

25th December 2017

The cracker broke apart with a satisfying snap and a brief scent of gunpowder. Did I let Sandra win, or did she beat me fairly? Either way, she looked pleased with herself.

'Yay, I won!'

'Yes, you did. What did you get?'

She reached into the cracker and pulled out a purple paper hat and something wrapped in a plastic wrapper.

'It's a compass.'

'Ooh, could come in handy.'

We both laughed.

'What's the joke?'

Sandra pulled out the thin strip of paper. 'What do Santa's little helpers learn at school?'

Pause. 'No idea.'

'The elf-abet.'

I couldn't help but laugh. It was so bad it was good.

'Here, I've got another one. You've gotta win this time. Don't worry, I'll let you.'

We pulled the crackers and this time I came out victorious. After pulling out a yellow hat and a miniature sewing kit, I read out a joke that was equally as terrible. Dad lay on the bed beside us, still in his coma, but alive. I felt like the beeping of the heart monitor was his way of laughing along with us.

'Thank you for being here, Sandra. Really. You didn't

have to, but it means a lot.'

'Of course. I wanted to. Besides, it gets me out of another year with my mum and brother. She'll drink too much sherry and start bad-mouthing Dad, the same way she does every year.'

Sandra spoke about her family a lot now. It seemed to help her as much as speaking about mine helped me. Getting it off our chests, as if we were decluttering our houses. Throwing out all the rubbish we'd accumulated over the years.

'Come on, let me treat you to a Christmas coffee,' I offered.

We made our way into the main hospital cafeteria that had become our second home. I'd worked several Christmas Days in the past, but spending one there as a visitor had a completely different feel to it. Suddenly, I felt part of a much wider group. One comprising all those people who'd had to swap their usual Christmas barbies and beach trips for medical emergencies and hospital food. I was in their club now.

I passed Sandra her coffee, and we sat down at one of the few empty tables. It really did mean so much that she was there with me. Dad should have woken up by now, so my anxiety increased with each day that passed. I was hoping he'd be home by Christmas, but that just wasn't meant to be.

'Are there any updates?' Sandra asked as she gently blew on her coffee.

'Nope. Just that he's stable and should be awake by now. Dan's not sure what's wrong.'

'He's in great hands though. Dan's one of the best

surgeons we have.'

'He sure is.'

'So, seeing as it's Christmas, maybe you can tell me about Christmas Day, 1997?'

I had a feeling she'd bring it up. We hadn't talked about the past for a little while, and I had got as far as Christmas in my narrative. Considering the date, it seemed appropriate to tell the story now.

I took a deep breath. 'There isn't much to tell, really.'

'Did you finally get your car?'

I shook my head. 'Of course I didn't. I knew I wouldn't. That's why I stopped asking. But he did give me something else.'

25th December 1997

Jeremy tore away the red and green striped paper like a dog with a bone. He'd been staring at the gift all morning, but Dad insisted on us waiting. That had been our tradition when Mum was alive, so we adhered to it. We'd wake up, check the carrots had been eaten by the reindeer and the sherry drunk by Santa. Then we'd help prepare lunch, before sitting at the table and demolishing it. Once our plates were finished – down to the last sprout – we'd finally be allowed to open our presents. But before we had a chance to play with them, we'd head out on our afternoon walk. They had probably wanted to leave something for us to do on Boxing Day.

My brother's excitement had been visibly brewing as we finished our Christmas pudding. He hated the dessert, but he polished off the lot, squirming in his seat as he stared at the tree. Or, more specifically, what was underneath it.

Dad finally gave in as he cracked open his third beer. 'Go on then.'

Jeremy ran over to his present, which was enormous this year – a big rectangular box. Perhaps its size was to compensate for getting only one present each. Mine was also pretty big and square, but much flatter in comparison. It definitely wasn't a set of car keys. Not that the car even mattered a whole lot at this point.

Scraps of shiny wrapping paper and tape quickly

accumulated on the carpet as Jeremy pulled out a toy monster truck. 'Wow!'

Sometimes I wondered if the anticipation was more exciting than the gift itself, so I was glad that it was something that Jeremy would actually enjoy. 'Thanks, Dad!' he said as he tried to pick the box open.

'Don't you mean, thanks, Santa?' Dad tried with all his might to keep the magic alive.

'Thanks, Santa!' Jeremy said, playing along.

Dad smiled down at him, pleased that Jeremy was happy, perhaps because he knew it would keep him quiet for the rest of the day.

Now it was my turn. I'd already accepted I wouldn't be getting a car, so I'd made peace with that and prepared my reaction. Now all I wanted was to rewind to when Jake and Kylie were in my life. Before everything had gone so horribly wrong. Before I'd fucked it up, like I always do. But of course, that wasn't something I could open under the tree.

'Yours is a little bit more sentimental this year, Seb. Hope you like it.'

Now I was intrigued.

Tearing away the wrapping paper, I was met with a large photomontage. There were dozens of photos of Mum, Dad, Jeremy and me. Photos of Mum and Dad when they first met. Photos of both Jeremy and me when we were in our cribs. A photo of Dad holding me as a baby that I'd never seen before. Photos of us smiling. Laughing. Happy. Not one of them on the farm. Not one of them in The Nowhere.

Then it hit me, like a tsunami crashing against the coast.

Destroying everything in its wake. The tears welled up in my eyes and rolled down my cheeks. I tried with all my might to stop it from happening. To stop Dad from seeing any weakness in me. But it was too late. The floodgates were open. The montage had touched me in such a way that I was crying with both joy and sadness. The car I so desperately wanted suddenly seemed unimportant. All I needed was right there on the farm. I wasn't the only one for whom happy memories existed before The Nowhere. It was the same for Dad. It was the same for Jeremy. If I ran away, all it would do is create more sadness for the pair of them. I realised it was my responsibility to create happy memories with them too. So that's what I planned to do. That would be my New Year's resolution.

'Jeez, Son. I didn't expect you to get upset.' Dad was visibly surprised, but also proud that his gift had had some impact. 'Do you like it?'

'I love it, Dad,' I said, wiping away my tears. 'I really do. It's the greatest gift I've ever received.'

It really was.

'Seb's a big cry baby!' Jeremy laughed as he finally got into the box and began pulling his new toy out of it.

'Shut up, J.'

But I didn't mind, really. Crying in front of them hadn't felt half as bad as I thought it would. Perhaps showing a bit of vulnerability was exactly what I needed to do.

'Not yet, Jeremy,' Dad said, suddenly stern. 'We go for our walk first, remember?'

Tradition was always prioritised. And for once, I didn't

mind at all. I'd take any chance to create new happy memories, especially at Christmas.

25th December 2017

I stared down at the empty coffee cup, considered getting another one but decided against it. The last thing I needed right now was to get the jitters. When I looked up, I immediately noticed Sandra's glassy eyes.

'Sandra? Are you okay?'

She wiped her eyes, looking embarrassed. 'Yeah, I'm fine. It's just… that's the first time I've heard you talk about your dad in that way.'

'In what way?'

'With… compassion.'

Silence. Nothing but the mumbling sound of nearby hospital visitors nervously chatting over their coffees.

'Yeah. It was definitely another side of him. Or at least, a side I hadn't seen in a very long time. Or maybe I was just growing up, you know? Not being so selfish.'

'I don't think you were ever selfish, Seb. Quite the opposite.'

Another silence, but I knew what she was thinking. Her thoughts were of Dad lying in his hospital bed three floors above us. Her thoughts were wondering whether he would wake up on Christmas Day.

'Come on. We should go back to your dad; he could wake up any minute.'

That was optimistic.

The lift pinged and we stepped out onto the third floor.

'I've been doing a lot of thinking,' I said, 'about what you said about getting in touch with Kylie.'

'Oh yeah?'

'Yeah. I think you're right. Life is too short. And closure is important. I want to try and get in touch with her.'

Sandra's face lit up. 'That's fantastic news, Seb. I think you're making the right decision.'

We returned to Dad's ward. He still lay motionless, the heart monitor beeping in the same monotonous, unforgiving way. We took our seats next to him.

'You know, he'd be glad to know I'm reaching out to her. He always liked Kylie.'

'Well, you can tell him all about it when he wakes up. Who knows, she might even get on a flight herself to come visit.'

That was unlikely. Kylie had made her attempt to reach out, and I was doubtful she would still care. I was the one who'd rejected her. I hadn't been open to healing old wounds, so why should she? She didn't owe me anything.

'Well, first things first. I'd have to work out how I'm even going to get in touch with her. You know me, I'm a digital dinosaur. I don't have any social media accounts these days.'

'That's okay, I do.' A wide grin spread across Sandra's face. 'Hey, why don't we look her up now? See if she's still living in Melbourne at least?'

A punch of anxiety. Was I even ready for this? The idea was fine in theory, but part of me was terrified to dig up the past.

'Uh, I guess? There's no harm in having a little look, I suppose. Doesn't mean I have to reach out yet.'

Sandra laughed. 'Well, you'd have to figure out a way to do it that doesn't involve using my profile. She might find it a bit weird if some strange woman suddenly messages her out of the blue claiming to be contacting her on your behalf.'

This made me laugh too, which eased my nerves slightly.

'Okay, come on then. Let's do it.' Sandra pulled her phone out of her handbag and began tapping away. 'What's her surname?'

I took a deep breath and told her. So many thoughts whirled through my mind. Would she even want to hear from me?

'Here we are!' Sandra soon said. 'I think I've found her – it's the right name, the right location, and she fits your description.' She passed me her phone.

Reaching out and taking it from her grasp, I stared at the brightly lit screen. Blue and white filled the page, framing a small square picture of a woman who was undeniably Kylie. She looked as beautiful as the day she left the farm. Her red hair was smoother and more refined, and her freckles were covered by makeup, but her smile was as sweet and innocent as it had always been. Her pearly white teeth on show. Her eyes squinting slightly. Sure, I could see the years on her face. But they'd been kind to her. Kinder than they had been to me.

I scrolled down and saw another picture of her, this time with a man by her side. In her arms, she held a newborn baby. It couldn't have been more than a few days old. Below the picture was a comment left by a woman with a sweeping smile. I read it in my head: *Congratulations guys! She's beautiful. Looks like she's got her daddy's eyes, so let's hope she has her mummy's brains! Xxx*

Beneath this were countless more comments left by friends offering their compliments. I beamed as I read through them. Of course Kylie had met someone by now and settled down. Why wouldn't she? She was a beautiful woman with so much to give. I felt relieved. She deserved to be happy. I stopped when I noticed a note left by Nicole, who hadn't aged a day either: *Welcome to the mummy club!*

'That's her, right?' Sandra asked, pulling me back from the virtual world in my hand.

I nodded and passed her the phone. 'Sure is. Looks like she's just had a little baby too.'

'Adorable!' Sandra gushed. 'What a beautiful little girl.' Then silence as she proceeded to read the comments.

'So,' she finally asked, 'what are you going to do?'

'What do you mean?'

'I mean, how are you going to reach out to her? You can't do it with my account, remember. That would just be weird. Want me to help you set up a new one?'

I realised that as soon as I'd seen the picture of Kylie with her happy family, I no longer felt the need to reach out to her. Of course there were things I would love to have said. How I was sorry for everything that happened when we were young and inexperienced. Dumb and naive. I would have loved to find out whether she would have ever forgiven me. But what good would it do now? She was happy and that's all that mattered.

'No, that's okay,' I said. 'I think I'll just leave things there.'

Sandra looked perplexed at first, but her expression was soon laced with realisation. 'I understand.'

All I could think about now was how much I needed Dad to wake up so I could at least tell *him* everything I needed to.

You can't keep it secret forever.

14th January 1998

'You're looking much better, Son.' Dad had a sincere smile on his face as he spoke. His kindness caught me off guard.

'Thanks, Dad.'

He was right. I *was* looking better. Perhaps it was the summer sun. Perhaps it was because I was finally eating properly again. But mostly I put it down to my Christmas present. The montage of happy memories had put everything in perspective. It had flipped a switch within me, triggering a release. There was still no car. There was still no Jake. But I had my beautiful brother. And, despite being far from perfect, a father who deep down had my best interests at heart. Everything else would sort itself out. Everything else would fit into place.

'I can't believe you're turning eighteen next week, Seb. You're all grown up now. Officially an adult.'

Was this it? Was he finally going to tell me I was getting my car? I didn't care anymore, and perhaps that was exactly what I needed to do. Stop caring about it and it would find its way to me.

'Why don't we throw a little party for it?' Dad said, raising his brow. 'It's a pretty special event, right? We could invite Jake and his parents over.'

'Seriously?' He had said I wasn't banned from seeing him forever. Maybe he'd now decided enough time had passed.

'Seriously. I'm proud of you for coming through this situation and turning yourself around. That's a sign of maturity. That's a sign of strength. Just in time for your eighteenth birthday, too.'

Is that all this was? A test? Had he been testing me? It wasn't the time to question Dad's motives.

'It'd be nice to have the party on your actual birthday,' Dad continued. Let's get our chores done over the weekend so we can celebrate on Tuesday.'

'Thanks, Dad! That sounds great. It'll be nice to see our neighbours.'

Scampi barked. His usual tactic of letting us know break time was over.

'No worries, Son. Now come on. The day's passing us by.'

I spent the rest of the day in a daydream as I rode my quad bike alongside Dad. It was great he was happy for me to reach out to Jake now, but would Jake even want to see me? He hadn't tried to contact me since he'd sent his fist flying into the side of my face. One way or another, I needed to find out what he thought of me. If he didn't want to see me, I might as well get it over with. Rip the band-aid off quickly in one go. I'd make the call tonight. If I waited, I'd just feel worse.

As soon as Dad fell asleep and Jeremy had gone to bed, I strolled into the hallway to call Jake. I picked up the receiver and took a long, deep breath.

'Here we go,' I said to myself, warming up my vocal cords.

It felt like the phone rang for a lifetime. I was about to give up and put the phone back down before I heard a click.

'Hello?' Alison's voice. It felt good to hear her syrupy tone again.

'Hey, Alison. It's me, Seb.' For some reason, I felt the need to say who I was. Perhaps I thought she might have forgotten the sound of my voice.

'Seb. Hello, dear. How are you? It's been so long.'

I was relieved. I didn't know what I'd expected, but I was grateful she didn't hang up on me.

'I know. It's been way too long. I've missed you.'

'I've missed you too, darl. We all have.'

Did that really include Jake? I found it hard to believe.

'I'm having a little party on Tuesday, for my birthday. I'd love for you guys to come.'

Should I have waited to speak to Jake first? What if he didn't want to come but felt obliged to? Just like last year. I couldn't go through that again. It had taken so long to break through his barriers.

'Oh, darling, that sounds wonderful. We would love to. We'll be there. Hang on – let me go get Jake so you can tell him about your party yourself. I know he would love to hear from you.'

A burst of fear. 'Okay, cool.'

'I'll just warn you though, Seb – Jake hasn't been himself lately. He's been quite down. But I'm sure speaking with you will lift his spirits.'

Jake had been down? Surely he couldn't have felt as low as I had these past few months. Without him in my life, my world had become as dull and meaningless as it had before he came into it. There was no more fun. No more excitement. No more anything. Just endless days on the farm. Just like it had been before. And no matter how much I tried to kid myself that I was better off without him in my life, nothing could take away the emptiness and longing I felt without him.

'Hello?' It was Jake. He'd actually come to the phone. That was a big enough shock in itself.

'Hi, Jake… it's me. Seb.'

'Hey.'

That was it? That was all I was getting? A single word, without a shred of enthusiasm. Not even anger or resentment. Nothing. No emotion. Just an empty word, sent spiralling out into existence like a small boat lost in tumultuous seas. I would have to guide the conversation.

'It's my birthday next week, so I'm having a party. Do you want to come?'

'Sure. See you then.'

The phone went dead.

That was it? No mention of the punch? No telling me how he was or asking how I was? He didn't even ask when the party was. It was all too strange. My mind swirled as I ambled towards my bedroom. At least he'd agreed to come. That was something.

Lying down on my back, staring at the lone crack that ran along the ceiling like an artery, Alison's words played back in my mind: *Jake hasn't been himself lately. He's been quite down.*

He hadn't sounded down to me. He hadn't sounded any-thing. Just blank. Numb. Maybe that was it. Perhaps he was just over it. Maybe he'd reached the point I'd reached by the time he met me last year. Perhaps now I was just closer to ac-cepting my fate of spending my life in The Nowhere. Where I belonged. Maybe it was just starting to dawn on him that that's where he belonged too. No more dreams of becoming a surfer. No more dreams of anything. Just a life spent under the baking sun on the barren grass and red earth. Where the windmills never turn. Where the rain rarely falls. Where only the strongest survive. Was he strong enough? Of course he was. I pictured his defined, tanned torso as I closed my eyes, unzipped the fly of my denim shorts and reached my hand beneath.

29ᵗʰ December 2017

Hey Seb. Arrive in Perth on the 10th. Hope we can still grab that coffee.

I stared down at the words on my phone for about five minutes, glaring at each letter individually until the words lost all meaning. Finally, I processed them. It was really happening. After two decades, Jake was going to be back in my life, albeit for a fleeting visit. How much had I accomplished in that time? I had a good job, although it probably wasn't as good as it could have been. I was well aware that I should have moved a bit higher up the ranks, but somewhere in my mid-thirties, I'd stopped trying. I'd stopped pushing. With Dad at home, I'd simply become complacent. There were no kids to think about, so I didn't have that extra incentive to work as hard as I possibly could. I also had a house, even if the mortgage did keep me awake at night sometimes.

Then there were the negatives. Dad had been living with me for more than a decade. How lame would that look to Jake? Especially considering how long we'd talked about escaping The Nowhere and leaving our parents behind. Dad's failing health also took up a big part of my time and energy, and I'd taken on the role of nurse both at work and at home. And now with him in hospital, would I even have time to see Jake?

Then there was the fact that I didn't have anyone in my life. I hadn't even thought to ask Jake whether he was seeing anyone, but I assumed he would be. There was no doubt he would have aged well. Sydney would have made all his wish-es come true.

Great. See you when you get here.

I sent the message and felt my throat go dry.

20ᵗʰ January 1998

A slither of light grew across my bedroom door as dawn broke. I'd already been awake for at least an hour anyway, but the light confirmed the day had officially arrived. I was now an adult. How had that happened? It seemed like only yesterday I was waking up on my seventeenth birthday. So much had happened in a year. My life had been changed forever. I wasn't the same person I was back then. Nor did I want to be. I still wasn't sure exactly where I was going, but somehow I felt different waking up eighteen. Just knowing I was legally considered an adult filled me with a sense of empowerment, despite my situation being much the same. I wanted to hold onto that feeling for as long as possible. For now, though, I needed to get up and get on with the day. I had to help Dad set up my party. That would be enough to keep my mind distracted from having no idea how Jake would act towards me later. Would he still be pissed off at me? It would explain his ambivalence over the phone. But if he were, why would he have even bothered agreeing to come? Surely he could have made up some excuse to get out of it. His voice didn't sound pissed off either. It just sounded... vacant. I replayed the few words he spoke to me over and over again as I climbed out of bed.

*

'So you didn't even set a time? What sort of idiot doesn't set a time for his own party?'

Dad was getting more and more irritated. He had every right to be. I don't know why I hadn't arranged a time for Jake and his parents to arrive. Perhaps I'd been so caught up in the fear of getting back in touch with Jake that the logistics had slipped my mind. But it wasn't the day for an argument. It was a miracle I was even being allowed to have a party on a Tuesday.

'I'll call them now, hang on.'

As I made my way towards the phone, there was a knock at the door. I sighed with brief relief before the anxiety kicked in again. Fuck. He had actually come.

Jeremy got to the door before me. 'Hello. It's my brother's birthday.'

I winced at his stating the obvious.

'Yes, it is.' Alison's warm words. 'He's all grown up now, isn't he?'

I took a deep breath as I heard the sound of multiple footsteps entering the house.

'Well, go on then, Son. Aren't you going to greet your guests?'

Reluctantly, I paced into the hallway. There they were. Alison. Rob.

Jake.

'Happy birthday, Seb,' Rob and Alison said in unison. Alison had a huge smile on her face as she passed me a silver envelope.

'Jake mentioned you're saving for a car. It's not much, but here's a little something to put towards it.'

It was a nice sentiment. It was also good to know Jake still hadn't given up on the idea of escaping The Nowhere with me. It didn't matter if he'd be using me to do it. I'd be using him too.

Jake stepped out from behind his parents. He looked just as miserable as he had the first time he'd come around for the barbie last year. Except something was different this time. He looked even emptier. Like there was no electricity behind his eyes. His body had changed too. He'd lost weight and his appearance was ragged. Could there have been more darkness living inside his head than mine?

'Happy birthday, mate,' he said without a slice of enthusiasm.

'Thanks, Jake. It's good to see you.'

We made our way through the house and into the backyard, where Dad and I had put out a spread of cheeses, cold meats, biscuits and party pies on the outdoor table, which was covered with our best tablecloth. Thankfully, Dad hadn't made his fairy bread. Rob walked ahead with Dad as Alison chatted away to me, asking if it felt different to be an adult as she picked up a piece of cabanossi. How much had Jake told her about what had happened? Probably nothing at all. She must've known something was up. But Jake had a way of getting around things, so he didn't need to give much information away. This would have been no exception.

Dad had pulled up the large umbrella at the centre of the table, and we were blissfully protected from the midday sun. Alison offered to make lemonade, but Dad insisted she didn't.

'Alison, I like your lemonade a lot. But you guys are the guests today, so sit back and relax. Not to mention it's a day for beer, not lemonade.'

Everyone except Jake laughed, while I took the signal that it was time to pop inside and grab the grog.

'I'll give you a hand,' Jake said.

We both walked inside, Jake a few footsteps behind me. I took the bottles of beer from the fridge and handed them to him.

'Jake, I'm so sorry…'

'Don't be, Seb. Let's just move on from what happened, yeah?' He didn't look up at me as he spoke. As if stacking the beers in the esky required all of his concentration.

Looks like I wasn't getting an apology. It was just like Jake to sweep everything under the carpet and pretend it didn't happen.

'No worries. Thanks for coming.' I cringed. He must have thought I was such a pushover.

'It's cool. It's your birthday, isn't it?'

We made our way back outside with the beer. Was he still pissed off at me? It was hard to tell. It wasn't the time to get to the bottom of it. I'd wait until he'd had a couple of beers first.

We sat down on the bristly grass. A murder of crows could be seen covering the bush at the end of the yard – as if they were waiting for something.

'So, how've you been?' I knew the answer to my question already and wasn't sure why I'd even asked it.

'Pretty shit. I didn't think it could get any worse living out here. But somehow it has.'

His words were hollow. Transparent. His voice was monotone and his face expressionless.

'I'm sorry to hear that, Jake. I really am.' Did I come off genuine? Would it even make a difference?

His dull eyes looked to me, framed with dark rings. 'Have you heard from Kylie?'

There it was. The question I'd been waiting for. Perhaps that's the only reason he came. To find out whether the girl he fucked had been in touch and whether there was any hope of her coming back for round two. The anger boiled up inside me, so I took a deep breath through my nose before managing the words, 'Nah, nothing.' Then, a long pause.

Jake finally broke the silence. 'I'm sure she'll come round.'

Was it up to her to come around? Or was it up to me? Did I even want to see her? Maybe it was better for Jake to believe that. At least he didn't seem to be mad at me anymore.

'Yeah, maybe.'

'So I take it you didn't get a car for your birthday?'

I shook my head. 'Nope. Not for Christmas either.'

Jake looked pissed off. 'Those fuckers really do want to keep us here forever, don't they?'

'I take it you haven't got one yet either then?'

'No.'

The silence returned. This time it was even more profound.

'It's okay,' Jake finally said, picking a bull ant up from the ground and watching it struggle. 'We're just going to have to think up a Plan B.'

A Plan B? What did he mean? What possible alternative could there be for us other than getting a car and driving as far away from The Nowhere as possible? Something about the way he said it made me uneasy. His voice was devoid of all emotion. Jake had never been the most compassionate person, but he'd grown even colder. Frosted over.

'What do you mean?'

'Are you boys gonna eat some food, or what?' Dad interrupted at the worst possible time. Or possibly the best. It was hard to tell.

Jake smeared the ant between his index finger and thumb.

As I tucked into my third hotdog, I noticed Jake had hardly eaten a thing. No wonder he looked so drawn. His cheekbones so angular. It was also clear that Alison was aware he hadn't eaten as she swapped her plate with his when Rob was looking the other way. A sense of sadness came over me. Not just at the thought of Jake being so depressed that he'd stopped eating, but also at the act of mother-son care. It was something I'd longed for ever since losing Mum. Something I knew I'd never again experience.

'Is the food that bad, Jake?' I knew I could count on Dad to put focus on what was obviously an uncomfortable situation.

'Oh, we had a big brekkie,' Alison said quickly.

'Don't lie, darling. He hasn't been eating properly for

months – you know that.' Rob's words were so blunt and honest I could sense that Dad was just as stunned as I was. Had The Nowhere started to take a toll on Jake's parents, too?

'I'm just not hungry, okay?' Jake dropped his fork on his plate.

'It's all right, mate. I'm just playing.' Dad could see he'd touched a nerve.

'Well, all the more for us,' Rob said, reaching for another burger.

Dad's face lightened. 'Plenty to go around, mate. Plenty to go around.'

We tucked into what was left of the food. Out the corner of my eye, I could see Jake feeding his scraps to Scampi under the table, much to the dog's delight. That had been me not so long ago. It was a relief to have my appetite back.

Dad disappeared for a few minutes before reappearing with a cake covered in lit candles.

'Happy birthday to you, happy birthday to you…'

Everyone started singing, including Jake, although he looked less than enthused.

'Happy birthday, dear Sebastian…'

A memory of last year's birthday. At least there were more voices singing to me this time around.

'Happy birthday to you.'

The cheers followed. I blew out the candles and made a wish.

Jake knew exactly what it was.

After we'd eaten the entire birthday cake, Rob and Alison started talking about how slowly their crops were growing since their fruitful November harvest. It had been a dry summer so far, so it was unsurprising that little had grown recently. As expected, Dad appeared to take satisfaction from this. His smug face had 'told you so' written all over it.

Jake and I left them to it and headed out the front of the house. We perched on the porch, each with a cold bottle of beer in hand. It was clear he wanted to talk some more, though I knew the process of getting anything out of him would be like extracting teeth.

'Your parents. Are they okay?' It was nosey and possibly inappropriate, but the question just fell from my lips.

'Not really. I think they're probably as unhappy as I am. They argue all the time these days. I think if we weren't stuck out here in this stupid place they would have probably just split up by now, but they don't have anywhere else to go. But then, it's this bloody place making them argue.'

That was sad. Jake's parents had always appeared to be the epitome of a happy marriage. Not like mine had been. They would argue all the time, and I often wondered whether Mum would have ended up walking out on Dad if her life hadn't been cut short. They just weren't a good fit. Not like Alison and Rob. They had always seemed so... good. I guess I'd been wrong.

'That sucks. I'm sorry to hear that, Jake.'

'It doesn't matter. I kinda hope they do just split up, to be honest. Then if Mum moves back to Byron, I can go with her.'

Another blow. A reminder that if Jake got the opportunity to leave, he'd go without giving me a second thought. I couldn't even pretend it didn't hurt.

'So, is that the Plan B you're hoping for?'

Jake shook his head. 'There's no point waiting around forever for that to happen. Mum will probably just continue to put up with his shit. Nah, we need to think of something else. We need to get creative.'

Creative? He'd lost me. I was relieved to know he didn't genuinely think he'd be leaving the farm without me, but whatever other ideas he was contemplating couldn't be good.

'What do you mean? Like, drive off in one of their cars or something?'

'Nah, we don't wanna get in any trouble with the police for stealing a car, even if it is just from our parents. That's not saying we *can't* break the law... we just can't get caught.'

Now I was really confused, and a little freaked out. What was Jake implying? How far was he willing to go to escape The Nowhere? A chill crept down my spine. I didn't even know why, but something felt wrong about everything he was saying. Something felt wrong with *him*.

'I dunno,' he said. 'Maybe it's stupid. Let's just have a think – there's nothing wrong in that, is there?'

'I guess not.'

'You want another beer?' The corner of Jake's lip rose.

'Sure. It is my birthday, after all.'

22nd January 1998

The faint sound of the telephone ringing came just in time to stop me starting up my bike. It had to be Jake. I'd been secretly listening out for his call since my birthday. All I could think about was what he'd said. What sort of Plan B did he want us to come up with? I could picture his withdrawn face and sunken eyes. I was worried about him, but it had also been so good to see him. I just wanted to make him feel better. To think of a Plan B. But one that didn't involve breaking the law.

'Hello?'

'Seb, hey.'

'Jake, how're you going? It's good to hear from you again.' There was no guarantee we'd go back to the way we'd been before, but I'd held onto hope. What more did I have?

'Listen, Seb. I've figured it out.'

'Figured what out?' I was slow on the uptake.

'Our Plan B. I've figured out what we need to do.'

My stomach dropped. A bad feeling brewed inside me, but I was still trembling with curiosity.

'Really? What-what is it?' I tripped over my words.

'I can't tell you now. Not over the phone. Listen, can you meet me tomorrow? In our usual place, as soon as your dad leaves? I'll be there waiting, so we have as much time as possible to discuss it.'

Whatever he was plotting, was it something I wanted to get myself into? The Jake that had turned up to my birthday wasn't the Jake I'd known before. He was something else entirely. Like he'd had all the life sucked out of him. Like he was possessed. But how could I not listen to what he had to say? There was no car in sight for either of us. There was no escape route. It was just this. The Nowhere. Every day, for who knew how long. Perhaps forever. Perhaps we'd be there until our parents dropped dead and we'd take over the farms and live in complete misery. Or, if we ever did manage to finally escape, we would have grown so accustomed to life in The Nowhere, we wouldn't even be able to adjust to the outside world. Surely I owed it to myself to find out what his idea was. Surely I owed it to Jake. Maybe it was what we'd both been waiting for. Maybe my birthday wish would come true after all.

'I'll be there.'

The line went dead.

5th January 2018

'Hey, Seb, it's me. I know you're avoiding me. But you can't hide from me forever. Please call me back. Bye.'

Sandra hadn't stopped trying. It was me who had. It started when I stopped visiting Dad in the hospital. That way she couldn't find me. Then I stopped going to work and kept the lights off at home. Even on the evenings she turned up unannounced, I could just pretend I wasn't in. It was pathetic. I was disgusted with myself. I was disgusting.

You can't keep it secret forever.

I could give it a bloody good go.

The truth always comes out eventually.

Not if I had anything to do with it.

But the harder I tried to resist, the lonelier and more depressed I became. So much so that I eventually decided to give in and return Sandra's calls. She deserved that at the very least.

'Seb, hi. How are you going?'

'Yeah, okay.'

'Good. I've missed you.'

'I've missed you too.'

'Wanna get coffee?'

'Sure. That would be nice.'

*

A giant cockatoo squawked boisterously as it bounced through the trees beyond us. The evening air was warm, but not as unbearable as it had been in recent weeks. It was a reminder that autumn would soon be on its way, ready to relieve us of the long, scorching days.

'Seb, listen. I understand why you've been avoiding me, okay?'

'You do?' I could still feel the caffeine buzzing through my system. I knew I should have had a decaf at this time of day.

'Of course I do. You're approaching the part of your story you've been dreading to tell me from the start. But that's all right.'

'You don't know that though.'

'I don't know what?'

'You don't know that it's all right. It's not all right. It's fucked up. It's always been fucked up.'

Sandra could see the sadness in my anger. She wasn't going to give up here. She'd come too far.

'Seb, whatever it is... whatever it is that you've been carrying all these years... it's time to let it go. It's okay to let it go.'

She grabbed my hand and squeezed it tightly, before whispering: 'I give you *permission* to let it go.'

For some reason, that's what it took. The permission of someone who I knew deeply cared for me. After all those years of harbouring my pain, I was finally ready to just let it go.

I took a deep breath and shut my eyes.

23ʳᵈ January 1998

The shrubs brushed against my bare legs, scratching shapes into them as I walked. Perhaps they were warning signs, telling me to stop. To turn back. But I couldn't stop. And I couldn't turn back. I'd promised Jake I'd meet him at our usual time in our usual place to hear his Plan B. So that's exactly what I'd do.

It was a bone-dry morning. The hot air clung to me as I paced through the bush, getting closer and closer to our meeting place. Getting closer and closer to him.

My mind went into overdrive. What could he possibly be plotting? It had to involve stealing one of our parents' cars. He'd denied it, but I couldn't envision another way. Unless he wanted me to get back in touch with Kylie. See if she could come and pick us up. Maybe that was why he'd asked me whether I'd heard from her. She had to have something to do with it. The wait would soon be over. I'd meet with Jake and he would finally put me out of my misery. Or breathe new life into me.

I stopped in my tracks. There he was. Standing directly before me, his eyes transfixed on mine. Like he was in a trance. Like he was made of stone.

5th January 2018

Sandra focused her eyes on mine intently. She knew she couldn't press me. She needed to listen to the silences between each word. She needed to sense how I was feeling from the pace of my breath. But I couldn't be rushed. I had to get there in my own time.

The swarm of cockatoos broke through the trees, screeching deafeningly. It was as if they'd heard us. It was as if they'd heard me, even before I spoke. Like they were listening to my thoughts. Listening to my memories.

'Do you have anything you've carried inside you your whole life? Something that forever weighs you down, that you can't even bring yourself to put into words?'

Why was I even asking her this? Maybe I was looking for even ground. Perhaps I wanted to feel less alone in my guilt.

Sandra thought for a moment. Long and hard. Before she finally nodded her head.

'Of course I do, Seb. Everyone does. And if I tell you, will you promise to share your secret with me?'

I nodded. 'I promise.'

Sandra drew a deep breath before beginning her story:

'Well, when I was about eleven years old, I was helping my dad clean the car in the garage. Earning my pocket money for the summer. There I was, in my little red crop top and denim shorts, innocently splashing away, music blasting out from the radio. Making a soapy lather and getting every last bit of dirt off so the car would be sparkly and clean. I was having so much fun that I hadn't even realised that Dad had stopped cleaning the car. He was watching me.' She stopped speaking momentarily before continuing. 'Now, all dads watch their little girls, right? With pride, with love. But it wasn't like either of those things. I could see his face in the reflection of the car. It was a look of lust.'

'Oh, Sandra,' I interrupted.

'That was just the beginning. I tried to ignore it, forget it ever happened. Convinced myself I must have been imagining things. It wasn't until Mum went away with my brother to visit my grandmother a couple of summers later when I saw that look on my dad's face again. By now I'd reached puberty. So my body was starting to take its shape. But I still wasn't a woman. Not by a long shot. I was a girl. A girl playing the part of a woman. A girl playing the part of a woman to impress her father. But he wasn't just impressed, was he? So he deemed it appropriate to let himself into the bathroom and watch me shower. It got worse from there.'

Tears welled up in my eyes. I shut them to prevent them from spilling down my face. I'd had no idea about Sandra's abusive past. There I'd been, going on about how strict Dad had been, but he would never do anything as disgusting and perverse as that. It was surprising Sandra was so well adjusted.

'Sandra, how awful. What a vile man. Please tell me you didn't have to endure it for long.'

'Well, the physical abuse stopped soon after that. Sick fuck, I probably got too old for him. But the mind games started soon after. He used to manipulate me, make me feel like I'd done something wrong and that if I told Mum or anyone, it would turn everyone against me. The sad thing was, I didn't tell anyone. Not for a long time, anyway. By the time I was ready to talk to a therapist he'd left the picture with another woman.'

'Did you ever tell your mum?'

Sandra laughed. 'Yeah, for what it was worth. She didn't believe me. She'd worshipped the ground he'd walked on for some crazy reason. Silly woman.'

There was a much-needed silence. But I knew what was coming. I owed it to her. She'd fulfilled her part of the bargain.

'But that was something that was done to you,' I said. 'You were the victim. This was something I did. I wasn't the victim.'

Sandra took my hand again. 'Sebastian, I'm not here to judge you. Or to compete with you about which of us is the better person. I'm here to listen to you, as a friend. Okay?'

I nodded. 'Okay.'

Okay.

23rd January 1998

'You came.'

'Of course I came. Why wouldn't I? I'm dying to hear what this Plan B is you've thought up.'

I was trying to make light of the situation with a breezy tone. Break the tension in the air. Shield my fear. That was it. I was feeling afraid. Afraid of the unknown. Afraid of whatever it was Jake had cooked up in his unhinged mind. Afraid of myself and what I was capable of.

'Come on,' Jake said. 'Let's sit down.'

Following his command, I crouched down next to him. It was the closest I'd been to him for a long time. So close I could smell him. That rusty, earthy scent. It was familiar and alien all at the same time. An image of the first time I saw Jake walking over to Dad and me on our farm filled my head. How he'd hidden from me. Avoided my eyes at all costs. We'd come so far, yet nowhere at all.

'Before I tell you my idea, I need to know that I can trust you. Fully.'

He'd caught me off guard. 'What? Of course you can trust me.'

'But I need to know that I can *really* trust you.'

A pause, before I said: 'Okay. How?'

'Hold out your hand.'

'What?'

'Hold out your hand.'

Without thinking, I obeyed.

Jake pulled out a switchblade.

'What? What the fuck are you doing?'

'Calm down, drama queen. It won't hurt, just a little scratch. Here look, I'll do it to myself first.'

'Jake, no! Stop it!'

Too late. He slid the sharp steel along the skin of his upper hand, drawing a line of crimson.

'Are you crazy? You're bleeding.'

'Now are you gonna hold out your hand or not?'

What had come over him? Jake had acted in reckless ways so many times in the past, but nothing like this. He was scaring me. But I couldn't resist. I just couldn't resist. I held out my hand and drew a deep breath. The corner of Jake's lip curled. He was smiling.

It didn't hurt. Perhaps it was the adrenaline, or that I was so focused on finding out about his plan. I just wanted to get it over with. My blood was slightly lighter than Jake's. And there was more of it. Maybe he'd cut me deeper. The blood ran down my hand and wrapped around my wrist.

'Fuck. Are you happy now?'

He grabbed my hand and held my open wound against his. 'Yes. Now I know that I can trust you.'

Did he really need to cut my hand open to prove that? Surely I'd proven my dedication to him countless times before.

Once satisfied that our blood had blended enough, Jake reached into his backpack and pulled out a roll of bandages and his hipflask.

'You came prepared.'

'Of course.'

It stung like hell as he poured the vodka onto my hand before cutting off some of the bandage with the bloodied switchblade. He wrapped it around my hand first and then tended to his own. 'Okay, now that's out the way, we can talk business.'

The pain had really started to kick in now. But I didn't mind. I liked the thought of Jake and I sharing blood. It made me feel special. It made me feel closer to him. Part of him. I cringed at how bizarre my thoughts were.

Jake jumped up and stared down at me. He was nervous. I could see it in the way he moved. 'Now, I thought long and hard about what we could do. And of course, in an ideal world, we'd get given a car by our parents and just take off into the dirt. Or we'd have enough cash to jump in a cab. But as you and I both know, that ain't gonna happen. So we're either stuck here forever, or we do something about it. We send a warning.'

I nodded impatiently. 'Yeah… so… what do you have in mind?'

There was a long pause. Jake's eyes locked with mine. It was strangely intimidating. Like he was trying to listen to my thoughts. Or predict how I would react to whatever he was going to say. With his hipflask of vodka in one hand, he reached into his pocket and pulled out his cherry red lighter with the other. He flicked it, creating a thin blue flame.

That was when it dawned on me.

'Are you… are you serious?'

He nodded slowly, the flame still burning.

'You're crazy. You're out of your mind. You'll get us all killed.'

'No we won't. Not if we plan it properly. Look, all it would take is a simple little fire to wipe this whole place out. No more bush. No more farms. No more Nowhere. Then we'd *have* to leave. They'd take their insurance money and leave. They'd have no choice.'

Was I really hearing this? It was as if Jake's words were paper planes, brushing past me and disappearing into nothingness. They were empty echoes in the night. They were as transparent as air.

'So this isn't a joke? You're really not kidding?'

'Do I look like I'm kidding?'

He didn't. Not at all. In fact, he looked more serious than I'd ever seen him.

A sharp pain in my hand. A reminder of Jake's insanity. He'd gone too far this time. And I wasn't going to be part of it. Not for a single second.

'Well then, I'm sorry, Jake. But you're on your own with this one. I don't want to be involved with something that will either get us killed or thrown in jail.'

'I thought I could trust you, Seb. I thought it was you and me until the end.'

A different kind of pain. This time down my spine. Was that really how he saw it? Him and me until the end? Or was he just manipulating me? Playing with my heart to get his own way? Either way, I couldn't agree to take part in this.

'I'm sorry, Jake.'

His expression changed from disappointed to frustrated. He put out the flame. I exhaled.

'Well, Seb... I'm afraid I'm going to be carrying out my plan with or without you. And I can't guarantee the safety of you or your family if you don't join me.'

Was he threatening me? I felt sick at the thought of what he was suggesting and how he'd cornered me. If what he was saying was true, the only way I could attempt to keep both my family and me safe was to take part in Jake's sick plan of destroying The Nowhere.

But was it even that sick? Maybe it *was* the only way. Maybe it's what both my dad and Jake's parents deserved. Maybe it's what The Nowhere deserved. To burn in bloody hell.

I shook my head. What was I even thinking? There's no way I could go along with something so dangerous. So sadistic.

'No, Jake. This is a bad idea. I won't.'

Jake's expression changed again. This time I couldn't read it.

'Seb. If you don't do this with me, I'm gonna tell your dad exactly who you are.'

His words cut into me deeper than any blade could. It was as if I was the person he'd set alight. What was he saying? That he knew I was a fag? He obviously thought *he* wasn't. I was the freak. I was the sicko. I felt ashamed and I felt alone. Jake wasn't my friend. He just wanted me as an alibi. So what was worse? To risk burning alive alongside my brother and father, or to risk being exposed?

'Okay,' I said finally, shaking my head. I couldn't look him in the eye. 'Let's do it.'

I looked up. A huge smile broke across Jake's face like flames through a forest.

'Good choice, mate. Good choice.'

He held his hand out and took mine in his palm. 'You and I, until the end.'

I forced a smile. 'Until the end.'

I'd never hated him more. I'd never hated myself more.

5th January 2018

Sandra shifted her focus from my eyes to the ground. It was hard to read her thoughts. She had to be judging me. She didn't even know the full story, but I could just imagine how she would be busy making up her own ending in her mind. Perhaps she had multiple scenarios. Whatever she was thinking, it was enough for her to avert her eyes from mine. Maybe I was just being paranoid.

'I think I've said enough for today.' I wanted to break the awkwardness, bring Sandra's focus back to me. It worked. She looked up and met my gaze once more.

'I understand. It must be emotionally draining... going back there. You can finish your story another time.'

Was it weakness? Was I defeated? Either way, Sandra was right. It *was* emotionally draining. And it was enough for tonight.

'Thanks, Sandra. For being so understanding. You're a true friend.'

The warmth of her smile calmed the tension and bought me a bit more time.

She reached out and rubbed my arm. 'That's okay, Seb. I'm here for you, no matter what.'

Those last three words. She knew what was coming was going to be bad. And no matter what it was, I would have her support. But would she be so sure when she found out? Sure, she'd probably say that. But what would really be going on behind her eyes?

My phone lit up. A message from Jake: *I'll be free next Friday. Still on for that coffee?*

My throat turned dry. I couldn't even swallow.

'Are you okay?' Sandra sensed my anguish.

'It's Jake. I haven't told you yet. He's coming to Perth next week. I'm seeing him next Friday.'

She looked visibly shocked. Tucking a strand of hair behind her ear, she chose her words carefully. 'How do you feel?'

If only I knew myself. 'Numb. Anxious. A little like not even responding.'

'Only you can make that decision, Seb. But I know deep down you want to see him. You need closure.'

I nodded, wishing she were wrong. Wishing Jake hadn't reached out to me at all. Why reopen the wound? Hadn't I suffered enough?

'Come on,' she continued. 'Let's go home.'

Without words, I got up and followed, like a zombie, making its way back to its grave in the dark.

Sadness spiralled through me as I pushed the door of my empty house open. I was alone. Alone with my secrets. Alone with my memories. Alone. Why had I been avoiding visiting Dad? What was wrong with me?

Sandra's engine started up outside. I turned and ran towards the car.

'Sandra.'

She stopped the car and wound down the window. 'Seb,

are you okay?'

'Tomorrow, I'm going to finish telling you my story. Once and for all.'

'Are you sure? There's really no pressure.'

'I know. But I need to. I want to.'

'Okay then. Sounds good.'

'Do you want to stay the night? I'll make brekkie and coffee in the morning, and then we can head somewhere quiet where I feel comfortable talking.'

Sandra turned off the engine.

'Sure, Seb. You had me at brekkie.'

My smile said it all. I was grateful to have Sandra in my life. I was grateful to be telling her my secret after running from the truth for so long. And I was deeply grateful not to be alone. Not tonight.

26th January 1998

The days that followed our conversation had drifted past like ghosts in the fog, the first colliding softly into the next. I'd gone back and forth with my decision, wrestling with it. Could I really go through with Plan B? Were we willing to risk our safety? And the safety of our families? Something had to change, but surely there was another way. There had to be.

My t-shirt stuck to my upper back as the sweat thickened. It was hotter than it had been all summer. Drier too. There had been fewer storms than usual, meaning less rain. The grass, which was always a golden hue, had been sun-bleached almost white. As I rode my quad bike with Scampi running alongside, I imagined the whole place going up in flames. Torched to the ground. Nothing left but midnight-black dust embellished with dancing embers and a reddened post-climatic glow. These were the perfect conditions for a bushfire.

Dad and I parked our bikes next to our usual lone, dead tree, which stood like a skeletal hand reaching up into the sky, barely providing enough shade to keep us from overheating. Rolling his cigarette, Dad looked at me more intently than usual from under the rim of his hat.

'Something's on your mind, Son. I can tell.'

No matter the state of our relationship, Dad always had good foresight about these things. He knew when I was unhappy, when I was distant or when I was mad. You don't spend that much time with someone and not pick up on their moods.

I took my time with my words. Perhaps this was my chance to change fate. To avoid the devastating outcome Jake had planned. Maybe I'd give Dad one more chance. One more chance to prove he loved me by giving me the only thing I'd ever asked of him. The opportunity to escape.

'Dad, I'm sorry to bring this up again. And I promise it'll be the last time. But is there any chance at all that you'll ever buy me a car?'

As soon as I spoke the words, I regretted them. Dad didn't say anything at first. He just stared at me blankly. His expression quickly turned into one of disappointment. And then into one of fury. His nostrils flared as he puffed away on his cigarette. His moustache began to twitch.

'You really are an ungrateful little bastard, aren't you, Seb?'

Closing my eyes, I drew in a deep breath. I could sense the presence of that thin purple vein on his neck. It was the answer to my doubts. My fate, clear as rain. There was no other way around it. I was never going to win. He would never let me. I would have to take things into my own hands.

As he stamped the cigarette out on the whitened grass, I imagined what the ground would look like ablaze.

'I'm sorry, Dad,' I lied. 'I don't mean to sound ungrateful. I truly appreciate everything you do for me.'

He shot me a doubtful look. 'Now you're just taking the piss. Come on, get on with it.'

As we climbed back onto our bikes, I realised it could be

the last time we ever did.

'Is everything okay?' Jeremy asked observantly as he dried up. I'd been virtually silent over dinner and finished my meal faster than usual. Jeremy had slopped and slurped his own as if to compete with me.

Scrubbing the bubbly water over a plate, I nodded while looking out the window to the bushland in the distance. 'Course it is, J. Everything's just fine and dandy.'

Satisfied with my answer and clearly not picking up on my sarcasm, Jeremy eagerly patted the plate down once I was done rinsing it.

We finished the remaining dishes without speaking, while I played out the plan in my head. How quickly I'd have to run to get back to the house and alert Dad and Jeremy about the fire – if they didn't already know. How I'd focus on getting to Jeremy's room first.

Once Jeremy was in bed and I'd triple-checked Dad was asleep, I strode into the hallway and picked up the phone. I said a silent prayer he would answer straight away so I wouldn't have to speak to either of his parents. My prayers were answered before the phone had a chance to complete a single ring.

'Hello?'

'Jake, it's me,' I whispered.

'I thought it might be.'

'Are you ready? Tonight?'

'Tonight? Wow, I'm shocked you want to do it so soon.'

'Well, I've made up my mind. So there's no point waiting,

right?'

'You're right… I guess.'

Was he having doubts? It was *his* idea.

'Are you sure you want to go through with this, Jake?' I lowered my voice again after I noticed myself speaking louder. 'Because we can't do this unless we're both sure.'

'No, no… I'm sure. Believe me, I'm sure.'

'Good.'

'Shall we meet at midnight?'

'Midnight sounds perfect.'

'See you then.'

The call clicked to a close. It suddenly felt real. We were really doing this. We were really setting The Nowhere alight.

6th January 2018

I woke with a burning knot in my stomach, knowing today was the day. The day I'd be attempting to set myself free by telling Sandra my secret. The day I'd finally stop running from the truth. The following hour passed slowly, and I decided to stay in bed. I didn't want to wake Sandra. She was in Dad's room down the hallway, but the walls were thin. And she'd need all the energy she could get for what I was about to tell her.

Lying in silence, my mind darted back to that fateful night. It was etched in my mind. One of the hottest and driest nights of the year. And what would become the worst night of my life. The smell. The heat. The speed of the flames. The look in Jake's eyes. The hatred in his heart. The hatred in mine. I'd never forgive myself for my lapse in judgement.

The sound of Sandra stirring shook me from my thoughts. Soon, I'd be reliving it in its gruesome entirety. Speaking it out loud for the very first time. I'd make the most of the next few hours of not having to be back there. It felt like waking up on death row, and knowing it was my turn on the chair. Once showered, I wandered into the kitchen to prepare breakfast, but Sandra had beaten me to it and was frying a couple of eggs with a pot of fresh coffee on the go.

'Hey, I said I was gonna do that.'

'It's all good. You take a seat and relax. It's a big day

for you.'

It was a sweet gesture. And it was the truth. It was a big day. Bigger than I could even comprehend.

'So where do you want to go? To talk, I mean.' Sandra piled the fried eggs on toasted sourdough. They were cooked to perfection.

'I was thinking we could drive a little further out of town today. There's a little beach I know that will be empty. It usually is. It'll be easier for me to talk.'

'No drama. I understand.'

I wasn't hungry, but I finished every last bit. I wanted to show my appreciation. We filled a couple of flasks with water, packed a few snacks and set off towards the beach. Towards the truth.

As we pulled into the car park, relief washed over me like the crashing waves before us. The beach was completely empty, as I knew it would be. We approached the sand and took off our shoes. It felt warm against my feet, but it didn't yet burn the way it would in a few hours. We'd have to seek refuge under the trees behind the beach once the day warmed up, but right now I wanted to be as close to the water as possible. As if sitting next to the foamy waves as they collapsed on the sand could extinguish my words – and the memory.

We sat down on a small slope that led to the sea. Our bare feet were close enough for the waves to lap against them. After a long moment, Sandra took my hand.

'Are you ready?'

I wasn't. I never would be. But still, I said: 'I'm ready.'

27th January 1998

Twigs snapped beneath my feet, each creating a satisfying, dry crack as I made my way through the scrub. I kept my hand in the back pocket of my denim shorts, fumbling the photograph I'd taken from the montage Dad had given me. It had all four of us in. Dad, Mum, Jeremy and me. Jeremy hadn't long been born, and I cradled him in my arms, wrapped in a knitted blanket. The picture was slightly blurred because grandma had taken it on a disposable. The glow of her thumb was visible in the top left corner. But I loved it. It would bring me luck. And if we didn't have time to pack our things before leaving, it would be all I'd have left of Mum.

I felt like a chunk of metal being dragged towards a magnet. Did I have no conscience? Did I even have a mind? Free will? It was as if I'd been possessed. I was no longer a person. Just a shell, marching through the night. Like one of our cows to the slaughter.

As I walked, I stopped feeling the ground beneath me. I stopped hearing the chirp of the crickets and smelling the scent of eucalyptus. I became one with the moment. One with the darkness. I imagined myself floating out of my body and drifting up towards the stars. Towards the moon. Towards the sun. Floating closer and closer towards its burning rays until I could feel them scorching me. Blistering my skin. Melting it away, so nothing was left but bones. Then dust.

Then nothing. Just cold, empty silence.

When I finally reached our meeting place, I was surprised to find Jake wasn't waiting there for me. Wouldn't he be eager to turn his vision into reality? He'd shown signs of uncertainty. His words played back in my mind. Did he have cold feet? If only I'd brought a lighter with me.

He'll come, faggot. Give him time.

Time was all I had. It was all there ever was in The Nowhere. Endless amounts of time. An eternity. Lifelessly floating in an infinite universe. That was The Nowhere. That had been my life. But not anymore. Not any longer. It would all change tonight. It would all end tonight. It had to. There was no other way. No other option. We'd exhausted them all. It was time to take control and show The Nowhere exactly who was boss.

I laughed into the darkness. The crickets stopped, then laughed back. Had I lost my mind? Had I lost everything?

No, queer boy. Tonight you will win. Tonight you'll finally grow a pair and become a bloody man.

And then he appeared. Like a fallen angel. Or the devil himself. I wasn't sure. I never had been.

'You came,' I said.

'Of course I did. Until the end, remember?'

'Until the end.'

Thinning my eyes, I tried to decipher Jake's expression. He didn't give anything away, just as always. He'd give me something… enough to want more. But then he'd pull away and leave me with less than I had before. How was it possible to love and hate him so much at the same time?

Jake reached into his pocket and pulled out his lighter. 'Are you ready to do this?'

Taking a deep breath, I replied: 'I'm ready.'

Jake offered me a devilish grin that sent a chill deep into the marrow of my bones.

What were we doing? Were we able to comprehend the magnitude of our intended actions? Did it even matter anymore? No. It was too late. Too late for us. Too late for change. We had to make an impact. We had to be heard. There was no other way.

Jake had that dangerous glint in his eyes. But through his focus and the layers of venom, he still managed to look more beautiful than ever before. I wanted to be his. Solely his. I wanted to go up in flames with him, the smoke of our burning flesh rising from the ground and entwining. Forming an intricate connection that belonged to us, and only us. I wanted to see the trees burn, to see the birds boil. I wanted to see the farmhouse turn to embers. I wanted to see the sky turn purple. I wanted to be his. I wanted to be his. I wanted to be his.

Jake took a swig from his flask before pouring the liquid to the ground. It trickled to a finish. 'Come on then, mate. Let's do this.'

He flicked the lighter, producing a single dim flame. He lit a twig and dropped it to the ground. A gasp escaped me before the world went into slow motion.

It didn't take long before the flame had climbed across the dry ground and up into the trees, spreading its wings of silver and scarlet. We both stood for a few moments, perhaps frozen, perhaps shocked we'd actually gone through with our plan. But if we'd stood still any longer, the fire would have swallowed us. Engulfed us in its flames. After a brief moment meeting each other's eyes, we both spun around and ran. We ran as fast as we could back to our farms. Back to our houses. Back to our homes. To save our families. To save ourselves.

As I ran, my mind went back to the last time I'd run through the scrub. How different that had been. If the trees had been alight the way they were now, perhaps I wouldn't have even bothered running. Maybe I would have just let myself fall into their burning branches, letting them melt me like wax, so all that was left was my broken, barely-beating heart. A sorry state of an organ.

My legs moved independently from my brain. I let myself be carried along, soaring through the scrubland, racing to beat the fire. But it was running faster. Competing with me. Bigger and hotter. The back of my body was reaching boiling point as the flames stretched out to catch me. The choking mass of smoke was beginning to cloak me as the rumble grew louder, becoming a ceaseless roar. The break in the bush wasn't far off. I had to make it. I had to make it through. Back to Scampi. Back to Jeremy. Back to Dad. I had to make it back. Would my selfishness be the end of us all? Is this what I'd asked for? Is this what I deserved?

I imagined the ruthless flames wrapping themselves around me, like the wings of a golden eagle. Burning through my skin like paper. Turning my white bones into black ash. Revealing my innocent intentions as pure evil. Was I evil? Had I always been? Had Dad been right to worry about me?

Had everything I'd done and everywhere I'd been led me to this very night? This very moment?

You're a filthy faggot and now you're going to burn, burn, burn in Hell for your sins.

The warm night air was a relief from the ferocious heat of the bush as I sprinted through the gap in the scrub. Like I was leaving the womb. Being reborn. But for how long? The fire had reached the grass behind me and was overtaking me. Fuck. How many times had Dad drilled into me how dangerous fire was out here? The blaze sped across the yard, rapidly hopping from one patch of grass to the next. Each flame splitting in two, before smouldering into even more flames. Would Jake have made it out? Would he have made it home?

The fire reached the windmill, its flames lapping the rusty metal. My eyes and mouth widened watching the destruction unfold in front of me. It was almost beautiful. An unnerving satisfaction swept through me as I watched my former prison being engulfed in a blaze. Until my breath stopped.

Scampi.

There he was, barking at the house. The flames had reached him, but he wouldn't run. He was sacrificing his life to wake us. To wake me. He was my most loyal, faithful friend. The one who had been there for me when Jake wasn't. When Kylie wasn't. He was risking his life to save me. The person who was about to get him killed.

'Scampi!' I screamed, the burning windmill towering over me.

It was too late. The fire had reached the house now. I had

to get to my brother and Dad. Tears drowned my eyes and stung like crazy. Was it the smoke or guilt? I could barely see. I blinked furiously. My tears dampened my vision, but they couldn't save Scampi. They wouldn't save my brother or father. They wouldn't save Jake or his family. They wouldn't save me.

What had we done?

Lurching towards the door of the house, I pushed through to be greeted by a thick cloud of toxic smoke. Holding my breath, I darted towards Jeremy's room in the darkness. I knew the route with my eyes closed. Four steps forward, three to the right. I ran my fingertips along the wall to make sure I didn't lose my way. The smoke travelled up my nostrils, like a plague making its way into my lungs. I wouldn't be able to hold my breath much longer. I just had to make it into Jeremy's room. I had to make it.

Just as I found myself gasping desperately for air, taking in a mouthful of smoke, an arm wrapped around my torso. Dad. I could just make out his silhouette through the black and deep-grey swirls. Jeremy hung limply over his other arm. Had he looked for me too? Within moments we were outside in the night air. We ran to the car. Dad threw Jeremy in the back seat. What was left of the windmill came crashing down to the ground less than a foot away. There wasn't time to process how lucky we'd been to survive the near miss. We weren't safe yet.

Dad started the ute and reversed out the drive with so much force Jeremy and I flew forwards. I reached over and pulled Jeremy towards me. As the vehicle twisted around and roared down the road, away from the fire, I checked to see if he was okay. He was unconscious.

'Put your belts on!' Dad bellowed from the front.

I obeyed, buckling my brother in first. Had Dad not realised Jeremy was unconscious?

'Dad, we need to get to a hospital.'

'Where do you think we're going?'

Merredin. That was the closest. Westonia had a flying doctor service that visited on a six-weekly cycle. But no hospital. It was Dad's fault. He was the one who brought us here. He was the one who thought it would be a good idea to move to the middle of fucking nowhere. Now he would regret it. Now he would pay.

'Jeremy,' I whispered into my brother's ear. 'Stay with us – we'll be there soon. Be strong. Be strong, Jeremy.'

I felt my brother's wrist. A faint pulse. He would be fine. He *had* to be fine. We just needed to get to the hospital fast.

'Dad!' I yelled. 'How much further is it?' He couldn't hear me. He was in a trance. Racing through the dusty, empty streets. A torpedo in the darkness. A spirit in the night. Leaving the flames behind. Leaving The Nowhere behind. Leaving Jake behind.

Wrapping my arms around my little brother, I whispered into his ear again: 'Stay with me, J.'

8ᵗʰ December 1989

'Here you go.' Grandma reached out her wrinkled hand and wrapped it around mine, her skin cold but comforting. I felt the hard lollies fall into my palm as she offered me a soft smile.

'That's for being such a patient boy.'

We'd been in the hospital for hours, but I was happy to wait. I had no idea how long it would take. But the excitement was bubbling beneath me.

'Thanks, Grandma!'

Just as I tore the wrappers off the hard, colourful lollies, Dad's voice echoed down the corridor. 'Linda! Bring Sebastian! Hurry, quick! He's here!'

A flourish of butterflies danced around my stomach. This was it. I was finally getting to meet my little brother.

Despite my excitement, I made sure to link arms with my grandma and help her down the corridor. Dad had quickly slipped back into the ward, unable to hide his delight. Although he'd said he'd wanted a daughter next, he quickly adjusted as soon as Mum had the gender revealed. 'Another little boy. It's a miracle. We'll save a boatload on baby clothes,' he'd said.

When we entered the room, a swarm of nurses surrounded my mother's bed – cooing sounds resonating between them. As soon as they realised Grandma and I were coming, they began to clear the way. That was when I saw him for the very first time.

Wrapped in Mum's arms, I could just see the top of his little head poking out. His face was beetroot-red, his hair a fine sprinkle of blonde.

'Isn't he beautiful?' Grandma asked in her calm, croaky voice.

'He sure is,' Dad said with a wide smile.

Mum turned to face me. Her hair sweat-sodden and tangled, her cheeks flushed. Unsurprisingly, she looked exhausted. 'Do you want to hold him, Sebastian?'

Unable to speak, I nodded my head.

'Come on then, Son.' Dad led me over to the seat beside Mum.

Slowly, she passed my baby brother to me. 'His name's Jeremy.'

'Say hello to little Jeremy, Sebastian,' Dad said, stroking my hair.

'Hello, little Jeremy.'

Staring down at his tiny features, I knew instantly I was in love. And I knew that no matter where our lives would take us, I would be the best big brother I could.

6ᵗʰ January 2018

Thick tears streamed down my face, mirroring the waves. Two arms wrapped around me. The arms of a friend.

'I'm so sorry,' Sandra whispered with a slight croak in her voice. She knew even before I said it.

'We lost him. We lost him before we even made it to the hospital. He didn't stand a chance. My poor little brother didn't even stand a chance. Why did I… My family, I…' But I couldn't get the words out to express the pain. The guilt.

Sandra knew all she could do was offer silence. Silence, and her embrace. My tears evolved into sobs. Sobs into utter despair. Hysterics. Finally, I was releasing it. All I had kept in for so long. The secret I knew I couldn't keep hidden forever. The truth I knew would come out eventually. And I was so relieved it had. I'd waited for the right time. For the right person. I didn't feel judged and I didn't feel evil.

'It's okay, Seb. It's okay.' Sandra stroked the back of my head as she hugged me tight. At that moment, I was hugging my brother. I was hugging my mother. I was hugging my father.

'How can I live with myself?' My words were barely audible. I inhaled deeply, trying to calm myself down. 'How can I live with myself?'

Sandra released her hold. She stared me directly in the eye and grasped my hand tight.

'You made a mistake, Seb. Okay? Yes, it was a huge,

terrible mistake. But you were so young. You were a kid. And you were influenced by the guy you loved.'

Sandra's words were shards of glass, scraping across my skin. I hadn't loved Jake. I'd been infatuated with him. I'd worshipped him. But it wasn't love. It had never been love. He didn't deserve my love.

She was right about one thing though. I had been a stupid kid who made an awful mistake I'd never forgiven myself for. But how could I? I wouldn't let myself. The moment I even entertained the thought of forgiveness, I would be letting Jeremy down. No, the guilt was the punishment I would be taking to my grave. It's what I deserved.

The waves spilt onto the soft, blonde sand as the water glistened in the sun. It was a simple yet beautiful scene. The antithesis of my complex and hideous story. But I somehow felt lighter. As if I'd cut away an anchor that had been dragging along the seabed. Guilt grew within me for allowing myself to feel any sort of cathartic release. What right did I have to feel healed in any way? Jeremy would never obtain such a privilege.

Sandra gave me time to sit in silence. Knowing she was there, with me, was what I needed.

'How do you feel?' she finally asked.

I searched my mind for the words.

'I don't know. Better than I did, I guess. In some ways it's made it feel more real, saying it aloud. But I know that's what I needed to do.' My eyes burned as the tears dried.

That familiar smile. 'Today is a very important day. It marks a new beginning for you. Your whole life is ahead of you. You can't let it pass you by any longer.'

She was right, as hard as it was to accept. I'd allowed the guilt to stop me living my life for so long. I'd felt I didn't deserve to be happy. Not only for killing my brother. But for never being punished for it.

Sandra wanted to hear what happened next. I could hear it in her silence. She'd been so patient – I wanted to tell her. I'd come this far. I recomposed myself.

'It wasn't until the investigation started that I found out Jake and his parents survived. He must have ran faster than me. We were both questioned by the police but neither of us said anything. And our parents didn't suspect anything, so they stepped in to defend us. The investigation was dropped soon after. Ruled out as just another bushfire disaster. An accident.' I looked down. I couldn't look Sandra in the eye.

'Did you see Jake again?'

'Only during the investigation. We were questioned together once by the police in Merredin. We said goodbye to each other afterwards and that was it. Dad got a small payout from the cattle we lost. Once we got back to Perth, Dad just wanted to cut out that whole part of our lives. To forget The Nowhere completely. We never spoke about the farm, the fire or Jake and his family ever again.'

I rubbed my eyes and continued: 'I thought about Jake a lot over the years. Played back much of what happened in my mind. The good and the bad memories, but mostly the bad. Mostly about what we'd done that night and how we'd never owned up to our actions. Never suffered the consequences. The thoughts come mostly at night. In my dreams, or in those lonely hours when I lie awake. I can still picture Jake's face so clearly. The look in his eyes as he put flame to grass.'

'I can only imagine how awful it's been for you, Seb. You must have tortured yourself so much over the years. That's the consequence you've paid. And I'm sure it's been worse than any prison sentence.'

She was right. In many ways, my guilt and regret had been the sentence. And it was one I'd serve until the day I died. But I hated myself for not owning up.

Sandra turned away and watched the waves for a few moments. 'Your brother wouldn't want you to spend your life suffering.'

It was a thought I'd never entertained. I'd always imagined Jeremy was angry with me, wherever he was now. That he hated me for taking his life before he'd had the chance to live it. All out of my own selfishness. My own impatience.

'You think?'

Sandra nodded. 'I do.'

Nothing but the sound of the waves.

'Where is he?'

'What do you mean?'

'Where is he buried?'

I told her.

'Do you want to go see him? I'd love to pay my respects.'

It'd been a long time since I'd visited his grave. He'd been buried next to Mum. Dad and I visited once a week for many years, but the visits grew less and less frequent.

'I'd like that a lot.'

*

Sandra's car rolled through the large iron gates of the cemetery. I'd offered to drive that morning but she insisted in case I didn't feel up to it after finishing my story. A huge weight had been lifted from my shoulders, but I was emotionally spent. It was as if I were nothing but a skeleton sitting there in the passenger's seat. But it felt right to visit Jeremy and Mum. It was the right time.

We meandered our way down the long, winding road through the graveyard. There was barely a cloud in the sky, and the sun shone brilliantly across the tombstones. I looked out the window at all their different shapes and sizes. Different colours, some old and some new. I'd never really taken in just how many headstones there were. Probably because I was normally the one in the driver's seat, sitting next to my father in silence.

'Are you okay?' Sandra interrupted my thoughts.

'Yeah, I'm fine. The car park's just up here on the left.'

We parked up and I led the way through the leafy grounds. We walked in silence. I was sure Sandra must have had many more questions, but she was right to hold them in. At least for now. It was time to pay respect. We each carried a large bouquet of flowers we'd picked up on the way. Sandra wrapped her arm around my shoulders as we walked. It was a kind gesture. She always knew the right thing to do and say at the appropriate times.

We finally reached the graves. My mother's headstone, grey granite that had aged well. My brother's, pink limestone that looked just as polished as it had the day he was buried.

A pang of sadness hit me at the sight of both the graves, sat lonely without any flowers beside them. It was a sadness I needed to feel. I felt grateful Sandra had suggested us coming here.

I gently placed the flowers down on my brother's grave, while Sandra placed hers on my mother's. She would have liked Mum a lot. Mum would have liked her. Some things in life you just know. I turned my attention back to my brother's tombstone, staring emptily at the dates engraved into the limestone. *1989-1998*. It just didn't seem possible. It didn't seem fair.

'What are you thinking?' Sandra asked softly, gently rubbing the top of my back.

'Just about... what he would have been like. If he was still with us now.'

'I'm sure he would have been very proud of you.'

Silence. I wasn't sure he would. And I wouldn't blame him for a second.

'He would have been twenty-eight. A grown man. How could I have taken that from him, Sandra? How could I have taken everything from him? His first kiss. His graduation. His wedding day. All taken away. Before he even had the chance.'

'Seb, you can't torture yourself. It's not what he would have wanted.'

'How would you know what he wanted? He'll never get the chance to tell us, will he?' My tone bordered aggressive.

Silence, again. I immediately felt guilty. Sandra was nothing but supportive. She didn't deserve that.

'I'm sorry,' I went on. 'It's just hard. I've never really spoken about this before.'

'It's okay. You don't need to apologise. It can only get easier from here.'

Would it get easier? It did feel like I'd made a huge step by telling someone the truth, after all these years. But it didn't feel like it would ever get any easier.

'So you never spoke about it with your father?'

There it was. The question I knew she'd been dying to ask.

'No, never. I could never bring myself to it. And it's killed me, every single day.'

'Do you think you ever will?'

Another question I'd asked myself far too many times over the years. One I still didn't have an answer to.

'I don't know. Perhaps. You're thinking it would give me closure, right?'

'I can't answer that question for you. But if I were you, I wouldn't give up on your dad. I would be by that hospital bed, waiting for the minute he wakes up.'

Once again, she was right. Sure, he'd had imperfections, but he'd also suffered his share of hardship. And he was my dad. I loved him unconditionally. I had no other choice.

'You're right. I will. Thanks, Sandra.'

But there was one more person I needed to find closure with first. And he would be arriving in town in less than a week.

Was I ready to be reunited with Jake?

1st February 1998

'Are you boys lyin' to us?' The cop's face cracked as he grimaced.

'No, sir,' Jake replied blankly. Dishonesty came so effortlessly to him.

'What about you, young man? Do you have anything to say for yourself?'

That I'd been involved in a murder? Of my own flesh and blood? I could never own up to what I'd done.

'No, sir.'

Both officers sat opposite us in the grey, windowless room, shifting their eyes between us, trying to figure out whether we were telling the truth. We'd already made countless statements, both individually and together, as had my father and Jake's parents. All saying the same thing. We'd been tucked up in bed when the bushfire started. We all escaped together. My stomach turned. I swallowed, worrying it would reveal my deceit.

'Well, I think we've questioned you boys enough,' the other cop said.

He was right. The exhaustion was visible on Jake's face, and I'm sure I looked the same. We'd been questioned for hours, but we hadn't budged. We couldn't. We had our story and we had to stick to it no matter what.

'Come on. We'll take you back to your parents.'

The interrogation was over. Surely, now, there would be

no more questions.

The cops led us back to where our parents were waiting. Alison was visibly distressed. Tearful, with her hair scraped back into a messy bun. Holding a crumpled copy of the Merredin-Wheatbelt Mercury, she looked like she hadn't eaten or slept in days. *Boy, 8, killed in Westonia bushfire* the headline read. A photograph of what was left of our farm accompanied the article. A blanket of ash coated what was once The Nowhere. Rob and Dad just looked distant. Vacant. Their dreams had been destroyed. An uncertain future lay ahead.

Jake told me in one of the few moments we'd had alone that the fire had also spread quickly through his farm, destroying any crops that had grown that season. He'd managed to get inside quickly and help his parents out to the car. They hadn't suspected anything, just like Dad. How low had we sunk to lie so terribly to our parents?

'Well?' Alison asked, slamming the newspaper down. 'What now?'

'We'll have to go back through everything one more time, ma'am,' the cop with the creased face said. 'But at this stage, it doesn't look like it's a case we'll need to pursue. It appears like it was just another unfortunate bushfire.'

My own relief was reflected in the faces of everyone else in the room. Were Jake and I really getting away with it? Was the nightmare nearly over? I didn't doubt it was only just the beginning.

The police said their goodbyes and made their way back to their offices. Dad stood up as soon as they were out of sight.

'Seb, I'll be in the car.' He turned to look at our once-neighbours but said nothing.

Was this it? We were leaving? We'd been staying in a motel near the police station in Merredin, but Dad was ready to head back to Perth. Nothing was left of what we'd owned but Dad's ute, which was now all we needed.

'Stu.' Rob looked Dad in the eye. 'If there's anything we can do. Anything, mate.'

Alison came over and hugged me, for which I was grateful. 'Take care of yourself.' She turned to my dad, but she had no words. She burst into tears.

'Come on, let's leave these boys to say goodbye,' Dad said, eager to get on the road.

Despite the unthinkable events that had played out, Dad understood Jake and I had been good friends, at least once upon a time. And it would probably be the last time we'd see each other.

'Come on,' Jake said. 'Let's talk out back quickly. There are so many cops in here.'

I followed Jake out the back entrance of the police station. Our parents were waiting out front, so he obviously wanted to speak privately. We stood beside the brick wall outside, where there was no one around.

'We did the right thing, Seb. Not speaking up, I mean.'

I remained silent. How would I ever see it as the right thing? We'd killed my innocent little brother, and now we'd have to live with ourselves. I'd have to live with myself. Would that even be possible? If only it'd been me who had perished in the flames instead of Jeremy. That's what I deserved.

'I guess,' I said. 'So, are you going back to Byron?'

He tipped his head. 'Yep. It's finally time to get back into surfing.'

I could have strangled him. All of this just for him to follow his stupid dream. Had it been worth it? Killing my brother in the process? Did he ever even want to escape The Nowhere with me, or had it always been about his own selfish goals?

'Bye, Jake,' I said frankly. It came out colder than I'd intended it too. But it was hard to mask how I felt.

Jake reached forward to give me a hug, which caught me off guard. I hated myself for wanting to hug him back.

It was then I noticed the tears welling in his eyes. As I hugged him, his body jerked from the sobs. But they were short-lived.

'It wasn't supposed to end like this,' he said, pulling away. His face was red and his nostrils flared. His thick lips turned pale.

Was that a real apology? It felt remorseless. Empty. Why couldn't he just take ownership of his actions? He owed me that. Although I had myself to blame for going along with his sinister plan, it was his idea. It would always hang heavier on his conscience than mine. Or would it?

Jake quickly wiped his face with the back of his palm. 'We better get going, Seb.'

We walked back to our cars without speaking. Through the rear-view mirror, I could see Jake waving, but I didn't turn back around. It was over now, and I would never stop hating him. Not until the day I died.

12th January 2018

Of course it was raining. It matched my mood. Thick layers of water crashed against the car's windscreen as I swung around into the car park of the café. Just as I'd hoped, there was barely a vehicle in sight. I'd purposely picked the quietest café I knew. Truthfully, I wished I could have arranged to meet Jake on the isolated beach I'd taken Sandra to. But that might have seemed strange. A café felt like neutral ground. Who knew how the reunion would go? At least it would be easy for either of us to slip away, should we need to.

My stomach churned as I climbed out the car, quickly opening my umbrella to keep myself dry from the late summer storm. Within seconds, the strong wind had turned it inside out, so I gave up and made a run for the building. I'd purposefully arrived ten minutes early as I figured I'd need a coffee to mentally prepare myself, to make sure my brain was sharp enough not to rely on my heart. Relying on my heart had always been dangerous when it came to Jake.

The dry, warm air welcomed me as I made my way towards a table in the corner. The café had always been slightly rundown, so I noticed straight away they'd given it a makeover. The plastic chairs had been thrown out. Instead, there were colourful stools, sanded down just enough to see the odd streak of metal beneath. The carpet had been stripped, nothing in its place but a couple of Persian rugs atop the concrete floor. A red, industrial-sized coffee machine was pouting for everyone to see. But as soon as I saw the waitress approaching me, I realised the staff hadn't been updated with the décor. I recognised her tired face, covered with far too much makeup, her bleached-blonde hair, scraped back into a dry, wispy ponytail, and her thin frame and leathery skin that had seen far too much sun.

She appeared bored and disinterested as she scribbled down my order. I had always liked the café, but perhaps it wasn't the best place to bring Jake. I was just grateful it was quiet. And the coffee was always strong. He'd appreciate that.

The sweet scent of roasted coffee beans filled the café as the machine steamed into action. I heard the door open behind me but resisted the urge to turn my head. The knot in my stomach tightened. What would he think of me now? Would he think I'd aged well? Would he even recognise me? How much would he remember? Would we speak about that fateful summer night? Would we speak about Jeremy?

Two young women walked past me and took a seat a couple of tables down. They were laughing and talking loudly about one of their friends. They obviously thought it was trendy to dress like it was the '90s. They both wore high-waisted jeans and chunky Doc Martens. One wore a crop top with a peace sign on it. It was exactly the sort of thing Kylie had worn when it was cool the first time around. It was kind of ironic. I'd spent my life running away from the '90s, but they had finally caught up with me.

The waitress returned and placed my long black down in front of me in a lime green cup with a mismatched yellow saucer and a collectable vintage teaspoon.

'Thanks,' I managed.

She half smiled, half grimaced, before heading over to the two hipsters to take their order.

I drank my coffee, staring at the rain as it pummelled the window, distorting the world outside. The usually quiet street was completely dead but for the occasional car speeding through the rain. I could just make out the shopkeeper in the op shop on the other side of the road. She was reading a book behind the counter, maybe it was a magazine.

The café door opened but I didn't look. This time it had to be him. The flames entered my head. The smoke filled my lungs. The ash coated my heart black. Was I ready? Did I need to do this? Was it too late to get up and make a run for my car? I downed the last of my coffee.

'Beautiful weather you have here, mate.'

There it was. The same voice I'd heard on the phone. Just like it had been in The Nowhere, but thicker. Raspier. Smokier.

Jake sat down directly in front of me. The face that greeted me was barely one I recognised. The chiselled jawline was gone, filled out with age. His skin, once smooth, was now worn and rough. His hair had thinned, his eyes dulled. Turns out time had been just as unkind to his appearance as it had his voice.

'It's been a while,' he began, drying the rain from his face with a napkin that had been placed in a tin on the table.

'It sure has,' I replied.

Jake reached out for a hug, which I hadn't expected. He

smelt of sandalwood and cigarettes. He obviously hadn't managed to kick that habit. He was wearing a business shirt with faded jeans. That's when I noticed his wedding band.

'You look good, Seb.'

'Thanks. So do you.'

He smirked. 'It's all right. You don't need to humour me. Life's been rough. I know it shows. But it's all good; I turned it around.'

Was it the right time to probe him further? Not just yet. One step at a time.

The moody waitress returned to the table. 'What can I get you both?'

'I'll have another long black.'

'Do you have any herbal teas?'

That was something I hadn't expected.

'Sure. We've got camomile, peppermint, ginger…'

'Ginger's great, thanks.'

The waitress slowly made her way back to the kitchen.

'She's a barrel of laughs, isn't she?'

'No coffee?'

'Nah, I kicked it a while back. I gotta watch my blood pressure – you know how it is.'

I thought about bringing up the smoking, but Jake beat me to it.

'I know. I should have ditched smoking over coffee. It's the one vice I haven't been able to kick.'

At least he was being honest. Hopefully that would continue.

'So, what are you doing with yourself these days, Seb?'

A single sentence acting as a reminder how long it had really been. Jake knew nothing about my adult life. And I knew nothing about his. The brief time we shared as late adolescents was a different life. Like we were completely different people.

'I'm a nurse. Have been for years. I lived in London for a while but moved back to Perth when my dad had a heart attack. I've lived with him since.'

I hadn't meant to blurt my whole life story out like that. Saying it so briefly and quickly trivialised it. But then, everything seemed trivial after the fire.

'A nurse? That's awesome, Seb. It really is.'

Jake was so different now. He'd never had social skills as a teenager, or if he had, he'd managed to hide them well. How different would it have been if he'd shown this level of empathy back then? Maybe the life experiences he'd hinted at had taught him a thing or two about how to be a decent human being.

'How's your dad doing now?' Jake sounded genuinely interested.

'Not so great actually. He had another heart attack recently and he's in a coma.'

The lines that ran across Jake's face were emphasised as his expression turned to one of sympathy. 'I'm sorry, Seb. I'm sure he'll pull through. Your dad's a fighter, always has been.'

This was the first indication that Jake was indeed the same person I knew on the farm. The first sign he remembered the past. My heart fluttered frantically at the thought of us discussing what had happened that summer. I had questions, but I wasn't sure I could handle the answers.

It was also an interesting choice of words, describing my dad as a fighter. Sure, we had fought a lot. But had Jake really been observant enough to my father's personality? He was right. Dad was a fighter. It was so easy to focus on the things in life I had to live without or hurdles I had to overcome. But Dad had faced these challenges with me, as well as many of his own.

'How about you?' I asked, deciding to switch to a different subject. 'You mentioned you're here with work, right? You're a marketing director?'

He nodded with a slightly smug expression. He was obviously happy with his six-figure salary. The smugness was more proof it was the same Jake I'd once known.

'That's right. I run a marketing consultancy back in Sydney. Started real small, but now we have offices in Melbourne and Brisbane. Perth's next, which is why I'm here.'

'Wow, Jake… that's great. I'm happy to hear how well you've done for yourself.'

The waitress put our drinks down with enough force to spill some of my coffee onto the saucer. She headed over to some newly arrived customers.

'Believe me, it hasn't always been so rosy,' Jake went on. 'Once we moved back to Byron, I was a lost soul. At first, I thought I wanted to get back into surfing. But I guess it had just been too long. I'd lost my spark. That's when everything started to fall apart. I got into a bad crowd and before I knew it, I was massively into drugs and spiralling out of control for a long time. I'm sure it was one of the main reasons my folks divorced.'

'I'm sorry to hear that, Jake. About your parents, I mean.'

'It's all good, mate. My folks' relationship was doomed for years. They're much happier now. Dad remarried, but Mum never did.'

It was a relief to hear Jake's parents were still alive and well. I was glad Rob had found someone new but wished the same had been true for Alison. She was always so lovely to me. I hoped she was happy.

There was a brief silence, the first since we'd been re-united. Did Jake want me to ask more about when he'd been hooked on drugs? Did I even want to know? It was no big surprise really. Jake had always been drawn to the dark side and certainly had an addictive personality. Not that I'd been a saint myself over the years.

'Anyway. All that turned around when I met my wife.'

There it was. Said out loud. The confirmation Jake had settled into adult life as a straight man. Even though I'd known all along he could never face the more confusing parts of his sexuality, it was still a strange feeling to hear he was married to a woman. It was as if it proved in one fell swoop that all the feelings I'd had for him as a teenager had been unrequited.

'That's fantastic, Jake. Congratulations.'

'Thanks, mate. Her name's Olivia. It's hard to believe we've been married nearly ten years already.'

'Wow, I bet it is. How did you both meet?'

'Through a mutual friend. He knew all about my battle

with addiction. Olivia had her life in order, but he knew we'd get along. He joined the dots. Thank god he did. She saved my life.'

It was a bold statement, but one I was authentically happy to hear. 'That's great, Jake. Really.'

'I know. Here, look. We even have a couple of kids.'

Jake opened his wallet to reveal a picture of two smiling boys on one side, the younger of the two missing his front teeth. The picture on the other side was of Jake and a woman I assumed to be Olivia. She had pale skin, bright green eyes and her hair was auburn and curly. Just like Kylie's.

'You've got a lovely family there.'

'Thanks, mate. Those boys are a nightmare sometimes, but we love 'em to bits. So, what about you?' He studied my fingers. 'No wife? No kids?'

Why did this make me angry? Was it because I felt Jake should have known about me? Or did he think it was just some teenage phase that would pass? I thought about blurting all this out but decided against it. 'No. It's just me right now.'

'That's a shame. I'm sure the right person will come along.'

Jake's words sounded as hollow as they always had as he downed the last of his ginger tea.

I finished the dregs of my coffee. Was that it? Would we simply go our own ways, perhaps never seeing each other again? Something felt unfinished. Incomplete. We hadn't revisited The Nowhere. Did Jake even want to? Was he waiting for me to bring it up? It was as hard to read him now as it ever was.

'I know it's terrible, but I'm dying for a cigarette. Mind if I slip outside?'

It had only just stopped raining, so he must have been waiting for the opportunity to sneak out. Or had he sensed the tension I was feeling?

'Course, go ahead.'

Once he was gone, I took the opportunity to pay for the drinks before following him outside. I had to get closure. I needed it now.

Jake was leaning against the brick wall around the corner of the café. He'd already lit up.

'Mind if I have one?'

Jake looked surprised. 'Sorry, mate – I would have offered. I assumed since you're a nurse and that...'

I smiled as I took the Marlboro Light from his hand. Suddenly, we were seventeen again.

Inhaling the smoke deeply, I shut my eyes. When I opened them, Jake was staring straight at me.

'You want to talk about it, don't you?'

'I don't know. Do you?'

'I don't really see what good it would do. It was such a long time ago. It feels like another life, you know?'

I nodded. 'I do. But there's not a day that goes by when it doesn't haunt me. It was my brother who paid the price, after all. Who got killed.'

I couldn't help it. I didn't care if it hurt or if it didn't. I wanted to get my point across. And now, finally, I had.

'I know, Seb. Do you think I don't know that? Do you

really think there's been a bloody day that's gone by when I haven't thought about it either? That's how I got into the drugs in the first place… to try and escape it. To try and escape what we did.'

What *we* did. Although he was right – we had committed the crime together – he should have taken more of the blame. It'd been his idea. Sure, I'd been a fool to follow him blindly, the same way I'd always done back then. But I was older and wiser now. I knew he should've taken ownership of what happened. He owed both Jeremy and me a genuine apology. But it was clear neither of us would be getting one. How young and gullible had I been? Everything looked so different through adult eyes.

'Besides, mate. That really is all in the past. You should focus on moving on. I know I have.'

That was when I realised I didn't like the person Jake had become. On the surface, he appeared successful. A good job and a nice family. But behind all that he was as heartless as he'd been back then. He had the same glint in his eye that he'd had the night we set The Nowhere alight.

'Yeah, maybe you're right,' I said flatly.

We stamped our cigarettes out on the wet pavement. I knew it would be the last one I'd ever smoke.

There was silence as we walked towards our cars. It was hard to figure out whether the meeting had been worth it. In some ways I felt a sense of closure, seeing Jake all those years on and knowing the feelings I'd once had for him had well and truly been buried in the past. There were tinges of sadness. I couldn't imagine finding friendship with him now.

And deep down I wondered if he was really being true to himself. But if he'd moved on, why shouldn't I?

'How long are you in Perth for?' As soon as I'd asked the question I realised it made it sound like I wanted to see him again. I didn't. There'd be no reason to.

'I'm not sure, to be honest. Probably not long, I'm just here to work out the logistics of setting up the business here. But I'll be back.'

The notion of Jake being a regular in Perth didn't sit well with me.

'Maybe next time I'm here you could show me around a bit? Show me some of your favourite haunts?'

I nodded and offered a smile that gave little away. 'Yeah, maybe.'

We hugged, tighter than before. I noticed Jake holding on a little longer than he should have. I pulled away.

'Goodbye, Jake.'

'See ya soon, Seb.'

We got into our cars and drove away in different directions.

I glided along the motorway with the windows down. It felt good to feel the fresh air on my face. The humidity had dropped after the storm and the tension in the air finally released. I thought about the meeting. It was shorter than I'd expected, but I was satisfied with how I'd handled it. It was empowering to realise how far I'd come from being that awkward seventeen-year-old boy on the farm. And I was never going back.

I intentionally drove past my exit on the motorway – I didn't feel like going home just yet. Where would I go? To the hospital? To see Sandra? Back to Mum and Jeremy's graves? I decided on the latter. Going with Sandra had reminded me of how important it was to visit them. After seeing Jake and opening old wounds, it felt like the most appropriate place to be.

Just as I changed lanes to make my way towards the cemetery, my phone started to ring. An unknown number. I answered and put it on loudspeaker.

'Hello, Seb speaking?'

'Hi Seb, it's Dan.'

It was good to hear his familiar tone. 'Hey, Dan. How's it going?'

'You should get yourself down here. Your dad just woke up.'

A mixture of relief and elation rippled through my body. It was just the news I needed.

'He did? How is he?'

In the two-second pause it took for him to reply, I knew something wasn't right.

'He's not good, mate. I'm so sorry to say this, but he's not got much time left.'

I suddenly felt the urge to vomit. I held it in, too shocked to process the sadness.

'Can I see him?'

'He's confused right now, but you should be able to in the next hour or so.'

'I'll be right there.'

I changed lanes again at the nearest opportunity. Mum and Jeremy could wait. Dad needed me now.

And I needed him.

*

Sandra's familiar form was visible, sitting in the waiting room. She was in her scrubs. She must have finished her shift and headed straight over. Seeing her was a reminder I had a true friend, someone with a pure heart who had my back. Without speaking, I walked straight over to her and held out my arms.

Sandra embraced me tightly. 'He's still with us, Seb.'

But for how long? It was worthless thinking about it. Right now there was still time. Still time for me to talk to him. To be honest with him. It was my chance to tell him the truth. My chance to ask for forgiveness, even if he'd never grant me it.

'How did it go?'

It took a moment to realise she was asking about Jake. I'd already pushed our reunion from my mind.

'I don't know. I'm not sure what I expected to gain from it. Or whether I got it. I just know I'm now where I'm meant to be.'

Sandra's smile said more than her words could.

'Seb, hi.'

Dan's voice. I turned around to be greeted with his forlorn expression.

'You can come in and see him now.'

Sandra gave my hand one more little squeeze, before

sitting back down. 'You're doing the right thing.'

I gave her a thumbs-up, took a deep breath and stepped into the ward.

Silence, except for the familiar beeping of Dad's heart monitor. Gently closing the door behind me, I paced over to the chair next to his bed and sat down. Lying on his back and staring at the ceiling, my father looked ghostly. His skin was almost translucent. His cheekbones sharp from the weight he'd lost. He was a shadow of the man he once was. Sadness sliced through me like a scythe. Despite everything we'd been through, everything he'd put me through, it was still painful to watch him fade away.

'Hey, Dad. It's me, Seb.'

He slowly turned his head to face me. 'I know who you are, Son.'

'I'm so glad you're awake.'

He made a noise that sounded like something between a grunt and a moan.

'Are you okay? Are you in any pain?'

'No.'

It was quiet for a few moments. Was he annoyed with me? Annoyed it hadn't been me taking care of him?

'I came as fast I could, as soon as I heard you were awake.'

Another grunt.

I bit my tongue, worried I'd say something hurtful. Someone or something out there had given me a chance to tell my father the things I needed him to know. I didn't want to ruin my opportunity.

'Where were you?' he asked.

I thought about making something up, but decided just to be honest: 'I was with Jake actually.'

I surprised myself with the admission. We had never spoken about Jake after the case had been cleared and I wondered if he'd even know whom I was talking about.

His milky eyes opened wider as he shifted his body around to look at me more closely. 'Jake?'

He remembered.

'Yes.' I nodded. 'I wanted... I needed closure.'

Slowly turning his head away from me, his expression went from shock to disdain. 'I see. And did you get it?'

'I guess so. Well, I don't know actually.'

'Well, that's a shame.' Another silence, until he spoke again. 'I suppose you want to find it from me instead?'

The scythe was back. This time it was after my beating heart.

'What do you mean?'

'Son, did it ever cross your mind that maybe I knew all along?'

The realisation dawned on me like the first time a child comprehends their own mortality. The flames were back and burning through the hospital. Burning through Dad. Burning through me.

'You... did?'

'Yes, Son. I did.' His pace picked up. 'But there was no way in hell I was going to watch you get thrown in jail and lose the last family member I had.'

My skin began to burn. I felt eighteen again. No, I felt

eight. Vulnerable. Guilty. Foolish.

'Dad…' I struggled to get the words out. 'I am so, so sorry.' The last words broke off into a whisper.

That was when something even more unexpected happened. Dad's hand reached out for mine. I placed it in his. He wrapped his bony white fingers around my clammy palm.

'I know you are, Son. I know you are.'

He turned back around to face me. Colour returned to his face as his eyes began to well up. 'And I'm sorry, too. I'm sorry you lost your mum. I'm sorry we moved to the farm. I'm sorry for everything.'

Tears streamed down my face. My throat went as dry as the Outback. My head throbbed.

'No, Dad. You have nothing to be sorry about. It's all me… it's all my fault.'

I reached out to hug him. He hugged me back and our faces pressed together, rubbing salty tears from both our eyes against our cheeks. Shaking uncontrollably, I had to find a way to hold it together.

'Now look, Son.' He spoke directly in my ear, holding me hard. 'What you and that kid did was a foolish, stupid thing to do. And it's pretty damn obvious you didn't expect what happened to happen. You were crying out to be heard, and you ended up losing your brother. I know how painful that must have been to live with. You've suffered every single day of your life, just like me. But the suffering has to stop. For both of us. You have to let go and move forward with your own life. Because we don't have a lot of time here, do we?'

Had I ever heard Dad speak with such wisdom? Where

had he been hiding it? Where had it been when Mum died? Where had it been when we lived in The Nowhere? Maybe if he'd shown this softer side then, things could have been different. Maybe Jeremy would still be with us. But I couldn't keep blaming him. I'd blamed him enough throughout my life. For Mum's death. For moving us to The Nowhere. For making my life miserable. I had to take the blame now. Own the blame and do what I had to do to let it go, just as he said. Just as Jake said. Just as Sandra said.

'You're right, Dad. Thank you.'

'I love you, Son.'

It was the first time I'd heard him say it. I was so stunned I could barely say the words back to him. But I pushed through my shock: 'I love you too.'

We remained in an embrace until Dan entered the room.

'You better let your dad get some rest, Seb.'

I pulled away from the hug slowly and nodded, wiping my eyes. 'You're right. I can be pretty tiring.'

Dad had an honest smile on his face, before turning over on his side.

'I'll just be outside if you need me,' I said. 'I'm not going anywhere.'

'Okay, Son.'

I reached over and gently kissed him on the head. Would this warmth towards one another last? For now, it didn't matter. I would make the most of every moment.

As soon as I stepped out of the room, Sandra launched over to give me a hug.

'Are you okay, Seb?'

I fell into her embrace as she rubbed my back. 'It went well. So much better than I'd ever imagined.'

I sensed Sandra's smile before I saw it. That loving grin I'd come to know so well.

'I'm so glad, Seb. Really, I am.' Sandra picked up her handbag. 'Come on, I'll buy you some dinner.'

'Sounds perfect.'

*

Over a dinner of slightly stale sandwiches from the hospital canteen, I filled Sandra in on the anticlimactic meeting with Jake and the conversation with Dad that followed. It was past eleven now, but we decided to order coffee anyway. I probably didn't need it with the amount of adrenaline pumping through me, but I didn't want to risk falling asleep.

Sandra blew on her coffee softly. 'You've had quite the day, haven't you?'

'I've had quite the year.' The familiar taste of cheap, filtered coffee burnt my tongue.

'So, what comes next?'

'What do you mean?'

'I mean, what comes next for you?'

I had an idea, but I wouldn't tell Sandra. She would try to talk me out of it. Despite the momentary relief I'd felt owning up, it hadn't made the guilt go away.

'I really don't know. Dad doesn't have long left, I can see that. He won't leave the hospital now. Once he's gone, I'll have no one.'

'That's not true. You'll have me.'

But no one who depended on me. No more responsibilities.

'I know. And you have no idea how much that means to me. Especially now you know my secret. I wouldn't blame you if you hated me. I hate me.'

Sandra placed her hand delicately on mine.

'Course I don't hate you, Seb. It's going to get better, okay? I promise.'

I managed a smile. 'What about you?'

'What about me?'

'What comes next for you?'

'Well, to tell you the truth, Seb, I was pretty lonely before you came into my life. So I'm just looking forward to our friendship. To watching you move forward.'

'That's very sweet. I guess I—' My sentence was interrupted by my phone vibrating in my pocket. Dan.

20th January 1985

mummy asked how old are you today sebastian and her voice sounded sweet like honey so i held out my outstretched palm and said i'm five and then she said that's right sweetheart which means you're a big boy now aren't you and i nodded and then daddy said we've got you something special so i asked what and i felt so excited and then daddy said come outside and take a look so i followed mummy and daddy outside into the hot summer sun and mummy rubbed thick white sunscreen onto my nose ears and neck as we walked and i tried to push her hand away because it wasn't time for that i was too excited to see what my present was and then as soon as we stepped into the yard i saw a blue bike and daddy pointed to it and said it's yours and my eyes nearly popped out because i was so surprised so i gave daddy a big hug and a kiss and then i gave mummy a big hug and a kiss but then i noticed there were no training wheels on the bike and i asked daddy why not and he said because you're a big boy now and i felt afraid because i wasn't sure if i was ready to ride without training wheels but he said you must be brave sebastian and you are ready and i asked if we could take it out right now and daddy said yes so he carried the bike to the car and we all got in and drove to the bush and when we got there we walked out to the pathway and the smell of eucalyptus was so strong and i could feel the sun against my skin and i could hear the birds singing loudly and i felt so happy because i was with mummy and daddy and it was my birthday and everyone was smiling and daddy wasn't mad at me or mummy and then i jumped on the bike with daddy holding me and i felt scared but mummy said don't worry we're right behind you and you're a big boy now and we're so proud of you and daddy walked with me pushing me along on the bike and i said please don't let go daddy because i'm scared and he said you will be fine sebastian you are brave and you are strong and then he started to jog and then he started to run and i pushed the pedals and i started to breathe quickly and i felt my heart fluttering like a butterfly and daddy said into my ear you can do it you can do it i said no i can't no i can't and he said yes you can you're doing it sebastian you're doing it right now and i hadn't even noticed he'd let go and i was riding without training wheels and it felt so good and i felt so happy and i felt so alive

12th January 2018

A crowd of doctors and nurses surrounded my father by the time I reached his ward. Dan pushed past the others when he saw me coming.

'I'm so sorry, Seb. We tried everything we could, but it was too late. He wasn't strong enough. We lost him.'

I flinched as my blood ran cold. Dad had waited to tell me he loved me before he was able to leave the world. This made me prouder of him than ever before.

'It's okay, Dan. Thank you.'

Sandra, who had been standing by my side listening, held back from reaching out to hug me or offer her hand. She stood waiting, as did Dan, to see how I would react. To see what I'd do next.

The doctors cleared the room and so did the nurses, one by one.

'Can I see him?' I knew the answer already. I was familiar with the protocol.

Dan nodded. 'We're here if you need us.'

'I second that,' Sandra added tenderly.

'I know. Thank you.'

Entering the room, I was greeted with the same frail man I'd not long been speaking to. Except this time he was without his spirit. An empty shell that his soul had shed. Sitting down on the chair beside him, I unclipped the thin, gold necklace I always wore and placed it on his chest. I held his hand, which was slowly cooling.

'Do you remember giving this to me on my seventeenth birthday, Dad? My eyes began to well. I know I didn't appreciate it at the time. All I wanted was that damn car. But I never took it off. I will keep it forever, okay? I will keep it forever, and it will always remind me of you.'

Silence. Not even the sound of the heart monitor to keep me company.

*

I stepped out into the warm air of the staff car park. Sandra had offered to spend the night at my house, but I refused. With Dad now gone, I knew exactly what I needed to do next. And I wasn't going to allow her to try and stop me.

Leaning against the side of my car, I took a moment to look up at the stars bathing in the pitch-black sky. The same stars I'd spent so much time staring up at during my time on the farm. Searching for something, anything. A meteor. A satellite. Anything that might be a sign that change was coming. It only took me a few seconds to locate the Southern Cross. There it was, shining away, as familiar as a freckle on a loved one's face. I traced its stars with my index finger. One for my grandmother. One for my mother. One for my father. One for Jeremy. And that little one for Scampi. I smiled to myself, knowing they would guide me in the right direction. They were all out there somewhere, finally reunited. Soon, I'd be joining them. And I'd be ready.

The night's silence was interrupted by a screeching sound. A pair of red-tailed black cockatoos soared through the darkened skies, cutting my line of vision. Reminding me it was time. I'd run from the truth my whole life, but where had it got me? Mum had told me to be strong and look after my brother and I had let her down. It was time to pay the price. Climbing into the car, I drew one last deep breath before starting the engine. Outside, the sound of the birds faded into the distance. Shrieking into the night like teenagers, wild and free.

About the Author

Although born in a seaside town in Sussex, England, Chris spent his childhood in New Zealand devouring countless books and penning his own short stories. This continued throughout his teens back in the UK, before he decided to broaden his craft by studying journalism at university in Hampshire.

After chasing the bright lights of London for a few years to pursue a career in writing, Chris decided to head back Down Under to be closer to his family and find fresh inspiration.

He released his dystopian debut novel, *Shell*, through his co-founded publishing company, PRNTD, in 2015. An underground success that climbed the post-apocalyptic charts in both Australia and the UK, Chris then released his debut poetry book, *Verses*, the following year.

Chris currently lives in Sydney with his husband and juggles a copywriting career with his fiction.

chrisgillbooks.com

CPSIA information can be obtained
at www.ICGtesting.com
Printed in the USA
LVHW091733120320
649865LV00004B/614